Night's Grasp

Written by Zachary Toombs

Edited by Taylor Martin

Cover Illustration by Nayla

Copyright © 2021 Zachary Toombs

All rights reserved.

ISBN: 9798464643567

For Andrea and Jack and Cooper. For Mom and Dad. For Justin and Kaitlyn. For Alex and Jeremy. For Vin and Matt. For Alex and Sophia. For Troy and all the Quinby's. For the Grandparents. For the Uncles and Aunts. For the cousins. For Mr. Alptekin and Mr. Harris and Mrs. Jordan-Parisi. And, of course, for all the cats running around.

A little piece of each of you lies ahead.

CONTENTS

	Acknowledgments	i
1	Him	1
2	The Pit – Five Years Later	8
3	The Land Below	18
4	The Half-Elf	29
5	Parasite	40
6	The Blood in the Sand	50
7	Flood	60
8	Fragments	74
9	The Girl	85
10	The Brute	96
11	What Remains	108
12	The Final Day	118
13	The Struggle	128
14	The Replacement	138
15	The Girl & The Elf	147
16	Fringes	157
17	Vultures	167
18	Gaunt	176
19	A Black River	185
20	Vespertine	196

"DEATH WILL COME, THEN A CLOUD OF LOVE"

~ EMILY SPRAGUE

1 HIM

The girl found comfort in the dirt. The way it gave her a shell, wrapped its arms around her, and kept her close. It was her pillow, blanket, and mattress. She could rub it on her skin, roll around in its embrace, dig her fingers into the grime, and cleanse herself.

Cariaah lived in a village house with her father. Fields of grain, pens of livestock, and wells of dripping water encompassed the group of homes. Their house was built with crude stone and slabbed together with a gluey clay. A lopsided chimney stuck out of the straw roof, constantly emitting fluffy, white smoke into the golden sky.

In the dusk, upon the nearby hill, she sat beneath a tree. It was late autumn, and the brittle leaves had piled below the bare branches, which twirled toward the strands of clouds. She had carved a nest out of the leaves, creating a cocoon around her. This way, if she got cold—which happened often, even in moderate weather—she could cover herself and escape, if just for a few, sacred minutes.

This oncoming winter would be her eleventh. The first snow hadn't arrived yet, but its whisper trailed through the bite of the wind. Her thin—borderline scrawny—frame could feel the tinge of frost in the air, stippling her skin with bumps. Each breath generated itself clean and crisp, so that all she had to heed was the sunset before her, and the dirt encompassing her.

All of this—everything surrounding the girl upon the hill—distracted her. It gathered her attention and hurried it away from the shrewdness of all else.

It distracted her from the bruises.

NIGHT'S GRASP

***

Dinner was one of the goats—one of her favorites, whom she named Eva—roasted over the fire. Her father had commanded this goat be served in its entirety for the next week, in very specific portions.

She was to cook the meat for her father, chop a vegetable alongside it and bring him a fresh pint of ale from the cellar. After finishing his meal, Cariaah could have what was left over for herself.

Once she had taken a cucumber from inside the cupboard, she brought it over to the table—where her father sat—to slice it. The rusted, iron kitchen knife rested on the table along with the cut of goat, its blade shimmering in the orange glare of the sun.

She took the piece of metal in hand. The girl inspected the curve of the blade, following the glint of sun all the way up that sharp edge. But just before she could get to cutting, something distant introduced itself.

Something that encroached.

Cariaah could feel it through the wood of the floor. *Hooves.* So many of them drove into the dirt that they turned into one, whole sound. An onslaught approached in a crescendo.

Her father rose from his seat at the table, taking the knife from Cariaah's tiny hand and pressing his face against the window.

She crawled to the furthest corner, digging her fingers into a bruise at her hip, and ignoring the cacophony. The symphony of villagers screaming, dogs barking, steel ripping through flesh, and fire consuming straw.

But drowning out everything was the snort of a horse at their very door.

She sat up, tears finally catching up to her.

Her father held the kitchen knife as if it were a longsword, flaunting it at the closed door. He ripped the front door open, unveiling the apocalypse that was their village. Corpses lined the dirt paths—some on fire, others ash—flames laced the homes, raging. And a thick, dark smog hung above.

It all served as scenery for one man.

Him.

His hair flowed like white silk, shimmering in the chaos, and framing his smooth, youthful face. Peering, his shrewd glare spewed at the girl's father, cutting into him. A sparkling gauntlet wielded a longsword, dripping with blood.

Cariaah's jaw fell agape. To her, this person—even though he was part of the chaos—glowed like someone out of a painting. Her eyes swelled with life, with curiosity, with *hope*.

He dismounted, presenting the sharpness of his blade to Cariaah's father. The man walked like a creature on the hunt, staring down his prey in a lurk. He spoke no words. Only glared.

The door closed behind him as he entered, muffling the outside death.

"Sit, oaf," the man commanded.

The oaf still held the knife like a buffoon. "Don't come into my house and order me around," he said.

The flash of the man's steel enforced his order. The strike was so swift—so unbelievably precise—that it removed the knife-wielding hand with surgical ease, spraying blood.

Cariaah's father hovered his only hand over the wound, trying to stop the pour of crimson in futility. His dried mouth refused to swallow. He couldn't even blink.

"I said, *sit*." He brought his sword to the boor's throat. The man looked to Cariaah.

She gasped, taken aback by the vivacity of his eyes.

"You may sit, too," he said, slowly and kindly, antithetical to his demeanor just seconds ago. He then smiled—so passionately that his eyes almost closed—even though he held a bloody piece of steel.

"Yes, sir," she said, her legs shaking as she stood.

"No need to call me that."

"I-I'm sorry," she said, languidly making her way toward one of the empty, forbidden chairs.

They all sat, the man's blade still pointed at her father's throat. "I'm not here to hurt you, child." He smiled, again, gazing into her eyes. "I promise."

She couldn't nod or agree. She just looked at him, still crying.

"What is your name?" he asked.

She glanced vaguely at her father, who sat, hand over his bloody wrist.

"It's okay," the swordsman said. "He won't hurt you either."

Cariaah's hands covered her arms. She receded. "I-I-I never got one," she said, fear soaking her words. "But I call myself 'Cariaah' in my head."

"A very nice name," he said, placing the blade onto the table and folding his arms. "Why that one?"

"People see me crying all the time. They mock me for it. So, it's 'Cariaah.' It sounds kind of like 'crier.' I guess they gave it to me, not myself."

His eyes turned a little narrower, like his smile was bigger than it looked. "Have you ever told anyone else that?"

Cariaah hugged herself, bringing her knees to her chest. She shook her head, burying her face.

"Tell me," the man said, looking to her father. "Would you like something to eat, Cariaah?"

"I'm not hungry," she said into her legs.

The man glared with raw, fervent disdain at her father.

The injured, paralyzed oaf gazed back, *trapped*.

He didn't scoff. The man didn't even flinch. "You're pathetic," he said, words falling out as daggers.

Cariaah removed her face from her lap.

"The fact that I have to sit at this table with an animal, lower than this piece of meat, here…" his head gestured to the cut of goat, which still sat upon the table, drawing flies. "It's abhorrent. It's despicable. It's *sickening*." His face writhed in disgust.

The girl's father still felt the urge to defend himself. "I-I'd tread careful—"

"I would heed your own advice." Even the chaos of the village was silenced at the behest of his sharp words.

Cariaah's father returned his attention to his wrist.

"Get me the ale," the man commanded, not breaking his vehement glare.

Cariaah swung her feet to the side of her chair, ready to land on the floor.

"Not you, child," he said.

Her father stared back, silently pleading against the intruder's command. Yet, the glare that was returned to him drove the order into action. It insisted. He rose to his feet, each part of him trembling in terror.

"Just one cup," he said. "I don't want to chore myself into having a drink *with* you."

He hobbled toward the cellar; his deflated appearance akin to that of an old man. He forced himself through the metal door, which closed with a squeal.

The clashing tides of two converse feelings paralyzed the girl. She could either sit and gaze at nothing or sit and gaze at the man across from her. The curvature of his face, the way his eyes glistened in the light of the decaying village, and how gracefully he breathed; the way he existed, simply, kept eyes as prisoners.

Her father never looked into her eyes. He never spoke softly. He never asked genuine questions. In the span of just minutes, the person Cariaah looked at, now, had done things her father never had.

The cellar door opened, once more, Cariaah's father spilling out, cup in hand. Blood poured from the other wrist, dripping onto the floor.

"Good," said the swordsman. His eyes never tore away. He took the cup. He slowly gulped. "Did you piss in this?" the man asked. "It's downright rancid." He threw the cup at whom he glared.

It shattered, a shard of pewter lodging into his skull.

Cariaah gasped from her curling position.

Her father growled as the ale dripped. He knew nothing he said would stop this person's torment, and nothing he did would stop the sting of alcohol or throb of his wrist.

"Do you hear that?" The swordsman asked.

The once present, albeit muffled, sounds of fire and blood and death had fallen away.

"My men have finished their work on this village." He stood, the chair skidding back. "Which means the only house left is *yours*."

"D-don't."

"Why not?" he barked, taking his blade again and flaunting it. "Who are you to me, oaf? You are nothing." He leaned toward his victim, a scowl upon his face. "And you deserve no more breath than that." The man drove his steel into the animal, pinning it to the wall of its own home.

Cariaah felt no urge to move. She felt no urge to run. She only watched.

Her father heaved, blood escaping with each breath.

"I can't wait to watch you burn," the man said, a spell of flame emerging from his gauntlet. And as the fire consumed its victim, it ravaged each piece of clothing, each drop of blood, each fiber of flesh. The flames hissed.

"My daughter, *please.* Please help me!"

But she simply watched her father die.

"You'll want to leave, child," he said, standing beside the girl and admiring his work. "Your home will be turned to ash."

"I *will.*"

The man smiled. However, his eyes didn't flirt with closing, nor did the previous warmth reside. It instead arrived with cunning. His lips turned narrow. His eyes sharpened rather than softened. And his teeth revealed themselves like fangs.

After a second of lingering, the man retrieved his sword from the charred corpse. He pushed himself through the front door, leaving the girl alone.

She leapt from her seat, inching toward her father as he burned. "I'm not going to cry again. Not over you. Not over *anyone.*" She furrowed her brow. "Never again." She turned her back to the lifeless, black corpse and walked away.

Her steps paused in the doorway, motionless. The girl knew that if she looked over her shoulder, placing her gaze anywhere within the only four walls she knew, she would be leaving a piece of her behind. So, Cariaah walked on—and the door swung shut behind her.

Nothing of her village remained, nothing but ash.

The man stood before his mare, ready to mount.

"Wait!" Cariaah yelled to him, falling to her knees into the ashy mud.

He turned to the girl and approached her, a smile upon his face. "All has passed, child." He knelt, placing a hand upon her shoulder. "Everything is taken care of."

Cariaah's figure froze at his touch. She only managed to say, "What is your name?"

"Zenira."

She gazed at the blade on his hip. How she longed to wield it, to even hold it within her tiny hands.

He rose to his feet, the adamant aura of kindness and sensitivity following him. Even though he turned away from the girl, he never turned his back on her. And when he rode through the bloody corpse of the village—through the haze—the girl's wondrous gaze lingered on that blade.

How she longed to wield it, then.

2 THE PIT – FIVE YEARS LATER

Listen to them she told herself. *All they want is blood.* Her breath trickled to a shrewd pace. *That's how you know you're right where you're supposed to be.*

The gate opened before her, squealing. The once muffled crowd cried out.

Cariaah was unveiled to the golden sky of the capitol: a canopy of light. It pierced through her fiery hair, warming the bits of exposed skin from that leather armor. From her hip came a blade, one she yanked from its sheath. She narrowed her eyes.

A tower of a man—large axe in hand—traversed the curtain of shadow. A beard clung to his jaw, falling to his fur-coated chest. All served to annunciate his ferocity.

No gasps came from the surrounding crowd. Instead, cries of encouragement sliced through the air, reverberating in a crescendo.

The initiating horn howled.

Fiery sparks zipped off the steel, hot. Nobles, peasantry, and the new wave of fighters who arrived, observed with fervency. Electricity encompassed the pit.

Cariaah ducked beneath the axe of her opponent, driving her blade up into his knee.

The oaf grimaced, showing teeth.

She drove her sword deeper.

He flailed with his hands, reaching for any piece of the girl.

Cariaah ripped the steel away from the flesh. She climbed him like a tree, using his armor's straps to hoist.

Her opponent writhed with his entire figure, struggling to support her weight on top of his own.

Cariaah shoved her blood-sheathed blade into his skull.

His panic ceased.

And with satiation came a smile through blood. She was beneath its spell, the one she craved. The culmination of all things lit a fire within her. The sounds and sights and feelings drove the girl into euphoria.

Roaring was the crowd, crying within that spell of blood right along with the girl. And within held the half-elf and dwarf, looking upon the girl below, her smile more visible than the mass of flesh she stood upon.

"Quite the girl!" exclaimed the dwarf over the cacophony.

"I can't believe it," the half-elf murmured.

"Looks like you're not the only young one around here anymore."

Snjick looked upon the girl, her beacon of a smile, and fang of a crimson-soaked blade. That flame-hued hair lit a fire within him. It tore his senses away from the pandemonium, isolating nothing but her.

***

Below the pit was a cavern-like basement. "The hole" as it was dubbed by fighters. And those two opposing "sides" were ambiguous, participants drifting to whichever one the present fight required.

As if such a thing mattered. A peasantry comprised of beggars and janitors and other unassuming walks of life had little else to do. Even the kids were permitted to watch, and fight if they were so willing, though those fights rarely got permitted by the arrangers.

Sitting atop a mountain of gold and blood were the owners of the pit district in the capitol. They could care less who fought in their death arena, let alone children. It seemed, however vague and generalizing, that the morality of the pit's staff improved as you neared the fighters. The owners—both known to be elves—were particularly disgusting folk. They lived in the mountains somewhere, their carts of gold delivered to them by dalaryn, and their gratifications satiated by the same beak-donning creatures.

Below these elves, hierarchically, were the financial staff. They had studies in the pit district, shuffling the mounds of bet-cuts, calculating other sums of gold, and so-forth. They too were devoid of empathy, according to fighter-culture, but they also didn't have an ocean's-worth of blood on their hands to deal with.

Below them was the arranger, quartermaster, or "pit-keep." He organized the matches and recorded the fights in books, which took up shelves upon shelves, dating back centuries. He sat at his desk, scrawling away.

And finally—the most difficult to describe—the fighters. For, it was in their label to be particularly whip-like, stubborn and trudging. Some came from distant lands, introducing exotic weapons, techniques, and even languages.

The pit, arguably a character within itself, was a cesspool.

Snjick watched her from across the hole as she took the coins from Dahl, the quartermaster.

"Ale?" asked Bauer.

"Sure, sure."

"Are you going to drink it this time?" he asked with underlying flummox.

"Bauer," Snjick began, averting his gaze from the girl, "I *do* always drink it."

"So, drink it, and stop eyeing!" he exclaimed, sliding the pint to him.

He held his tongue with a chug of ale, drowning his embarrassment.

"It's a shame she's on the opposing side. *You* might have to fight her, kid."

Snjick bit his lip, in lieu of his tongue. "I know."

At the desk across the hole, she pawed through the coins. "Fifteen?" she growled.

"What, that's not enough?" Dahl asked, his voice gruff.

"Did you see what just happened—what I just *did?*"

"I saw that you came out alive. I don't care *how* you did it. You could have run around the pit for hours until he dropped of exhaustion. Fifteen is the pay—*fifteen.*"

"Come on, you ass." She clenched her fists.

A hand greeted her shoulder.

She whipped around, dropping the coin purse. "Get your hands *off!*" she exclaimed, shoving whomever it was.

Snjick stood, unsure as to how to respond. He was overwhelmed by the sight of her close face and the sudden silence.

"What? I thought elves had sharp tongues," she spat.

"I—"

She snatched him by the collar, yanking him close.

His nerves tangled.

No matter how softly she spoke now, everyone in the hole would hear. "Don't you *ever* touch me," she whispered ferociously. The girl released him.

He stood idly.

After a scoff, and once she had picked up her dropped earnings, she continued her way toward the exit. She paid no heed to the surrounding heads that followed her out the door, turning in unison.

The hole grooved back into its natural cycle. Tankards clinked, conversations commenced in a crescendo, and the value of the air slowly returned.

Snjick stood, his back against Dahl's desk, jaw agape, body still, but mind dense with traffic.

"*Snjick,*" Dahl said, boldly.

He flinched, turning his head sharply, meeting Dahl's eyes before reading what they said.

Piss off.

"Oh, sorry."

Bauer found it difficult to rid his face of a grin once Snjick returned. They sat, the dwarf beckoning the half-elf to reciprocate a gaze.

Bauer chuckled. "Were you planning on saying something, elf?"

"I'm only *half-elf!*" he exclaimed. "Now shut up and drink your ale."

***

The girl drifted from that rooftop to an emerald plain. Above was an endless, golden sky which soaked everything in its fluorescent, utopic hue. Surrounding her were luscious trees, their branches flirting in the warmest of breezes.

Typically, in her dreams, she felt small. But not in this one. For, below her straddle she rode a mare of ice-white. It cantered as if navigating clouds, and the recoil of each hoof barely existed.

In her hands there were no reins. Merely the sides of Zenira in her gentle touch. And at his hip, glistening brighter than the sky above, was that blade she longed so vehemently to wield. Though no matter how hard the girl tried…

She couldn't picture it in her grasp.

But she could picture his face as he looked back to her with an infectious smile. The angelic curvature of his face, beauty of his sparkling eyes, and smoothness of his pristine skin. All vivid.

Cariaah rolled over. Perhaps this dream would follow her into slumber, rather than simply adorning a conscious thought.

***

"Who is it?" Snjick asked, his voice soft. "Who's my opponent?"

"That's for you to find out once you get up there." Dahl's head was buried in a book—filled with bits of haiku—only a shred of attention dedicated to Snjick.

He knew who inevitably awaited him. Numbness plagued his gut. Perhaps he could have steered the girl away from the gold-filled allure of blood, of fighting, of *conflict* altogether.

"Now, scram."

He parted from Dahl's desk with a shuffle, dragging worn boots toward the shadow-veiled staircase of stone, which led to a fight he loathed.

He had complete freedom to shed his dagger and walk away. Yet, in doing so, he would become a coward, even though he felt like one regardless.

Those thoughts fell into futility. And the day arrived before his face. The crowd, the inevitable arrival of his opponent. They all roared for him—for a *fighter*.

The crowd's voice drove into him like a flurry of arrows. Voices pierced and impaled and eviscerated as he waited for someone to arrive before him. The girl.

Then, an opponent's face.

Bauer.

Snjick's throat closed. He held the hilt of his dagger for comfort, though it only brought the promise of blood and the inevitable spilling of it. Gasping turned to panting, that slam of reality crawling up his neck.

The horn came too soon, its call yanking the boy deeper into the pit.

Bauer did the same, though, it was more calculated and deliberate. His axe was flaunted, its ferocious sharpness smiling.

Snjick yanked his dagger away from its sheath. Racing were his thoughts, leaping was his heart, and curling was his stomach. He gazed with as much coaxing as he could muster. *Why,* he asked the dwarf's eyes, *why are you here?*

Bauer—his gaze nor his lips—gave no answer. A swing from his axe said more.

Snjick evaded, strafing away. Then, he evaded again. Again. And again, *refusing* to commence a rebuttal.

"Kill me," Bauer muttered.

Snjick's eyes gaped, struggling to drain the thought.

Again, Bauer growled as he swung his axe, "*Kill me.*"

He clutched his dagger, now with more intent—with more rage. "Please," he said over the crowd's obliviousness. "Please don't make me, Bauer."

Another swing of the axe.

Another evasion.

"You must," he said, swinging again. "*You must.*"

He felt so selfish. Not because of the inevitable call for blood, or the payment he would receive after. Instead, it was all of those thoughts, the ones of the girl. They seemed so minute. Irrelevant. He loathed himself more than anything now.

A strike, swift as lightning, with the sharpness of a wasp's stinger, dug itself—no, Snjick dug it—into Bauer's gut.

"Make sure you say something to her next time, *elf.*" And with those words, his life evaporated into the crowd's endless lust.

"Bauer," Snjick whispered to no one. He pulled his dagger from the corpse, avoiding Bauer's lifeless eyes as he toppled over.

The dagger yelled at him. *Selfish,* it said. *What a waste. What a waste,* indeed.

***

Cariaah enjoyed surrounding herself with noise. The tavern—or any bar for that matter—satisfied this. Instead of croaking frogs, teeming insects, or the breeze—things rhythmic and predictable—she listened to the drunken antics of others. Whether it be a belligerent dwarf whine over ale prices, the inn-keep drone on about political affairs, or a pack of miners return from a long day's work. Everything warmed her, the more sporadic, the better.

Though, as she sat, teeth working at a slice of bread until it became soft and gluey, something interrupted her. It made her next bite vitriolic. Her teeth ripped through the flesh of the dough.

That *elf*. His steps were bouncy, each one a hop toward the bar, through a cloud of pipe-smoke.

"Dammit," she uttered to herself.

Out he came from the swarm of folk, traversing the fogginess. In his fists were two pints of ale, brimming with foam.

A knot formed in her stomach as he approached. She grabbed her hip in that spot.

He flopped into the chair across from hers, placing the drinks down. The settling liquid was the only moving thing between them.

She pursed her lips.

Snjick relaxed in his seat, resting his forearm on the back of the chair. His eyes wandered, inspecting the tavern's high ceilings. "I like this place. Hate the ale."

She sat; lips still pursed. "So, why did you bring two cups of it?" she growled, staccato and rhythmic.

"There're two of us, aren't there?" he asked, but expected no answer. "Consider it the price for your name."

She released the pressure on her lips. "Why?"

"Am I not allowed to ask what it is?"

"It's," she hesitated, digging her fingers into the bruise at her hip. "It's Cariaah."

"Cariaah... strange."

She raised an eyebrow.

"You must not be from around here."

She coupled her hands in her lap. "No, I'm not."

"I haven't seen a girl like you. Not in the pit." His shifting in weight made his seat groan.

"Because I'm young? You know, you're not too much older than me, *elf*." She found it hard not to have a thorn.

"It's not that. Kids have fought in the pit before, younger than us, even. It's just they don't typically survive, and if they do it isn't because of strength." He peered into the frothiness of the ale. "But you *dominated*."

She made a fist around her blade's scabbard. "Well—"

"Also, I'm *half-elf*."

She scoffed. "Whatever."

"That's probably why half the time my tongue isn't so 'sharp.'"

"That doesn't make you any less of a bastard."

He resorted to his ale, sipping to disrupt the ensuing silence. "You gonna have some?" he asked.

"I don't drink."

He took another swig, a longer one this time.

"What were you going to say?" She clenched her jaw, eyes glued to her lap. "When you touched me on the shoulder?"

"I was just—" He thought of Bauer, so briefly but so shrewdly, it hit like a fist to the stomach. "I was baffled by what you were able to do." His eyes got lost somewhere—somewhere amongst the reel of thoughts in his head.

"Thank you," she said, quietly.

Now, his eyes met hers, only for the briefest of moments.

***

"Tell me why, Dahl."

He looked up from his book.

"Why did I fight Bauer?"

"The dwarf came to me," he said bluntly, "to propose a change."

"I don't understand."

He leaned back in his seat, gazing aside. "I think," Dahl began, hesitating.

"Tell me."

The pit-keep sighed, running fingers through his silver hair. "Just let me think."

"I need to know. *Please*."

"Do you remember those nights, Snjick, when you would be away?"

He nodded.

"Well, when it was quiet, here, Bauer would pull up a chair; you know, where you're standing now. We'd share a drink, maybe two, maybe more."

Needles pierced him everywhere. They crawled about his skin.

"Snjick, Bauer *wanted* to die."

All of the noise in the hole escaped the boy's focus. He ignored it, perhaps to make room for his mind to wrap around the old man's words. The dwarf, the one he knew—or thought he knew—and laughed with, wincing at the taste of ale as Bauer taunted him, was an illusion. Why wasn't he told what Dahl told him now? Was he too young and naïve to be hearing such darkness?

Snjick recalled a certain evening after a string of fights. He wasn't sure why this was. It could have been his attempt to escape, climb or leap into a time where things were familiar.

"This ale is *terrible*. By the gods, why did you drag me here?" Bauer had asked, tightening the face behind his beard.

"Well, it's a nice place. I mean, the high ceilings—just look at them."

"You know, it's pretty sad that the fucking *pit* could do better. And what did you pay for these pints? Fifteen?"

"Fifteen, twenty, twenty-five, who cares? It's not bad to me." Snjick reached for his cup and gulped down as much as he could, cringing through it.

Bauer laughed, maybe a bit painfully. It came from his gut.

And once Snjick had finished choking, he chuckled.

Dahl's gruffness interrupted Snjick's recollection. "I'm sorry."

The smile—the one he maintained for a brief moment—had faded at the solidity of the air. The cyclical noise of the hole—the conversations, pouring of ale, clinking of steel—was the finality. Bauer was gone, and the half-elf could do nothing to change it.

"He left this," Dahl said, presenting a piece of folded parchment. "He asked me to write it for him. I already know what it says—so, if you want me to read it to you, I will."

Snjick had learned to read when he was very young but was unsure if he had the ability to read Bauer's words. He sighed, yanking an empty chair from behind him and sitting down. His legs shook. He dug his nails into his palms. He nodded, though he knew he didn't need to.

The old quartermaster unfolded the parchment, reacquainting himself with the words. He cleared his throat, though it didn't alter the rough timbre of his voice. "'Snjick, I'm sorry that I've had to leave you, my boy, especially in the way I did. The pressure—what

I've forced you to do—is not something you deserve. You've been like a son of my own since you've stepped foot into the pit. I've told you of the son I used to have, though I never told you how he left me. He was killed, he and his mother—murdered by that group of assassins the peasants speak of. I have been living in so much pain since that night. That awful, *terrible* night. There was nowhere to turn for vengeance, only the pit for violence. So, please, accept my thanks for what you've done to ease my pain. *Thank you.*'" Dahl exhaled sharply, leaning back into his seat, struggling to look at the fractured boy before him.

3 THE LAND BELOW

In the evening, the stars were her blanket, which she pulled closer as the breeze cooled her skin. That cyclical night of noise added to her calmness as she lay on the rooftop.

But as she brimmed on slumber, as her eyelids grew heavy, something sliced through her lines of defense: clashing blades.

The girl darted upward, snatching the sword at her side, and leaping to the adjacent, lower roof. She landed in a tumble, collapsing onto her knee. Her balance abandoned her, feet skidding toward the edge. She clawed at the roof to get a grip. To save herself from the inevitable fall.

Smacking onto the cobblestone, her back cried to her. Cariaah's lungs recoiled with a deep cough—an almost-gag—as she scrambled to regain control. Her breath burnt, singeing her lungs with each inhale.

To her rattled frame's dismay, she sprung to her feet, those clashing blades her prompt. She hurried down that street, limping. The sound's constant, urgent rhythm encouraged her to push her knee—in all of its stiffness—just a bit further.

She rounded the corner, searching for the sound's cry. It resided in an alley, behind the veneer of the night, beckoning only shadows and sewage.

Though she halted before the alley's shadows.

"Snjick?"

He stood, dagger flaunted, and crimson irises bestial beneath a black suit of armor.

A group of men encircled him, their weapons glistening.

"Leave, *now!*" he exclaimed, warding off a flurry of strikes.

In a hiss, she ripped the blade from its scabbard, tossing the sheath away.

"*Now!*" he repeated.

A pair of them raced toward her, one with an axe, the other a longsword.

But as she raised her steel, prepared to strike, a blaze of fire grew near.

Just as the casted flame approached her amber gaze, she heard the half-elf call her name, ever-so-faintly.

***

Darkness. It, in all of its blackness wrapped a cold embrace around her.

Her left eye throbbed. As if someone peeled away her skin and unveiled the muscle and bone below.

Sharpness impaired everything. It started within her temple, branching out in thorns behind her left eye.

Cariaah laid on stone. Its roughness poked through her thick armor, rubbing away at her spine. She felt about, waving, reaching. But the girl couldn't find her sword's comforting hilt.

She felt a morbid urge to touch her face. A restricting quilt of angst wrapped itself around her, tightly in certain places—her throat, wrists, and torso—but irritatingly loose in others.

In a languid motion, she brought her fingers to the eye.

She panted, sucking in air through the narrow tube of her throat. Then, finally, she made contact.

Her eyelid was seared shut.

Unable to bear any thoughts, she darted her fingertips to the other eye. She felt her eyelashes as she blinked, making the heat of dread a tad more bearable. She knew now that she could trust her sight, albeit half as much.

A metal door squealed open, flooding the room with warm light. But that light held serrations within. It not only amplified the harshness of pain behind her vision but drew a grimace.

It sunk into the girl.

Half of her vision had vanished.

The next stallion of horror came over her. It had duality. Half patronized the loss of her vision, and the other carried terror of the unknown.

She resorted to that spot on her hip again, mauling the bruise with her nails. She winced, trying to comfort herself as the door opened further.

"Cariaah?" asked the familiar voice.

"Snjick," she said to herself.

He approached her in a ginger shuffle. A lantern's hinge groaned with each step.

"T-turn it off."

Snjick obeyed, the vapors from the freshly dormant lantern swirling. The half-elf gazed, paralyzed.

"Where are we?" she asked, digging a finger into her temple.

Snjick paused, inspecting her eye. The burn's vacuum had ravaged her eye, sealing it shut, leaving no pigment. The skin was smooth, foreign, raw.

"Now that you're here, there's someone you must meet." He guided the girl to her feet, gently escorting her through the darkness and into the light—into a new room.

A collection of people—all donning the same shade of unrelenting black—greeted her. Their attentiveness brimmed with ice. It made Cariaah shiver.

Elves, dwarves, orcs, humans, and even dalaryn—their beaks yellow and feathers puffed—all stared.

The violence of her eye's tenderness emerged. Her fingers clawed at the flesh of her hip, lacerating.

In the space mediating her and the crowd, a swirling, dark mist arose.

The girl stood, paralyzed.

A dark, cloaked figure traversed the shadowy portal. Sewn crimson stripes darted about the cloth.

They dropped their hood.

Cariaah's heart flipped.

It couldn't have been anyone else. By the curvature of his face, by the chiseled, refined structure of his bones, but moreover by the grace of his demeanor. *Him.*

Zenira's smirk radiated.

She stripped the pain away as she ran to him.

He accepted her embrace, holding the girl's head to his chest.

Snjick buried his gaze elsewhere.

Everything—where she was, the crowd who watched them, the worries in her mind—all fell to the wayside. His warmth spoke to her. *I knew you would come*, it said, *I knew you never truly left me.*

But the image of him which had manifested over the past five winters became a different reality. The man before her was Zenira, yet little things looked alien. His eyes were a shade lighter; his cheekbones were a touch too high, and his lips weren't as full as she had remembered.

"This is your new life," he said. "Amongst those who stand around us, you will find a home." He let go of Cariaah, though his warmth remained.

She surveyed the room. On the stone walls, banners hung—all black. Under them sat stone tables—though they reminded Cariaah of alters—hosting candles that dripped with gluey wax.

"There is something I cannot bear to tell you, however."

She looked to him.

"What you have tangled yourself in is *not* ideal."

Perplexity arrived in a flood.

"This order—this group that you see, here—are not just people."

She looked at the crowd of black, again.

"They are assassins. Each of them serves under one mission." Zenira took a step aside, allowing the girl to observe, wholly. "To rid the land above of its filth."

Cariaah's ears couldn't dissect much. The fact that Zenira *wasn't* this image of purity and white—solely and entirely—offset her. Zenira, the one she remembered, wasn't a knight, but an *assassin*.

"Many people masquerade themselves with a life they wish they had. However, behind this façade they live a life of darkness. We have sought out this darkness. And when I say, 'darkness,' I do not mean brokenness, sorrow, or even anger."

She swallowed.

"But evil."

She backed away, her steps slow and careful.

"You, Cariaah, are a gift to us."

The value of the air changed.

"You can become a Vantaknight." He sighed. "However, if you

decide against it..."

Snjick looked to the floor. He bit his lip.

She shivered.

"I'm afraid I cannot change your fate," Zenira said. "You are forever intertwined with darkness."

Feelings and thoughts and undercurrents of fears smoldered. Everything culminated into a drape which choked her. Though despite this darkness, she snickered, then chuckled, then laughed. "I'm being asked if I want to fight?" the girl asked.

Zenira smiled.

"It's all I've ever done."

The room carried a low buzz. Whispers emerged.

"Then follow me, my child," Zenira said, offering his hand to her.

Cariaah retraced those steps she took backward, allowing his hand on her back as a guide.

The group of knights parted, allowing the pair to traverse.

She took note of their collective demeanor—a congruent stature amongst them. Their weapons—primarily small blades and bows—shimmered. Little designs were etched into their steel weapons as patterns were into their leather armor.

As they continued, her eye wandered to Zenira. She searched for a hilt at his side, or one poking out from his cloak, though she saw none.

"This order is the greatest influencer of peace in the land above. For a hundred years, wars between nations have ceased."

She raised an eyebrow.

"The conquerors filled with greed and envy—it is they who need rightful punishment. They deserve no place in such a beautiful land."

"So, you decide?" she asked.

"On what?"

"To kill those with such power."

"I never said, 'kill,' Cariaah. I only said, 'punish.'"

She bit the inside of her cheek.

"But I understand your question. There is a council, the X. I, as well as four others make up this council."

On the walls, man-slaughtering weapons sat, mounted as antiques. Other trinkets—objects that couldn't be placed—sat on adjacent shelves.

"We're at the heart of it all, child," he said. "The home of the *Vantaknights*."

She stood before a pair of doors, a castle tall, painted red. Her jaw dropped.

Then, a groan echoed. It chewed on the air. The sound of hinges became masqueraded by new pandemonium, the sensory feast the doors once hid.

That room was a towering beast. Ceilings as tall as the sky—adorned in intricate paintings—peered at those below. Long wooden tables stretched across carpet of crimson, black-armored knights crowding them. Black banners—long and thin—hung from the back wall.

However, above all else was a loft—the ultimate pair of eyes—seated in the back of the hall. Five chairs—no, thrones—rested upon it, all of them filled.

Cariaah widened her eye, looking to where Zenira had stood just a second ago.

He was sitting down in his throne, a smile upon his face.

In the remainder of those seats were the remainder of the assumed council. An elf—her ears perky and features sharp—a dwarf—his face hidden behind a beard—an orc—her face round and teeth jagged—and even a dalaryn, whose black-beaked face and white feathers encompassed him.

The former cacophony of noise had subsided, for only whispers remained. All eyes—the knights that sat at the tables, the ceilings, the council, and the loft on which they sat—honed on Cariaah.

A black flame appeared in the center of the room, erupting from the thinness of the air. Every ember—every incidental crack made her skin crawl. Perplexity, flummox, *horror*. It all came in a tidal wave.

"It is the step you must take," said a deep, growling voice from the loft. It was the dalaryn, speaking through the cracks in his beak. "Cariaah, if you truly are set on your decision to join this order—to kill in the name of the lands above and below—then you *must* step forward."

Her fingers and throat tingled. She dug into her hip—into the bruise that refused to obscure all else.

"Fear not," said the orc, softly. "All you must do is take the step, and the flame will carry you."

An invisible hand wrapped around the girl's throat, carrying an anxious pressure.

She took a step forward, heel-first on the carpet.

Zenira's smile hadn't faded—and it wouldn't—as she continued her trickle of a walk.

In a great ascent, a rhythmic chant ruptured the silence. All at those tables called it: that unknown tongue.

Her eye darted about the room, searching, trying to make sense of it.

And that fire pulled the girl slowly, right to its face.

In she stared, finding no light.

That chant fueled her fears. Her thoughts. Her feelings. It all came down in a marinade of broken glass, coursing through her as images and sounds and memories. How Zenira looked on that day—how distant he was from her—how much higher.

And that final thought—of wanting to get closer—caused the girl to leap.

Cariaah felt herself drifting.

A flurry of voices—of scattered words—echoed.

"Your face...the way it curves, the way your gaze simply *is*."

"A bird of *fire*."

"To rid the land of its ocean."

She woke, ripping her head from its slumber. Silence hung in the air, and smoky vapors surrounded her. Her skin—besides her eye's scathing—remained untouched. Her once racing heart turned rhythmic in its slowness. She looked about, unsure where to move or what to do. However, her eye eventually met Snjick's, who leaned against the wall at the opposite end of the room.

A smile clung to his face.

Cariaah made a meager attempt to reciprocate.

"The flame—now that it is no more—has allowed you to stay," said the dalaryn from the loft. "May darkness be your companion, kin anew."

The room broke, conversations shooting off the ceiling and walls. Relaxation swept through the hall.

She looked to the loft, beckoning Zenira's eyes. Yet, no council members resided there.

After a moment of puzzlement, the girl meandered toward Snjick in refuge.

His smile had abated.

"Are you okay?" she asked once she stood before him.

"Yeah, it's just," he hesitated, falling back onto something else. "I've got your sword." He unclipped it from his belt, handing it to her, thereafter.

She had forgotten. As she took it, the weight felt familiar. She smiled internally.

"I can't help but feel responsible," he said, hurrying along through his thoughts.

"Responsible?"

"I shouldn't have brought that spar into the streets. I shouldn't've—"

"You can't blame yourself for my intervening."

"I still should've been more careful," he said, avoiding her eyes.

"I don't blame you, Snjick. I'm just confused. It's so much—everything is just so much."

He took an initial step toward her, only resorting to words. "It was either bring you here, or—"

"I know it was hard," she interrupted.

He smiled, if not to comfort her, then to comfort himself.

"I heard voices in there." She made fists at her sides.

Snjick raised his brow, placing a hand upon hers on impulse.

She flinched, raising her shoulders to her ears for a brief moment. Ultimately, though, she settled. Cariaah looked to him, the perplexity in her gaze all-the-more apparent.

His heart leapt, sending tingles. "Don't worry," he said. "It's just a spell."

"It felt so dreamlike."

"I know. It's strange, but you're going to be alright, Cariaah. I promise."

She mustered a smile, just for him.

***

The night embraced her as she lay in an assigned cot within a likewise room. She felt no breeze, saw no stars, heard no endless orchestra of noises. She only held her blade tight, burying her cheek into its hilt. She hoped that its coolness—the leather of the handle and the steel of the pommel—could resurrect some comfort.

The voices—the ones from the flame—echoed within her,

bouncing off other thoughts and fears.
A bird of fire…
Your face…
To rid the land of its ocean…
She hid behind her sword, trying to preserve its coldness for the remainder of the night.

***

She brought her fingers up to the flesh encircling her left eye. She shuddered and almost gagged as a shiver traveled up her beaten figure.

She stood from the cot, pulling herself up by the hip. She clipped the blade to her belt.

She turned the knob of her door, its stiffness startling her. "What?" she said. "Hey!" She slammed her fist into the solidity of the door. She reared back another strike, ready to pound the unmoving steel once more.

It groaned open, the lock turning in unison.

Before her stood a brute of an orc, his jaw sprouting flurry of jagged teeth. "The hall, *at once*." He reached for her bicep with a tight claw.

"*Don't*," she growled.

After she had traversed the orc and his broodiness, Cariaah maneuvered through a labyrinth of corridors, lost and fretful. She wandered aimlessly, her eye dissected her surroundings. The ceilings were high, surprisingly so for an underground corridor.

Candles, masks, pendants, and paintings juxtaposed war-axes the size of the girl who looked upon them.

"What?" said an echoing voice from behind her. "You don't understand the layout of this place within a *night?*" he asked once more through a smirk. "Perhaps you aren't qualified after all."

She turned to the voice, acquainting her eye with an elf she hadn't recognized.

"Isaac," he said, bowing like a buffoon. His right hand clasped a vial, filled with amber liquor. A black robe, stippled with violet, wrapped around his figure. He couldn't have been less than ten years older, despite his ridiculous demeanor.

Her brow remained unmoved. "Cariaah."

"Please. Everyone—and I do mean *everyone* knows your name," he said.

"Really?"

"Nope." He chuckled, as if he were keeping a shark in a jar. He pulled her along on an escort. "Being new isn't all that new, just so you know." He uncorked the vial, gulping down its contents, swiftly. "These sorts of things happen often. Maybe not under *your* circumstances; but regardless." He stuffed the vial away. "Like, for example, you've come all the way down here—tip-toe, tip-toe, tip-toe—*all the way.*"

She sighed.

"This place has been here for how many centuries—seven, eight, twelve? Well, my point is, it's new to *you,* not the land." His hands were electric in aiding his mouth. "That really is *something,* isn't it?"

The crimson doors into the hall arrived before them, two towering beasts.

"Well, you're *riveting,*" he said. "I'm sure I'll see you once more, Cathara."

"It's Cariaah!"

The elf had already departed.

Through the redness of the doors, an echo propelled itself to the loft. The hall was empty, only hosting an undercurrent of whispers from where the X sat.

"Come up," said a councilmember.

She flinched as the doors closed behind her, obeying the order once she spotted the adjacent stairwell.

As Cariaah traversed the steps, the weight of the hall's air slammed into her. She clawed at that spot again, warding off any danger.

Their seats lined the loft, symmetrical in their spacing. The X's robes all matched, and they fell to the stone floor like fluid.

"This place—all of the knights—are a garden," said Zenira. "A gardener must understand what it is he is planting in order for it to flourish and ripen. To serve our god with the blood he desires."

"We have all killed," said the dalaryn sharply. "All of us have been smothered by the flame, shrouded by the darkness of our armor, and faced the evil within ourselves." He interlocked his claws before his beak. "You will have to kill. Not for personal gain or survival, but instead for the sake of this family. *That* is the most important thing, child. Know that we are not a guild or clan. We are a family."

Silence clung to the air like a curtain—one Cariaah had no chance to speak through.

"Your mind is young," said the dwarf through his beard. "It still needs a lid. This line of work requires patience, control, and most importantly, a clear understanding of people and how they work."

"The fact is, we don't know anything about you," said the orc.

Cariaah's eye darted to Zenira.

He was silent, though his eyes spoke to her. *They don't know*, they said.

She was grateful. She didn't want these people to know what she was—the pitiful existence she arose from.

"So, we must ask you, what evil have you faced?" the orc inquired.

No matter how sharply her fingers dug into the flesh of her hip, sending pain like a beacon, the density of the air wouldn't flee. It was a monumental thickness, one that didn't even allow for the crawling sharpness of her angst.

Zenira took over. "She—"

"It doesn't *matter*," interrupted Cariaah.

Zenira's brow raised at her blunt ambition.

"What I was, *who* I was, means nothing now." The thickness of the air shifted in her favor. "If I was a street urchin, a nobleman's daughter, or a warrior-in-training, it holds no weight. All that matters now is the shedding of who I was, in order to grow and 'rid the land of its filth.' That's your mission, isn't it?" she hissed back at them.

Zenira's smile sharpened with the newly bred silence.

4 THE HALF-ELF

The setting sun rippled hues of orange on the sea, eclipsed by the encroaching city of Mira.

The city's beloved nature came from its ancient, unmoving presence. It sat not in rolling green pastures but on the powder of a beach. It hummed as a beacon of torchlight, beckoning ships of all sorts. Citizens from the near fishing villages conglomerated to sell their abilities and product to willing buyers.

Mira's walls framed two tapering stacks of mossy brick, which were stippled with bits of light. The elegant structures brought many nobles who traveled to see the landmarks and drink pretentious wine.

On one of these cargo ships—its hull groaning with each crash of the tide—many sang and whistled their way toward the city. The crew had no other way to waste time besides drinking and harmonizing in antics. Even the saltiness of the air served as a drug to warm their insides.

The hull, from the cabin outward, also served as a hub of light—of life. The captain intermittently looked to the stars through a lens of wobbliness, checking on their course every-so-often.

It produced a cycle of noises.

Noises which reminded Snjick of the hole below the pit—of the drinking, laughing, and reminiscing with the bearded dwarf. And as he sat in the crow's nest, his dagger's face reflecting the moonlight, he whispered his name. He thought of their conversations that ran deep into the night, their hypothetical fights, and who would win them. He, finally and loathingly, thought of the battle Bauer had been fighting on his own, and how he had done nothing to help him.

His attention trickled to the dagger. He thought of the things he'd done with it—from the inception of his skillset. It all came with the crash of the tide.

***

The snow had finished falling. It left behind nothing more than a land-encompassing sheet. On the mountaintop overlooking Yuria—a city known only for its muck—the two elves marched through the thick powder, clenching their packs tightly.

Snjick's eyes continued—with each monotonous trudge through the snow—to adjust to new bits of the season, as it was only his eleventh winter. Whenever a flake of snow fell onto his glove, instead of tightening his fist and crushing it, he held it close and inspected the intricacies.

"You can see it now," said his father, pointing through the post-blizzard haze.

Snjick scanned the cityscape, dissecting the castle's colossal presence and its surrounding city-homes. All of it seemed so small and minute, even to him, a little half-elven boy. As he stood, his jaw agape and eyes filled with the picturesque scenery, his mind flirted with the idea that he could crush Yuria like a snowflake, too. "How much further?"

"Well, we're not going into the city itself."

"We're not?" he asked with an undercurrent of disappointment.

"There's a sewer entrance just outside," his father said quickly, before speaking with more sternness. "Snjick."

"Yes, father?" The boy's wonderment had transformed into a narrowed attentiveness.

"I told you this already. You *need* to pay better attention." His father turned to him, shuffling a bit closer. "It is no training exercise—not out here."

Snjick lowered his gaze. "I'm sorry."

His father clenched his jaw. "And that's the other thing."

Snjick picked his head up again.

"Don't ever be sorry. You can't tell your opponent that once he's dead." He then continued, swiftly leaping topics. "We need to stop here before it becomes too dark. We'll start a fire—not a big one, but just big enough to keep our asses warm."

The boy giggled, quietly, fearing what his father might say if he had heard him.

"I wanted to talk to you about something." He reached into a pant-pocket, unveiling a piece of flint. "Something very important."

"What is it?" Snjick asked, that stomach-knot he commonly got returning.

His father had already gathered a small clump of kindling, digging at the snow with rigid fingers. "It's about Zenira—what he's teaching you."

Snjick made an affirming grunt, afraid to speak.

"You won't be going to those classes of his—not anymore."

"What?" Snjick blurted out. "Why not? I'm *good* at it!"

"That's not the point, Snjick. This practice— 'dark magic' as he calls it—is evil."

"*Evil?*" Snjick yelled.

"Think about it, son." He stood from his work on the fire, pivoting to the boy. "Right now, if I had this 'magical' capability, I could rise to my feet and look you in the eye."

Discomfort smoldered within the boy.

"And with the tightening of my fingers," he began, forming a claw with an empty hand at his side, "I could have complete control of your body."

Snjick widened his eyes.

"Every thought you've ever had—every memory—is at my disposal. I can move every limb in your body. I can *force* you to stop breathing."

The boy paid attention to his lungs, struggling to take his mind off the air.

"But, ultimately, with the clenching of my fist—something you do to wipe your tears, or cope with being scared—I can kill you."

He looked to the distant cityscape, settling on its shape as an escape.

"So," his father said, coming close and putting a hand on his son's shoulder. "I need you to promise me something."

He nodded, his gaze remaining on the distant city.

"Are you listening?" he asked.

"Yes." He still didn't avert his eyes from Yuria's allure.

Upon a sigh, his father instructed, "Promise me you'll never use it again."

"I promise."

***

The ship anchored alongside the dock with a drunken crash. The antics of the crew had officially spilled into their work, as well as the night.

Snjick, with a final look into the steel, slid his dagger into its scabbard. As the traffic below dripped into a teeming cluster of noise, he exhaled. With a strong toe, he leapt from the nest, grabbing onto a suspended rope. It bounced, accepting his weight, albeit coarsely. He flailed his legs about, and the fall onto the deck he'd premeditated appeared much graver.

His abdomen revolted against him, prompting a decision.

He hurled himself into the salty darkness below. And with a splash—one with more heft than he would've liked—Snjick plummeted beneath the surface, swimming for shore.

The muffled, distant sounds of the crew intruded his ears as he resurfaced.

"You're losing my supplies, dammit!"

"That—that wasn't a container, Captain."

The greasiness of the water clung to his armor, weighing him down ever-so-slightly as he came to shore—mere feet away from the city's outer wall. He patted his hip, ensuring the promise of his dagger as he commenced a dash through the sand. Mira's outer shell greeted his back, its moss and fermented salt giving him plenty of texture to ascend.

His wrists trembled with each hoist upward. Every movement proved to be a chore, jamming his toes and fingers into tiny crevasses. He peeked above the wall, scanning the perimeter of the parapet. Little orbs of light—the lanterns of guards—danced in the distance, hopping along. He prepared a final pull, bouncing on his toes.

But something metallic and heavy echoed on the stone.

Snjick ducked below the veil of the wall.

They were the steps of a guard, surely. However, this one held no lantern.

Their march halted, directly above.

Snjick had his balance to attend to. Particles of dust shed from the brick where his fingers dug and bits of seaweed fell away from where his toes were curled. His tongue came out as if it could help him in this crusade.

As his abdomen cried to him and his muscles absorbed more weight by the second, the steps marched away. Monotonous. Slow. Heavy.

The half-elf yanked himself up—perhaps a moment too early—falling onto the parapet. Aches echoed within, an obstacle for his breath. He picked his head up as the heaving continued, eyeing his eventual target: the chapel. Its bell tower stood illuminated, not only beneath the moonlight, but within the hub of life that was Mira.

***

The sewer grate beckoned the pair of elves with its spilling noises. The sky had dimmed, unfurling a dark cloth over the city and its subsiding noise.

"Armor up," he commanded Snjick.

The boy nodded, undoing his pack's fastenings. From inside, he laid his cuirass and greaves onto the snow, which had been turned a shade of brown from the sewer's overflowing muck. As he reached for the crude shiv he had packed, his father interrupted.

"Snjick."

Snjick looked to him.

His father held a dagger, one that shimmered despite the oncoming night. "Before I give this to you, boy, there is something I need you to remember, especially tonight."

Snjick's jaw fell agape at the piece of steel he hadn't fully inspected. He struggled to focus on his father's eyes, tempted.

"This is the first of your many contracts. This one may be easy, but not all of them will be."

He knew his father was serious. This wasn't the level of deliberation he had gotten used to during regular scolding. It was a cut above.

"Your identity is stripped away the second you carry out a contract. That doesn't just mean who you are. You have to forget who I am, too."

The words his father said, he had heard them before, but the way his father said them now introduced a level of legitimacy.

"Remember to forget *everything*," he said to him, "except how to kill."

This was something he hadn't heard.

The elves then dressed, strapping their armor onto their tight frames, and slipping their masks over their pointed features. As they both stood outside the sewer, the sky revealed its true darkness.

The night officially took the land into its thrall.

Snjick looked to his father, already dressed.

The cape framed him with grace. Its ripples and flirtation with the wind never ceased in drawing Snjick's eye. It was more than the cape itself. The piece of fabric that framed the assassin with a converse looseness also brought balance to the blades at his sides.

The boy wished he had asked him about getting a cape sooner.

As Snjick finished dressing himself, his father faced him, working his eyes all the way down the boy's tiny physique. "The armor suits you," he said.

Snjick clipped the dagger to his belt, the hilt peering. Its steel was encompassed by gold and blackness—and as Snjick awaited his father's first order, he couldn't remove his hand from the hilt. It drew him in. However, when he brought his gaze up, the smirk he didn't even know he had fell away.

His father glared shrewdly, slicing through the cold. He nodded, the fog of his breath a vague veneer.

Snjick felt his breath climb and bring his heart along with it. He watched the warmth leave his lungs, swirl into the air as a vapor, and fade away.

His father pressed on the sewer door, a metallic squeal following suit.

Snjick picked through a tide of memories. The fundamentals of his stance—wide and solid—where to keep his hands at all times—at hip level—and how to think—*not at all*.

This contract's details had been relayed to Snjick through his father. Beneath the city of Yuria—in all of its muck and disease—sat a specimen of vermin more tattered than a stray mutt. His name was Wallace, a pathetic excuse for a ninety-six-year-old human.

After a lifetime of necromancy—of capturing people from the streets and conducting experiments on their bodies—he carried out a lonely, helpless life. Frail and near senseless, his crooked fingers worked constantly to mix a solution for immortality. His surroundings were filled with vials and other ornaments, though not much protection. The man's focus had narrowed on the end of his life, and how he would delay its inevitability.

The plan: simple. Snjick's father would lead, and they would search solely for torchlight. When they would approach Wallace's back in his sewer-hole, Snjick would take the lead and spill the blood on his father's command.

The blanket order over all of this: Snjick was to remain vigilant for anything his father told him.

So, when they commenced their creep through the murky shadows, Snjick's ears were open dually: one ear was attentive for orders, the other for impending danger. His eyes looked only for the morbid warmth of torchlight.

The sensory overload fueled a slow drip of sweat, collecting behind the boy's half-mask. While his face gathered with moisture, his mouth turned dry. Whenever Snjick tried to swallow, it would take him a second attempt to do so.

The sewer donned a layer of green—one that masqueraded slippery stone. It hissed its hiss, dripped its drippings, and hugged them with an increasingly tighter embrace as they continued their work.

They followed the curve of a narrow corridor, each minute noise around them amplified with an echo. As they bent a little further, a flirt of torchlight met the moisture of the wall ahead.

Snjick looked to his father, reality falling before his eyes and dropping into his gut.

His father nodded, anticipating his son's eyes. *It's okay,* that nod said. *You'll be alright.*

And so, Snjick latched onto the idea and the comfort it gave him. *I'll be alright,* he repeated to himself. *I'll be okay.*

They inched closer, the hues of torchlight and moss clashing in a skirmish.

His father unsheathed his pair of blades, their reveal slow and groaning.

Snjick pulled his thorn of a dagger from its scabbard. His mouth built to such a dryness that he abandoned trying to swallow, instead focusing on his breath.

They traversed this bend, unveiling the first look of the dwelling.

Clutter piled high, crawling about the floors and up to the ceiling. Tomes sat open with their spines ripped. Crumpled parchment served as a foundation for everything else. Cracked alembics and retorts—some spilling with purple liquid—fragments of skull and bone—turned to flakes—and carcasses of mice—some older than others—marinated.

Then, of course, Wallace. He faced away, but his frame corkscrewed into a haunting figure. His back slouched so harshly that his head couldn't be seen. His hands worked on a crowded tabletop, one scrawling in a tome while the other held his stability.

Snjick could almost hear the faintness of his heartbeat, pleading for someone to bring its inevitable demise.

There ran a cleared path through the clutter—from the dwelling's entrance to the table where Wallace worked. They crouched through it, honing their focus on the necromancer.

They stood a longsword away.

Snjick's heart thumped, slamming against his ribcage as if it were a drum.

"Now!" shouted his father.

The boy shifted weight between toes—prepared to lunge forward—before a flash of steel barreled through his father, its wielder appearing from behind the jungle of surrounding garbage. Snjick looked—his eyes wider than his agape jaw—at the one who had done a lunge of his own.

An orc—massive and primal—stood before the boy with a war-hammer, a canvas for his father's blood.

Dad, he thought.

"Dad!" he screamed, turning to where his father lay. Yet, the boy wasn't anticipating such a curled, crumpled appearance. Snjick ran to his side, flipping him onto his back.

His throat closed. "Dad," he said, softly. The boy peered heavily and vehemently, searching for any trickle of life within the fallen elf.

Though his father's eyes were in a place where Snjick couldn't decipher their openness or closedness.

A metallic stomp cut through his terror.

He looked to the orc, who was a step nearer than before. Snjick's eyes had flooded, shedding a couplet of tears as he whipped his head around. Despair sank its claws into him, propelling futility.

The orc's razor of a glare put the boy's feelings into words. *You failed*, it said. *You did this to him.*

His father's voice rushed into Snjick's mind, replacing the despair.

The boy rose to his feet, his eyes saturated with the color of blood. *Remember to forget everything,* he thought, *except how to kill.*

The orc heaved the hammer at the boy's skull.

Snjick dropped his dagger, forming a claw with the empty fingers at his side, unfazed.

The orc—in all of his movements and thoughts—became still. Paralyzed.

As he maintained that grip, the orc's entire soul scrolled through the boy's conscience. His friends, his wife, his cottage in the country, and the rest of his now-memories drove themselves into the boy's mind.

"Don't," the orc coughed out.

The fears of his opponent infiltrated, one of them being of the battlefield—of death.

This made him consider his opponent's life—just for a brief moment, making his grip loosen.

The orc gasped for life.

However, at the sight of the orc's war-hammer—which had fallen to the floor in a crash—and his father's blood upon it, there was no other decision.

Snjick closed his fist, crushing the skull of the colossal beast before him. Everything the orc was slipped away.

***

The moon served as his guide. It shone through the stained glass, filling the darkness with ripples of color. Even in the attic where he dropped, tiny blips of ornate light spilled through the little windows. They had no glass, thus allowing a stream of salty air to flow through with the fluorescent breath of the moon.

Crates, barrels, and cupboards brimmed the attic, gifting Snjick ample cover. This crowdedness muffled his tiptoes, coaxing him to be even quieter.

The contract had detailed a priest—that of whom slept in a bedroll within the church—who slaughtered those he didn't deem worthy of the gods' protection. The people loved him, trusted him, and regarded him as a saint. This made his presence in Mira all-the-more dangerous.

As people disappeared from the streets and their very homes, they came to Father Gavin for consolation. The gods would then flip a coin. If the person seeking support from him were "righteous" in his eyes, they were to be spared. Otherwise, they were to be killed by the same man they came to for divine protection and guidance.

Through the attic door—which held a scrawled mural upon it—Father Gavin's reaping grounds unveiled themselves. A sea of pews sat below, obstructing any possible bedroll, or sleeping priest therein.

Snjick vaulted to an assortment of rafters that split the moonlight. One beam supported his rat-like scurry. His eyes hunted.

There it lay. The bedroll's vague shape rendered barely visible beneath the glow of the moon.

Snjick leapt to an adjacent rafter, the wood settling with a groan. His vision adjusted, singling out the cloth's presence from the moonlight.

Nerves crawled up his throat, *pinching*.

In the bedroll there lay a priest.

His body was strewn in several pieces—some on the bedroll and some on the nearby pews. A trail of blood followed, appearing in more places the longer Snjick looked.

Then, with the electricity of that very thought coursing through him, a sharpness shot up his calf. An arrow. It threw him off the rafter, into the murkiness below.

The stone greeted his side with a slam, and the pain in his calf cried.

Snjick corkscrewed to his feet, yanking his dagger from its sheath. He stood at the behest of something else—something he didn't understand. His head throbbed, his back pulsated with each movement, and his leg drained. He peered into the darkness before him, awaiting the ripples of light to unveil his assailant.

He panted.

His eyes widened.

Arising from the shadows, hoods drawn and faces abyssally distorted, were five hooded figures. Amongst them stood a bow-wielding marksman.

A dalaryn came forth, his beak jutting from the shadow of his hood. "The half-elf," he said. "What a stench you give off. And always so quick to prance around like a *rat*."

Snjick bit down on nothing. "*What?*"

"You forget who you are—what you have."

The commands Snjick sent to his muscles were interrupted—halted by the grip of this dalaryn's dark spell.

"Why *should* we prance around like rats?" His torturer's steps echoed on the stone.

Snjick's throat narrowed into a straw.

"You are so very talented, and you don't even know it—or at least you refuse to acknowledge it." He flaunted his claw-formed, casting hand.

Snjick fought back just enough.

"It would be shameful to lose someone like you. So, I suggest you heed the words I recite. Fall in with your dark talents," he growled, "or meet an inescapable death. In the end, it won't matter if your little elven heart beats, or not. All that matters is the bird of fire—the one who is promised."

Snjick felt the dalaryn's grip tighten, pulling his vision into a vignette. He could only fight for so long before a curtain of darkness fell.

***

Wallace limped into another room before Snjick's grip found him as well. His hand had just come to a fist when his ears caught the tail-end of his father's deep groan. He let the wizard's corpse fall with a crack, running to his father's side.

Struggling to push words into the air, he coughed through blood. His face had befallen to paleness, brimming on lifelessness. "*I'm sorry.*"

The boy's bloodlust ceased.

"On something as simple as this." He scoffed, blood in his throat.

"Don't," Snjick said. "Don't leave, *please.*"

His father's sob erupted. There was nothing to stop it from coming—no strength, no dexterity. Those tears fought the inevitability of the scenario, the reserved despair, and the sorrow of his son's words. "I made you use the spell. It's my fault. Everything—it's my *fault. I'm sorry.*"

"Dad…" Snjick whispered, helplessly. "I won't use it again—I won't, I promise you. I *promise*."

The exhaustion—emotional and physical—overrode everything. His father's trickle of life fell away, spiraling into oblivion.

5 PARASITE

Dimness crawled up the walls and filled the room. Only the languid, meandering light of the dripping candles showed what laid within. Clutter—stacks of parchment, inkwells, tankards of ale—surrounded the five of them as they rested in their seats. Their conversation picked up where it left off, like the removal of a bookmark.

"How many does that make?" asked Raquel, stroking her pointed, elven chin.

"Thirty," answered Zenira.

"That many attempted—and failed—assassinations?" Geneva asked, his feather's puffing.

"It's intentional," Duke said swiftly, from behind his beard. "They want us to know of their presence."

"Yes—well, I believe we *know* now," Raquel said. "The question remains: who lies within this group?"

"They're from the inside is my answer." Duke's stout, dwarven fingertips drummed the table's smooth mahogany. "The breed of magic they're using was brought to life by *us*—Zenira in particular." He shot the wizard a glance.

"That narrows it down," said Raquel. "Are there any suspects, Zenira? Any students that seemed rebellious?"

"None come to mind," Zenira said deliberately. He sorted through his words. "But these pathetic rats… they have no idea what they've begun."

"*We* don't," said Raquel. "Their motive is still unclear, whoever they are." She snickered. "For all we know, they could be from

Dunarch, that fantastical dalaryn land. What do you think, Geneva?"

He found no amusement in considering such a fairy tale. "It's still too early to raise any sort of alarms. Our family is more than capable of fighting a few rogues."

"All whose contracts have been interrupted only reported three hooded figures amongst—"

The doors burst open, allowing a tide of torchlight to spill inside. It singed their vision, all of them cringing in discomfort.

"Hassai?" Zenira said, peering over his shoulder to the newly arrived dalaryn.

"Get your servant out of here," said Korbin, waving her clawed, green hand through the air.

"I apologize," said Hassai. "But there's been another incident, and the survivor is here." Hassai stepped aside, allowing the person to pass and stand before the council.

Iz stood no taller than the chairs her audience sat in. Her hair fell to her waist, pin straight and ice white. Her youthful glare—which scanned the room purposefully—matched the hue of the shadows.

Raquel's brow tightened. "This young girl was—"

"Out on a contract, alone—yes." Hassai nodded.

"To which trainer does she belong?" asked Duke, stroking his chin.

"Isaac," Geneva said.

"That drunken elf?" questioned Korbin, scoffing.

The girl continued to gaze at nothing, unfazed by their remarks or their clear inspections of her.

"She's a savant with the blade," said Zenira. "And even more so with the spells of fire and ice."

"Let her speak," said Duke, holding his hand up from its armrest.

She stood, idly—coldly. Silence clung to the walls, usurping the dimness. The dripping wax of the candles spoke in lieu. "There were six of them."

Duke raised an eyebrow.

"One with a bow, one a hammer, and another a blade." Her voice found individual words tedious, droning through them as if they were one. "The remaining three were spellcasters."

"Why send six?"

"They were trying to kill me." Her icy inflection froze the room.

"How do you know?" asked Zenira.

"They wanted to send a message by casting their dark spell." Iz made a fist. "But it didn't work on me. They couldn't take control of my body."

"*What?*" Raquel blurted out.

The room jumped into motion, the chairs groaning alongside the chorus of gasps.

"I could see them trying—time and time again—to stop me in my tracks. But it didn't work. So, they turned to the steel and bow."

"And?" asked Geneva.

"I killed the three of them." Her words froze solid.

Zenira gripped the armrests of his chair, clenching his jaw. "Have we identified them?"

"I didn't have time to check their faces. I know its cowardly, but I *ran*," she said, a squeal of emotion leaking out.

"No." Zenira eased himself. "You were braver than we could've ever asked."

"If you'll excuse me," Iz said, "I need to go find my trainer." She pivoted toward the door and walked through its openness. As the girl marched out—her figure rigid—her back unveiled the fang of a blade strapped to it.

Zenira curled his toes and gritted his teeth, still clawing at the wood of his chair.

***

The training room buzzed with the rhythm of steel. A sea of knights—some accompanied by trainers, others alone—swung their weapons, their focus restrained to their respective targets.

Cariaah showered the sea of darkness until she found a familiar face.

Isaac leaned against the back wall—perhaps the only idle person in the place—sipping on a vial of liquor. He offered a glance as she approached. "Ah, I've seen you before, haven't I?" Isaac asked, corking the vial, and stuffing it away. "Or am I thinking of someone else?"

"Where's Snjick?" she interrogated, evading his fluff.

"He's out on a contract. Mira, I believe?" Isaac frantically patted his robe. "Should be back by now." He shoved his hands in the various pockets. "*Shit.*"

"Hey."

"Where did I—"

"*Hey!*" she yelled.

His eyes darted to her. "I don't know where he is. I'm sure he's fine. Why are you looking for him?" His words were staccato, separated by hiccups.

"He wanted to meet me here."

"But he's not here. I see your dilemma," he said, dismissively, walking toward the middle of the room. "My student's back. So, if you wouldn't mind, Carmen, I have responsible things to take care of." He tried to shake the liquor out of his walk—to no avail.

Iz—with her white hair and black eyes—stood amongst the percussion, awaiting her mentor's arrival. Her blade's hilt peered at Cariaah from over her shoulder.

But something else beckoned from the edge of the room: Zenira. His silhouette, painted by the faintest torchlight, pulled her on a string, drawing Cariaah's languid steps toward him.

The rhythm of the room fell away into obscurity, isolating him as the only presence. The floating sensation—from riding with him upon that white mare in her dreams—returned with grace.

Only to be ripped away by a stiff hand.

She was tempted to yell, only she was silenced by a pair of eyes that ripped through such an urge.

The white-haired girl gripped Cariaah's wrist with a black gauntlet and cut into her with a black stare. Her irises had no separation from their pupils, massing into one entity within her eyes. They pulled Cariaah in.

But that string from across the room took hold of her again, reeling her away from Iz's grasp.

Zenira presented a joyful smile, with slender eyes and lips. "You seem to be searching for something."

"*Someone.* Snjick."

That smile clung to Zenira's face. He escorted her out the room with a gentle hand. "A talented boy. I used to train him quite some time ago."

"I didn't know you—"

"Oh, yes," he said, nodding. They split off into a corridor.

Cariaah raised an eyebrow. "Aren't there still people who still don't believe in spells?"

"Correct. However, the spell I teach isn't fire like you've seen or even ice."

The ceiling cascaded as they continued, inching closer to the tops of their heads.

The girl's perplexity silenced her.

They reached a door—small and iron—cut into the stone wall. But it wasn't the purposefully placed brick like the rest of the land below. Only crude, precipitous rock served as a frame to the unpolished, metal door. Its handle flaked with rust. The hinges were turned a burnt orange.

"Open it," Zenira said.

Her brow curled. And as her hand neared the door, it shook. Bits of rust fell away when her fingers touched the handle. She pulled, only greeted with stiffness. Again, and again, she yanked. "It's locked."

"This door opens only to those who can uncover the darkness within themselves."

She shook her head.

"The things that have happened to you, all you've ever been, and what pulls at your everyday climb. These are the things this door requires for your passage."

She went through this list.

Most situations she'd faced brimmed with despair, though none held the weight of looking up to her father in futility. Of trying to find something within herself to fight. Every time. But she never could, always resorting to the morbid comforts of fantasies—fantasies that made her hellish reality his.

Cariaah was an escapee—a fugitive on the run. She found the task of curing herself hauntingly daunting. Even if she faced who she was, how would she go about it? The blade was her primary coping mechanism—along with her hip's bruise—satisfying her lust for blood, but never extinguishing the scars from her past. She couldn't unveil herself—her filth—to Snjick. It would taint their relationship. Its future.

Cariaah simply wouldn't allow it.

But in the end, *she* prevented progress. Cariaah knew she wanted to fight—to swing her blade. Yet, it all sparked a looming question: if her father was nothing but ash—long since dead—why did the urge to swing the blade still remain?

The door opened, giving into her weight.

Zenira smiled.

The unveiled room echoed as vast. Its ceilings were carved as high and cavernous. The walls held no visible end. Stacks of tiny, metal pieces tapered high, making mountainous heaps of sparkles—like a jungle of reflection.

"Life exists to be manipulated—to be changed."

She still fed on the visual feast of the room.

"All of this," Zenira said, "is the beginning—the foundation for every sorcerer that conjures this magic."

"What are these?" she asked, cautious around the heaps of metal. They towered like statues, placed together in intricate puzzles.

"These pieces were once blades, now fragmented into bits of steel." He approached the one she inspected. "Knights of our family used to be their wielders. But now that they have passed, their souls remained trapped within them."

Her lips parted and her eye widened, dichotomizing the idea.

"The blade they lent the Vantaknights is who they were." Zenira's words were soft. "They were born here, trained here, and died serving our order. It is life." He brought his fingertips to the metal. "And it is malleable."

The metal shifted, flowed, and folded onto itself like water.

Her eye was a subordinate to all before her. Her gaze traced the bits of steel as they danced, transfixed.

The fragments halted, balancing to their initial state.

"It's beautiful," Cariaah admitted.

"It took many decades to perfect channeling lost souls into something useful."

She looked into the smoothness of his skin, the sharpness of his bones, and the youth that adorned his eyes. *Decades?*

"It's daunting to think of all the darkness we've extinguished," he said, pivoting away from her. "There must be a way to hone this morbidity, I thought." He scoffed through a grin. "It was just before my eyes, at the foundation of the Vantaknights. Everyone has darkness within them, Cariaah—*everyone*. And you can use that darkness to control."

Control. The very word piqued her interest, though it didn't do so without raising an alarm. "You don't mean…"

"With the tightening of your empty hand and the curling of your fingers," he said, imitating what his words illustrated. "You can take someone's body under your own command."

Cariaah's eye gaped once more as he warped into something more alien than the knight she remembered.

"Some don't have the capability, I've come to discover, but those who do…"

She clenched her jaw.

"It's an incredible thing to behold."

Her hip beckoned her grasp.

"It is the fire that fuels dark magic." His fingertips brushed another metal heap. "And I believe that you will be prodigious."

She grabbed her hip, clawing. "Why me?"

"A bird of fire is promised, Cariaah. One to rid the land of its ocean—one to cleanse the land of its *filth*."

Her muscles felt so light, like they too floated. Her stomach fled her insides, and her heart plummeted. "I know," she said. "I know."

***

The private study of the X converged in solitude and dribbled with quiet conversation. The stacks of parchment grew large and mountainous, and pitchers of wine replaced the typical tankards of ale.

Zenira's posture conversed the rest of the X, rigid in his chair. Yet his hands remained relaxed in his lap, coupled.

"The half-elf hasn't returned," Duke said.

"Which one is that?" Raquel asked.

"Snjick," affirmed Duke.

"Is it possible that—"

"It's always possible," said Korbin. "We lose a handful of our children every season. Though this case may be different."

"And if that *is* the case," said Geneva, "why would they go after him in particular?"

"Nothing is certain." Duke's deliberation sliced through the pondering. "But this group, marked by a truly *odd* sigil…" He held a piece of parchment before his eyes, "I can't help but wonder what it means."

Upon it, that mark was drawn in crimson ink. It was an eye

within a star.

"For centuries, our order has remained tight and coordinated. If these people *are* from within our family," Geneva said, chewing on his words, "I'm baffled."

"I have a solution."

The room's undercurrent of whispers stopped.

"The girl." Zenira commanded the room. "Cariaah is the answer to our mission."

Raquel leaned forward in her chair, "I don't believe I understand."

"She is an extremely talented individual." He clenched his fists beneath the fabric of his robe. "It is a true display to watch her work."

The room stopped for his words.

"She needs to complete her first contract."

"Sure, Zenira. But alone?" Raquel asked.

"Nobody goes alone." Duke returned with sharpness. "Not until this matter is settled. I don't care *who* it is."

"Agreed," said Geneva. "This is ideal for one of our upcoming contracts."

"The large one?" Raquel asked, her interest piqued according to her eyebrows.

"Aye, but if the girl is to be a part of it," began Duke, "then she'll need something light to start with."

The door blasted open, slamming into the stone. A silhouette panted, their shoulders rising and falling.

"Zenira," said Duke. "Get your servant out. I'm fed up with the interruptions."

"That's not the dalaryn," said Geneva.

Raquel twirled her lips into a smile. "It's the *half-elf*," she uttered.

***

The wall held Cariaah's back upright as she sat in the corridor, the absence of stars keeping her awake. Mounted on the stone across from her sat a plethora of ornaments. A dagger—adorned with a hilt-embedded ruby—sat amongst them. Its crimson hue beckoned her eye. And her hands beckoned her attention, clamoring to form a deadly claw. Whether she gave in or not, they felt different on her wrists. For, if her blade ever left the girl's hip, she had a weapon in them.

But they struggled to detract from the intensity of her eye's pain and its curtain of black. If Cariaah stayed up for too long during nights like this or didn't drink enough water, that sensation returned. The boiling, crawling pain that only vanished if she could manage to fall asleep. And without the night's breeze or canopy of stars above, it proved a difficult task.

Cariaah's fears leaked into her sleep, as well. If she fell into slumber, yes, the excruciation of her eye would fall away— albeit until the following evening—but then she would have to dream. And while it wasn't the same dream every night, there were four or five scenarios that played out on permanent repeat.

It could've been her father's inescapable power, returning and driving her under the illusion that he was still in fact alive. Or the loss of sight in her other eye and how helpless she would be wandering in darkness. Regardless, the dreams haunted her with the promise of returning, and the nature of the nightly dice-roll tormented the girl.

No matter how many fingers she dug into her hip or how tightly she hugged her blade, it didn't matter. All became futile.

And as Cariaah sat in that corridor, eyeing the red jewel embedded in that dagger's hilt, it reminded her of that day. When she stood, peering at Zenira's steel as he parted from the ash that was her village.

It reminded her of how badly she wanted to fight.

The distant echo of the hall's doors called out. She sprung to her feet, sprinting as she clipped her blade to her side.

Cariaah rounded corner after corner, desperately trying to navigate the labyrinth.

Please, she pleaded to no one. *Snjick!*

Upon one final scramble around a corner, the crimson doors asserted their stature.

They caved to her barreling forearms, the girl catching a glimpse of the half-elf as he hurried into a side-hallway—one unbeknownst to her.

She followed blindly, veering into that room where Snjick stood: a study, wherein all five members of the X sat.

Snjick panted. He limped further into the room, barely able to muster a walk. "I was," he said, "I know it was…"

Zenira barely turned his head, following Snjick's steps with his ears.

"Snjick?" asked Cariaah.

Zenira snapped his peering eyes to the girl.

Snjick stopped in his tracks, pivoting toward the doorway.

"What are you doing?" Cariaah asked. "Are you hurt?" She approached him, diverting the half-elf from Zenira. Her hand hovered over a broken arrow jutting from his leg. "What's going on?" Cariaah scanned the room for answers—in any form.

The X remained silent as they held their breath for details.

Snjick's posture fell. His meager focus struggled to hone on anyone. "Cariaah?" he whimpered, collapsing onto the ground in a thud.

She called his name, again and again, to no answer.

6 THE BLOOD IN THE SAND

Kenzik walked Temiragrad's streets as their kindest man. The slums couldn't hold his constant perseverance to keep everyone alive. At sixty winters old, his research in medicine was a formidable arsenal of defense.

He hadn't always lived in Temiragrad—with its dry, sharp winds and sandy drapery—which aided his abilities. Coming from the northern hold of Yuria gave the dwarf plenty of horrid images to fall back upon. Those abysmal winters stained his memory.

In Temiragrad, however, he spent his days beneath the scalding sun, tending to anyone who caught the sharpness of the wind with terrible luck. "Blood-grain" was a disease which took the skin first and heart second. It swept through the slums and peasantry—mostly dalaryn—like a typhoon, for the nobility and courtship in this hold maintained a dangerous level of isolation.

Kenzik, ultimately, had to face this crisis alone. Only a few young dalaryn tended to the wounds of the sick. However, one patient in particular displayed an array of hopeful signs. Jenn—grey and withered—fell victim to a smattering of sores which tore at her skin, plucking feathers away. Her pulse turned irregular, and her words nonsense. It was only as of late that the symptoms receded. After days of applying ointments and jade powders, her sores dried and reverted to the color of her skin, even sprouting new feathers.

Kenzik learned of her avid presence in the slums upon her diagnosis. She was a grandmother of three young children: Kim, Gregory, and Sam. And it was after her irrefutable progress that

Kenzik promised to show her something very important in the night.

***

The hive: a submerged, wide corridor flooded with knights. Large alcoves were carved into the walls, soliciting shopkeepers fronting them.

A wicked smell filled the air. An amalgamation of so many things—boiling steel, roasting meat, hot lagers, and the usual scents of people—brimmed the warmth surrounding them.

The pair stood before it all, perched on the steps descending into the beacon of life. Cariaah's senses, without her anxiety's consent, studied Snjick's every movement. She'd never seen him filled with such vitriol or try so hard to hide it.

"I think you'll enjoy this leatherworker," Snjick said through a grin. As he descended further down the steps, Cariaah prepared herself to help him due to his injury. Snjick's limp had improved from his wound's tending.

The noise of the hive consumed them, welcoming the pair into its arms.

Cariaah's eye danced between two places: Snjick, and anywhere else.

And there was plenty for her eye to feast on now that they were closer.

One merchant—his white beard long and thin—claimed to be selling a breed of ale that helped one stay awake, in light of "contract after contract late into the night." This held her attention until the aroma of pressed leather veered it another way. A dwarf—whose hair split into nine braids—sewed together pieces of tanned hide with a thick needle.

"Can I ask you something?" Snjick said.

Cariaah's curiosity turned to panic. "What is it?" She asked, fearing the question's contents.

He exhaled, biting his lip to try and avoid her eye's sharpness. "You know, it's okay, never mind."

Now it was angst. It was the sort that flooded her mind faster than the crowd around her. It remained a desperate, frantic, smoldering creature within her. It urged her to do something.

She didn't want to revert to the bruise—in fact, she deliberately avoided it. If Snjick had caught on to this little mechanism of hers, it would constantly reveal her stress level to him, thus exposing herself as deceptive. Then she would lose him. *Surely.*

"Okay," was all she could muster.

Snjick exhaled again, veering away from her.

Panic rushed to the surface, testing her tolerance for it. This time, her hip's beckon was mandatory.

"Are you coming?" Snjick projected over the crowd, standing before a particular alcove.

She nodded overtop a gulp.

A crowd of knights passed as a veil of intermittent blackness, one she maneuvered through to follow Snjick, who waited with a turned back.

The scent coaxed the pair of them to enter, rather than a solicitor. A jungle of leather adorned the shop, some formed into armor—pressed, stitched, and cohesive—and others still pelts. A row of wooden models towered in the back, showcasing finished pieces. This armor, converse to the browns and tans of the rest, had its fibers stained the hues of the land below. That black allowed no light and expelled no shadow.

Cariaah and Snjick—he of whom knew the basic layout of the store, though not the newest of stock—didn't have time to explore. For an orc—whose head almost scraped the ceiling—stood and stared at the girl.

"What?" Cariaah sneered.

He remained silent.

A voice answered for him. "Don!" it barked.

The orc backed away, turning to the voice's emission.

"Stop scaring away the coin," scolded the voice, its speaker emerging from a back room. She was an elven woman—wrinkled and hunched—who hobbled around with the help of a polished tree branch. It clacked on the floor with each step. "Make yourself useful. Go stain those *damned* gauntlets. My eyes hurt too much to do it."

"Yes, Ellen," the orc said, firming his posture but lowering his head. He scurried into the room from where elf had emerged.

"Alright, who've we got here, Snjick?" She made her languid journey across the shop, her breath scurrying. "A human girl?"

"Cariaah," the girl said.

"Pretty," Ellen reacted.

Cariaah smiled.

"You smell abysmal," said Ellen, her face tightening into a knot.

Cariaah's face returned to blankness.

"It's that terrible leather job on you." Ellen took the girl by the fingers, escorting her to the back of the shop. "I'll fix you up."

Cariaah looked about, picking apart as much as she could. Her armor looked embarrassing in comparison to the gallery before her. Plagued by cuts and grooves and imperfections, it had begun to peel away from her frame.

"You've outgrown that armor. But in a more genuine sense, while the leatherwork is *atrocious,* you just need something new—something progressive—not something you've been wearing since you were a foot shorter."

The girl smiled again, her lips pursed and eyes escaping.

Don's voice emerged from the back room. "Do you need help with that, because of your eyes?"

"What do you know about my eyes, Don?" she asked, her voice commanding. "Fool." The intent of her murmur was a whisper but came out much louder.

They passed the working orc as he stood at a large vat of black, steaming, scentless syrup.

"Alright, Ellen, they're soaking," Don said, wiping his brow.

"Sure, sure, sure." She waved her hand through the air, letting go of Cariaah's.

Three armored models stood before them, now. Total blackness scaled their figures. Most materials were leather, but some steel sprinkled itself in, right along the gauntlets of one suit and up the chest of another. Masks sealed the blank faces of the models—all but one.

That model's face, in all of its emptiness, peered into Cariaah's eye.

She tried to avert her gaze but couldn't. She paid more attention to the wound on her face, now, and how it appeared to those surrounding her. The shakiness of her fingers returned, as well as the narrowing of her airway, which tightened its grip as the seconds passed.

"One of these will be yours." Ellen nudged her gently.

"Do they need to be fitted?"

Ellen chuckled.

Of course, they do, thought Cariaah. *You peasant.* Her fingers reminded her of her place, and of the bruise at which she clawed.

"Fate fits the leather to the figure, not me." Ellen's lips formed a gentle smirk. "I just make. In the many winters I've been doing this, the armor on these three stands—whatever it may be—always suits a newly-shrouded knight." The sternness, bluntness, and sharpness within Ellen's demeanor peeled away. "Which one, of course, is for your hand to decide."

She couldn't ignore the gaze of the unmasked model. Even as her attention continued—time and time again—to drift toward the other two, the cloth of the mannequin's face brought her back. Upon one of these returns, she inspected the armor below the blank face.

It appeared pedestrian. With mostly leather encompassing the suit's volume, bits of steel snuck into the shoulders, gauntlets, and shins. It seemed like most every other suit. Ellen spun the suit on its rotating base, heeding Cariaah's deep inspection of it, and revealing its exclusivity:

A feathered half-cape, which fell to the lower back.

Cariaah's hand wandered forward at that moment, only receding once the absence of a mask revealed itself again.

"I can craft you a mask," said Don from behind them.

Had her demeanor been that telling? "No," she said. "That's alright."

"Then why don't we get it on you, darling?" Ellen asked.

She was led into the fitting cubby—a tiny, curtained cylinder carved into the stone—where she tried to undress. Despite her thorough inspection of the curtain's closedness, each time she went to undress she couldn't help but check again. She feared the inevitability of a question. Whether it be, "Are you alright in there?" or "Do you need help?"

But eventually, she managed to peel the old armor away, and replace it with Ellen's creation.

The cuirass's embrace held her tightly. As she secured it onto her torso, a wince slipped through her teeth. Its contour to her body harshly reminded her of the bruise. The greaves—arguably leggings with their thinness—slipped on like the gauntlets she had equipped prior. Everything was a puzzle piece, and the girl welcomed the shadowy perfection.

A deep exhale fluttered the curtain as she secured that final article: the half-cape. She couldn't be sure of who stood outside at this moment. Ellen, certainly, and perhaps the orc, too. If she walked out immediately, perhaps she could avoid a dramatic presentation to Snjick.

Cariaah pushed the curtain aside for her feet to meet the stone.

There the half-elf stood, his brow raised.

She avoided the gallery of gazes. Snjick's, Ellen's, and even the orc who looked up from the vat.

Silence clung to the air like the heat of stares.

"I'm proud of you," said Snjick.

A smile rushed to her face, one she couldn't hide.

They exited the fitting area and eventually the alcove, sending their farewells and thanks to Ellen and Don. Yet, as they left, about to assimilate themselves into the crowd of black once more, Cariaah said, "Snjick?"

"Yes?"

"I'll get you your gold back. I'll earn it back."

"It's fine. You needed a suit of armor—*badly*. Especially considering your contract."

She smiled.

"I wish I had a cape," he said.

"Why don't you have Ellen craft one?"

"I never got permission."

Cariaah didn't understand, but she dually didn't feel the need to ask any further, as Snjick smirked at his own words. She didn't want to disrupt his joy.

"Cariaah?"

"Yeah?"

He bit his lip and exhaled. "How did you meet Zenira?"

"I," she said, hesitantly. Where was she to begin? *He burned my village down, but he saved me. From what?* She would reveal herself by unveiling their relationship. "It's a long story, and it was so long ago."

"Oh," said Snjick, deflating.

It tore at Cariaah's insides. She had nowhere to escape and nobody to be consoled by, even as this new family of knights continued to hum around them.

***

The hall—in all of its grandness—teemed. Knights—a few dozen—chatted over tankards of ale and bottles of wine. They sat at a table that stretched toward the loft. As Cariaah and Snjick arrived, the crimson doors closing behind them, he raised an eyebrow.

"This is for my contract, right?" asked Cariaah.

"It is," said Snjick. "That was the arrangement." His eyes drifted to the loft, where only Raquel sat in her chair, arms crossed.

The elf whistled. And the room amplified the noise.

All fell silent as Cariaah and Snjick found their seats.

"As a council, we have decided to merge two contracts into one large mission. Due to recent incidents, we can afford *no* risks."

Snjick closed his eyes, fending off the flood of images.

"Thus, we have assembled the unit of knights surrounding you now."

Cariaah's ears had been more vigilant than her eye. However, she studied the table's occupants as Raquel finished her sentence. She hardly recognized anyone until she came across Isaac—to which she scoffed—and Iz—to which she shivered.

"There will be one to lead you through both contracts," Raquel continued. "Ashura, if you would."

A brute of a human rose from the table. With languid steps, he marched to the head of the table, directly beneath the loft.

Ashura seized everyone's attention.

Black hair dropped to his cheekbones, a large sword clung to his hip, and his breaths came out in a slow, visibly controlled trickle. With a tight, unmoving brow, his command impaled. "Now," he said, gravel coating his voice, "onto the blood."

***

The forest helped the pack of assassins remain as shadows in the night. The canopy of branches and leaves above allowed enough sky to guide them south, Ashura at the helm of it all.

Cariaah's skin—or at least, what skin was exposed—thanked the breeze for its loquaciousness. She had forgotten its gentle flirt, how charmingly cool its nibble had been. The stars above beckoned her gaze, but the urge to look up, even for a second, didn't exist. Her concentration remained on her surroundings, and more importantly—most importantly—on the blade at her side.

They eventually reached their campsite: a bald patch in the grass surrounded by curling brush. It created a nest for each to find their respective nooks and holes to rest for the night. Though, Cariaah wouldn't sleep. Instead, she would be granting it to someone else.

"Benoit, Grimes, and Roy, you're on the first round of watch," Ashura ordered, quiet but firm. "The squad assembled for Cariaah's first contract need to be *right* where I'm standing in five minutes."

Cariaah's firm posture stood out amongst the three of them; Isaac leaned, weight on one hip, and Iz sullenly stood, affirming her blade's security on her back with a gentle hand.

"Alright," said Ashura, sighing. "We don't need anything going awry in the first phase of this." His stare whipped to Cariaah. "So, listen to Isaac."

She bit her tongue, holding back an immediate revolt. But the girl managed a nod.

"As for you, wise ass," said Ashura, whipping around to Isaac. "No liquor."

"Yeah, yeah. The X likes making things as bemusing as they can."

"That's not the X. That's an order from me."

"Save it, Ash, *save it*."

"It's a shame that a twelve-year-old is better behaved than you," scolded Ashura, gesturing to Iz, who stood idle. "Regardless, trust each other. *Rely* on each other. Don't be a fucking hero. And most importantly, all three of you are tools. You are not people."

***

Jenn's balance corkscrewed about, even under Kenzik's guidance.

"There's a big step here," Kenzik said, referring to the lip before the dark shack he led her into. "Good job, good job."

"Are we seeing my cuties?"

"Yes, we are." Kenzik sat her down on the table in the shadowy abyss. "Lay down, just rest on your back."

"Okay," she said, obeying. But it hurt to relax. Those muscles had been knots for so many nights of battling. This evening's breeze—which channeled through the doorway—eased her. The darkness became an enemy of the past, even as she lay in it.

The door slammed shut.

Jenn flinched but couldn't sit upright. "Is that Kimmy?" she asked, oblivious. She only received silence in return, until a languid drip of wet liquid fell onto her cheekbone. "H-hello?"

A strike of fire which lit a hanging torch plagued the darkness with light.

Strewn about the shack, pinned to the walls by thick nails were corpses, some still twitching. One man was halved, hung from the ceiling by a pair of hooks that impaled his feet. Everything dripped. Kenzik stood above her, a blood-soaked dagger in hand and a smile pinned to his face.

Jenn was paralyzed.

Kenzik unleashed a cackling, howling, draining laugh.

But with one gust of morose wind the torchlight ceased, and the veil of darkness returned.

"What?" murmured Kenzik, clenching the dagger tightly. His eyes danced about the shadows, looking, *searching*.

Then appeared an amber glint in the shadows.

"Who are you?" he called, scrambling for words. "She's just a dalaryn. No one cares if a dalaryn dies, not here!" With a morbid flash, Kenzik plunged the dagger into Jenn's skull. Bone split.

Out leapt a figure from the shadows, poised for Kenzik's throat.

Cariaah pinned him by the neck to the blood-caked sand of the floor.

Isaac and Iz hurried in, halted by the sights.

Cariaah tightened her grip around his neck. She glared as a predator. "Do you enjoy controlling lives? Controlling when they end? *How* they end?" she growled.

Kenzik tried to gasp, to no avail. The man had no opportunity to resist.

"Maybe I do, too." She squeezed, burying her thumbs into the skin of his throat. "This is what it feels like to have *no* control," she barked. "Do you enjoy it? Go ahead, fight back. Fight back," she chanted. "Fight back!" she growled.

"Cariaah," said Isaac, his eyes as agape as his jaw. "Cariaah!" he exclaimed, hurrying to her side.

She shoved him away with a stiff forearm.

Kenzik couldn't breathe. His mouth oozed foam, his legs writhed against empty lungs, and his fingers clawed at his assailant's.

"You can't?" asked Cariaah. "You *can't* fight back?" She laughed. Her thumbs broke the skin, plunging into the flesh of his throat.

Blood rushed to the surface, spilling down the sides of his neck and onto the floor, adding another layer of crimson paint to the floor.

She kept digging, pressing, *forcing* her fingers into his flesh until she saw fit to release him. Then, with her empty, bloody gauntlet she tightened her fingers. The swirling feeling assaulted her as she tried to take hold of his slipping soul.

But before she could experiment any further, she was rammed aside, slamming into the table where Jenn's corpse lay.

Iz stood over her, that fang of a blade flaunted at Cariaah's throat. The child's dark pits for eyes said enough.

7 FLOOD

The day hummed quietly. The birds sang the tune they always did, residing in the tree that held their nest. The village children gathered beneath it, bouncing on their toes to get a peek.

The blacksmith's home—the largest of the settlement—emitted a smog. Welding, crafting, and hammering weaponry brought Lain peace. His work wasn't the best in the land, but it still beckoned the capitol's attention. Once a week, a pack of city guards would come to pick up their expected load of finished steel. They also—depending on the mood of their captain—would occasionally stay for a hot cup of tea.

Lain enjoyed more than his craft. For, his daughter Willa liked to sit outside at the furnace with him, observing.

At nine winters old, Willa fancied the idea that she could one day inherit the forge. She dreamt of creating a sword so large that only a god would be able to swing it. And after many conversations between them, the sword was to be named "God-bringer."

They lived a quiet life.
It was simple.
It was enough.

***

Cariaah sat at the edge of the camp against a rigid boulder, peering into the brush as it shook.

Out leapt a hare, its jaw working at a clump of grass.

Her hand turned into a claw, tightening until she could feel the animal's muscles stiffen in paralysis. The black of her pupil gaped, lingering upon the hare's struggle.

She closed her fist. The softness of her target's fur turned to mush. Fragments of bone and slurpy intestines swam about the stew of hot blood.

Though most of them slept, the encampment lingered with alertness. Ashura remained vigilant, leaning against the unmoving tree as he stood on the opposite edge.

"Hey," said a voice, high-pitched and elven.

Ashura reached for his blade until Isaac unveiled himself. "You know," he said, startled, "you're not the most graceful elf, stomping around the woods."

"Save it," said Isaac, closing in on him. "There's something important I need to talk to you about."

"What's there to discuss? Nobody spotted you three out there," he turned worried at Isaac's likewise expression, "right?"

"No, everything's okay in that regard."

"So, what is it?"

"It's the girl."

"What did she do?" Ashura asked, certain of the subtext's nature.

"I explained to her the exact plan—how we were gonna do things," Isaac articulated. "And to be honest, she was doing a fine job up until we got to the fucker's shack."

"Isaac," Ashura said, tightening his brow. "What is it?"

"I'm getting there, I'm getting there." His breath slowed. "Let's just say it surprised me."

"Get to the point."

"She pinned him down by his throat. Dug her fingers into his flesh. And the things she barked at him, well, I'm afraid I can't wrap my mind around it." Isaac raked his scalp. "It's like she held a grudge."

"I need to know what she said," Ashura spat out. He looked to the girl from across the woods.

Cariaah rose to her feet, spinning herself back toward the heart of camp at the sound of crunching footsteps.

Snjick stood, staring, his eyes incandescent beneath the moon.

She smiled but received no reciprocation.

"I heard what happened," he said.

Her face turned blank, perplexed. "What are you talking about?"

"I could care less about how he died. Kenzik deserved a slow death." Snjick climbed onto the boulder she once leaned against, taking a seat. "But your use of Zenira's magic…" He paused. "I didn't even know he was training you."

"Is it a problem?" Cariaah suppressed her feelings toward Zenira as to not taint her words.

Snjick treaded *very* carefully. "I just need you to know," he said, his voice deepening. "Zenira is different."

"What do you mean?" Cariaah gulped through a dry throat. "How do you really feel about him?"

"I know how *you* feel about him."

"That doesn't matter," she protested.

His breath escalated despite his attempts to slow it. "His magic," he said, "is filled with nothing but hate."

She clenched her jaw. She thought of her hands—how different they had become.

"When I was little, he was my teacher, too. I loved having those abilities."

"Zenira told me you can use them."

"I *can* use the spell, yes." Snjick sat, rigid. "But I can't." He turned away, averting the richness of her eye. "My father told me the truth when I was young."

She bit her lip.

"Every time you use it, Cariaah," he uttered, "a part of you diminishes."

She reached for the bruise.

"And if you use it enough, your soul disappears. You become nothing."

The thought fell into abstraction. To be an empty shell—to be nothing but a wandering corpse—horrified her.

"He was a wise man. He knew what was best for my sake." His eyes wandered over to her again. "I'm just trying to do the same for you."

She repressed the flood of feelings and trickle of thoughts. "Thank you."

He unveiled a leather waterskin—stained black—and uncorked its top. Upon a deep drink, he gestured to her. "Ale?"

"I don't drink."

"Oh, that's right," he said.

"It's just that the smell irks me." She sat on the grass, leaning against the tower of a tree-trunk. "It reminds me of my father." Her heart plummeted. She covered her mouth, as if she could prevent a leak that had already sprung. Cariaah refused to believe she allowed it to slip out. "It's complicated."

"Sorry." He adjusted his posture, recorking the waterskin. "You can talk about it, you know." He chuckled, nervously.

She exhaled. Her breath bounced in accordance with the pit in her stomach. "I was a little girl." Her voice sounded so alien. She couldn't believe the words escaping her lips. "I always remember being so cold. I was so thin, then. I don't know where he would get it—the liquor—but he always had that stench on him. And every time I smell it, I'm reminded of what he—" The lump in her stomach rushed to her throat. She closed her eye so tightly it singed her temples.

"Cariaah, it's okay."

"No," she insisted, the tears on her cheekbones reflective in the violet light of the evening. "I *need* to talk about this." She dug her fingers into the bruise. "This has just been shredding me alive. These memories of him; the nightmares." She wiped her face with the rough texture of her gauntlet. "I hate him. I hate the memory of him, I hate that he called himself my father." She buried her eye into the stars—a reminder of the comfort they used to bring her on those nights. "I fucking *hate* him."

Snjick isolated her figure—the sitting, vulnerable encompassment of sensitivity—allowing the rest of his surroundings to disappear.

She rubbed the scabbard at her side with a stiff thumb. "Over the past five winters, I haven't been able to live without swinging my steel. Fighting is who I am."

The teeming insects filled the subsequent silence.

"He forced himself onto me—onto his own *daughter*." Replacing the tears was a storm of anger. "And I can't stand to be touched anymore." She spoke through her teeth. Her stomach hurt. *Burned*. It reminded her of the wound on her face.

Snjick couldn't tackle it. He only thought of when he placed his hand on her shoulder in the hole. Then of when he did the same to her hand in the land below.

Cariaah sniffled, her gauntlets working to rid her face of any emotion. "I'm sorry," she said. "I didn't mean to explode like that."

He looked into the stars. "I'm happy you told me, Cariaah."

"Really?"

"Yes," he said. "Really."

***

The following sunrise brought serenity to her. The dew of dawn sparkled on every inch of foliage. A pearlescent, emerald gallery surrounded the girl when she awoke, hushing the noise between her ears. Her stomach rose and fell with the weight of her hands upon it. Her lungs filtered the coolness of the air.

Each person stirred as the sun continued its journey into the sky, inverting its color from deep violet to shimmering gold. They trickled awake, and the purity and exclusivity of the morning fell away.

"Cariaah." A toe nudged her. "Get up," Ashura said. "We need to talk." He parted from her, his silence commanding to be followed.

She did so, hoisting herself to her feet and marching behind him to the edge of camp.

"What was the last thing I said to you before you left?"

She spat defensively, "I don't—"

"What was it?" he repeated.

She turned silent.

"*You* are not a person. You are a tool."

She stiffened her brow.

"I don't know what kind of twisted fantasies you have with ending someone's life but let me tell you something." He drove a rigid finger into her sternum. "What you did out there—the *way* you did it—was disgusting." He inched closer. "Don't stoop to your target's level."

As Ashura withdrew his hand and left the conversation on those final words, her angst returned.

She thought of what Snjick told her. *The entirety of your soul disappears. You become nothing.* There was an inherent allure. If that's who she was—a lifeless person with nothing inside but a beating heart—then she would have no past. Or, at least, she would be completely unaware of it. *To be numb,* she thought, *perhaps...*

She also thought of how he reacted—*truly* reacted—after their conversation. If he had decided to alienate her, where was she to go? To whom would she go to for consolation?

Cariaah scanned the camp. Everyone—as they conversed quietly in their little groups—seemed foreign. To her, they were nothing but strangers.

She thought of Zenira. The mare. His blade.

A whistle emerged, beckoning attention. "Alright, this is phase two," Ashura called out from within the mix. "We go north, according to the contract's details. If we leave now, we'll make it by sunset."

The contract—and the plan within—served as a distraction for her.

***

Among another clump of trees a cluster of tents sat assembled and posted. Their fabric flapped in the steady breeze of dusk, the sun's orange cloak enhancing the greenery.

The group of traveling robbers, urchins, and bandits divided into their respective cliques, in which they would remain for the rest of the evening. A young fire swayed and crackled within a nest of stones, warming anyone who sat nearby. Tankards of ale traveled amongst the thieves, each man pouring a pint. This was their rhythm—one they fell into each night.

Lain sat alone. His gruff dwarven face—riddled with imperfections—framed a hollow pair of eyes. His gaze buried itself into the fire and his axe's hilt burrowed deep into the dirt.

Willem—his commander—circled the fire, the iron plates he wore reflecting the orange of the flames.

Lain glared.

The sun would eventually set behind the horizon's encompassment. The fire that once served as a hub for the troupe dwindled into dormancy. The dwarf sat as a shell, time moving through him.

Somewhere in the thicket, just beyond the encampment, a set of heavy footsteps accompanied another, lighter pair.

Lain's brow twitched into rigidness, the grip on his axe tightening.

Then, a yelp. Short, abrupt, and loud.

He lifted himself, taking the weapon with him. His steel boots sunk into the loose dirt, crunching leaves.

It grew louder as Lain approached.

"Oy!" called a voice from where he neared.

Lain emerged, his axe's steel dragging through the dirt behind him. Evidently, he deduced which footsteps belonged to whom.

Pinned to the trunk of a tree, an elven girl squirmed. The heavy footsteps belonged to the one who immobilized her: a large human.

"Lain," he said, continuing to push the girl into the tree. "You didn't strike me as the kind of dwarf to want something like this." He laughed.

The girl screamed, pleading to the camp's unmoving silence.

The weight of Lain's axe left the dirt and dug into the man's neck.

Blood sprayed. The girl stumbled onto the dirt.

"*Go,*" Lain commanded, the fallen man's blood tainting his voice.

The girl scrambled upward, shuffling frantically away from the scene and into the depths of the night.

Lain spun back around toward the camp. He returned his axe to his shoulder, spit onto the leaking corpse below, and found his seat before the dormant fire, once more. He sunk into it, reacquainting himself with the dirt until the sun returned with its golden buzz.

As they ate their breakfast—a lentil stew—Willem stood amongst them, circling. The remainder of the troupe broke down tents, fed the only three of their mares, and sharpened steel with stones.

Lain sat in his spot, hugging his axe with one arm, and glaring at Willem.

"This village will be an easy piece of work," assured Willem, loud enough so they all could hear. "Ryne and Thames saw only two men when they scouted. Their crops are going to be open for us to harvest."

They strapped the collapsed tents and excess equipment to the horses, which tailed the band of marauders as they marched through the strip of forest. The dawn's sky—brimming with greyness—hung over them, teasing a storm.

Lain walked at their center, the axe over his shoulder, its weight a comfort.

An undercurrent of chatter emerged.

"I do wonder how Glenn died. It's a damned shame. He sure knew how to make us bust a gut."

"Come to think, that elven girl went missing last night, too."

"Shit, seriously? What a *fine* lass she was."

They arrived at the edge of the trees, peering through the brush and toward the border of the village. The homes were made up of crude stones, supported by rough timber. Puffy, white smoke swirled into the air from the chimneys, marking a beacon for any travelers to visit.

They crouched behind brush, Willem at their helm.

Silence encompassed the village, which turned into a crescendo of laughter. A pair of children—an elf and a dwarf—emerged, one chasing the other in jest.

"Alright," said Willem. "Archers at my side."

"No," Lain said.

"I beg your pardon, peasant?" Willem asked over his shoulder, to the dwarf who squatted around his axe.

"I won't stand by this," he replied, plainly.

Willem scoffed. "That girl out there, running around to the tune of her death, isn't your daughter. She's *gone*."

Lain's brow turned even crosser now that his glare was detected. "You can't change that."

"But I can change *this*," he said quickly, disregarding what his commander had said. "I won't let you do to this village what you did to mine."

Willem laughed. "You seek vengeance? Is that what this is about?"

Lain didn't say a word.

"Fine, then." He unsheathed his blade. "I won't take away your opportunity. Don't get involved," he commanded the rest of them. "This is something I have to settle."

The remainder of the group formed a circle around them, giving the pair ample space.

Lain sharpened his eyes and readied his axe, its ferocity accompanying his compatible stance.

"Let him try," said a gravelly, foreign voice. "The dwarf deserves that much."

"What?" Willem asked no one, looking about frantically.

Another circle had formed around the troupe. This time, instead of crudely armored bandits, the outer ring belonged to abyssally armored assassins. They held their blades to the throats of the inner ring.

"How did—"

Willem had to parry Lain's strike. His perplexity split in half, falling away into unimportance. Willem managed to stay one step ahead.

The dwarf paid no attention to the unknown, only focusing on what his emptiness preyed upon. He growled—borderline roared—with each strike.

Willem continued to evade, strafe, and block.

"The traitor. The deserter. The coward," said the voice. "Willem. To think that *you*, in all of your abandonment, were once a part of our sacred order."

Willem controlled his breath, calculating each strike the dwarf threw at him.

"And now you've resorted to banditry. How pathetic."

Lain swung and swung, ripping the steel past the evasiveness of his opponent. Grass tore beneath the dance of the duel.

"This dwarf only wishes to rectify his cowardice," growled the voice. "Perhaps *you're* the peasant, Willem."

Willem prepared himself to finish the dwarf off, pirouetting away from the bite of his opponent's axe and impaling. His steel cut through Lain's back and escaped through his torso.

The dwarf coughed. His breath filled with the metallic pungency of blood. His life spilled onto the dirt in a stream, making an orangey mud at their feet.

"A shame," said that same, rough voice. "The gods have flipped a coin, deeming the victor."

Lain attempted to muster a swing of the axe—or, rather the strength to do so—but as the seconds passed, his body and stature continued to crumble. Dexterity disintegrated, turning his muscles numb. He fell into the muck with a squelching thud. The plates of his spaulders rattled with his weight's collapse, and his eyes turned into pits of blackness.

Willem's breath lurched at a heightened pace, only heeding Lain's corpse for a moment. For the rest of his men squirmed at the behest of sharp steel, which teased their throats.

Steel slicing flesh joined the birds in their song. And as the bodies fell into the dirt, their necks leaking crimson rivers, the vanity of such a duel was unveiled. Willem stood as the last member of his troupe.

"The gods aren't very kind, Willem," said the rough voice. "All of the looting you've done—all of the murder, pillaging, and raping—led to this moment. When you were born, this was your fate, even when you were a part of our order. It was your purpose to be purposeless."

His breath climbed, not from the demands of the duel, but the swirling cloud of the inevitable.

"Now that your death is here—your ordained fate—it is up to you on how to react," said the gravelly voice. "You can die with the honor of a Vantaknight, or the honor of a coward."

The power within him—to lash and erupt against all who stood near—existed. He could conjure anything at his disposal, use what the order had taught him in the beginning of his life, but those words cut through him. Thus, with an ever-loosening grip, Willem dropped his steel into the bloody muck below. He fell onto his hands and knees, staring into the swirling pool of red.

A girl, a tree stump tall, meandered over to him, her foot on the hilt of Willem's blade. It sank into the ground beneath her weight. Her icy hair fell pin-straight to her waist, and her endless, listless irises severed any remaining hope. There was nothing within her, nothing that Willem could cling to in his final moments.

She drove her dagger into Willem's skull, cracking the bone and freeing a fountain of dark red.

"Good work," said Ashura, sheathing his sword. "Let's head back."

Iz ripped her steel from Willem's skull. The weight of his corpse dropped with finality.

"What an eloquent speech, though, I would've—"

"Isaac," Ashura responded, watching the elf walk about the scene like a buffoon. "I'm not going to waste the breath."

Cariaah lingered on the edge, where she had emerged from the brush and spilled blood. She watched as the sea of red grew, immersing herself.

"You okay?" asked Snjick, approaching her side.

She was silent. Her mouth grew wet.

"Cariaah?"

Her eye snapped onto him.

"Are you okay?" he said again.

"Yes."

"We head south again," said Ashura. "Come on."

His troupe obeyed, sheathing steel, and commencing a march.

"Wait."

Everyone looked to the speaker, unsure as to who it was.

"Do you feel that?" asked Iz, who now had everyone's attention.

Ashura looked about.

Something distant—something percussive grew louder as the moments passed.

"*Hooves*," said Cariaah. "A lot of them."

"What?" Ashura growled, hurrying to the edge of the trees. "Fuck," he muttered. "Run," fell out of his mouth. "*Fall back!*"

They all commenced their high tail away, maneuvering through the forest.

Snjick caught a glimpse of the sight with a quick glance.

A horde of horses—at least forty, encompassed in black—supported riders cloaked in a matching color. They rode through the village, casting flames onto its homes. A banner hung above them, its sigil peering into the trees: the eye within the star.

The half-elf's heart sank. "N-no," he whispered.

The oncoming army's gallop raced for the trees, fire paving their path.

"Ashura!" he called, stopping his retreat. "We can't run faster than them! They're traitors, here to kill us!"

He spun around to face the half-elf, catching the sight of their oncoming trample. "Alright," he said, almost silently. "Hold your positions! We have to hold the line!" He unsheathed his blade, hurriedly. "I don't care who they were to you!" He struggled to submit to his own words. "What matters now, is that they're traitors!" Ashura chanted. "Kill them all!"

The traitors' charge ripped through the edge of the forest. A wave of flames followed, bordering the fight, forcing it to take place. They leapt from their horses as they assaulted, some crawling up trees, and others sprinting into the heart of it all.

Snjick yanked his dagger away from its scabbard. He had to

convince himself that nothing else existed besides his weapon. His *weapons*.

The wave of opponents became obscured by a broadsiding fear. He didn't look at the thunderous inevitability before him, instead at his hands. He could save so many lives, prevent a river's worth of bloodshed.

As he almost dropped his steel, his father—his face, sternness, blades, even his bloodied corpse—infiltrated all else. He thought of what he said to him that night, what he assured the lifeless corpse he wouldn't do.

I won't use it again—I won't, I promise you. I promise.

His reflexes took over—his instincts. The half-elf parried the strike of a dalaryn, cloaked in black with the crimson sigil painted onto his chest. Snjick's dagger worked on its own. The rhythm of battle—steel clashing with steel and corpses hitting the floor—had its advent. He summoned a fuel to continue slashing away. Whether it be steel, flesh, or the air, flurrying strikes always followed.

Iz—in another reach of the forest—sprinted. Her enemies resided in the trees above, seemingly everywhere, scurrying about branches and rustling leaves. She ignored the distant screams of her brothers and sisters. To run was to survive and surviving—as Isaac had told her—meant the opportunity to continue running.

Out of the trees they fell, landing on the dirt in a crouch. They framed her in a ring, similar to the one she was a part of, earlier. In their hands were notched bows.

Iz slid her blade out of its sheath. The steel hissed.

They stalked her, revolving around the girl's tiny figure. A dalaryn cloaked in red separated himself, dropping his hood to his shoulders.

Iz recognized the yellowness of his feathers. The smoothness of his voice once he spoke.

"It'll be easy to kill you, girl," he said, inching toward her. "But remember, it's for the land."

She lunged, her blade slashing in a furious strike.

The dalaryn closed his claw, trying to take hold of her very movements.

Unfazed, she cut through the spell's thickness, as well as his neck.

Phrases rippled through the ring. "What?" they asked. "She's just a girl."

Iz remained silent. The sharpness of her steel spoke on her behalf, dalaryn blood dripping.

"Kill her!" commanded one of them.

Iz sprung herself over the fleet of arrows and came down in a fury of steel. She slaughtered two of them, one by a stab in the chest, and the other by a slash of the belly.

"The spell isn't—" exclaimed her next victim, before being interrupted by steel in the throat.

She propelled her blade at another archer, throwing it like a javelin into their chest before they could release an arrow.

There stood only a handful, now, defensive and shaken.

Iz's palms casted sparks. They fizzled, sputtered, and built into little wisps of smoke. But when she didn't relent—when she unleashed the tides of flames upon everything, nothing but screams remained.

Ashura ran, too, his blade sheathed. But his enemies didn't scurry along branches. They chased him into a line of burning bushes ahead. Bracing himself, he held his stiff forearms out and squeezed his eyes shut, uncertain as to what awaited him on the other side.

The heat of those flames came in a flash, forcing him to push harder. And as he opened his eyes, the decline of a hill greeted him, which ended against a wall of jagged rock.

He flailed about, trying to delay slamming into ground. Once he did, he tightened himself, bringing his head and knees to his chest. Each rock, root and imperfection upon the slope jabbed at him, taking just a bit of breath each time. He slammed into the solidity of a boulder, which stole the wind from his lungs.

Ashura had no other choice.

He rose to his feet, ripping his blade from its nest, flaunting it toward the onslaught of cloaks. *Everything,* he thought. *Everything always has to end in an ocean of blood.*

Initial contact came in the form of a parry. Thereafter, he sliced his opponent open, the steel singing until it connected with flesh.

Why is that? he asked himself, the cries of the wounded calling his name. *Always... it's always been that way.*

His sword flew about, eviscerating, *killing.* Every face as they came about, he recognized. The memories, the distant ones, whether it be contract work or drunken antics, stung him as he killed.

"Grichuk."
"Floyd."
"Lee."

He said their names as he took their lives, staining his face so red that it masked the pigment of skin. *Does killing supersede us?*

"Sven."
"Ollie."
"Martin."

Even while I kill, as I know I must, I can't help but wonder...

"Willis."
"Daniels."
"Turner."

Am I failing?

The opposite corner of the forest became the half-elf's nest. His constant footwork created a trench. His arms ached so sorely that the beckoning shadow of that spell called his name.

He plugged away, reserving his focus only for the dagger he wielded. He ignored the tide of morbid temptation. "I won't use it," he chanted. "Never again."

***

Smoke and blood and rain. It created a hazy mist, one that floated about in a vapory greyness. The snapping of rain on burnt leaves created a whisper, saying a prayer for the dead. They were strewn about, blood and bone everywhere, giving texture to the pools of crimson muck.

Ashura's eyelids felt heavy as they opened. His figure was numb. The pain only spoke once he moved. The crusty veneer of blood encompassed him, and when a tear escaped his gaze it paved a thin line of life upon his skin.

Iz dabbed her sleeping teacher's wounds with a damp cloth, working through the thickness of each cut. Her gaze remained listless, and her red blade clung to her back.

Snjick burst awake, throwing a corpse off him as he heaved in a breath of smoke. "Cariaah," he whispered, surveying the landscape of death around him. "Cariaah!" he yelled, ignoring the needles of pain that introduced themselves. "*Cariaah!*"

***

Everything fell away.

All except for *him*.

Through the haze of smoke, his glow returned in all of its shrewd glory, drawing her near. His armor looked just like it did on that day five winters ago. His hair flowed its shimmering hue of ice. But it was the blade at his hip, the one she hadn't yet reacquainted herself with, that ultimately pulled her into his arms.

She felt at home, and all of her fears evaporated into nothing.

8 FRAGMENTS

Isaac, Iz, Ashura, the half-elf, and Benoit—a grey-feathered dalaryn—were the only ones who remained. They resided in a spacious circle, the weight of the battle upon them. Their wounds had been tended to, albeit crudely. The bandages turned sticky, blood seeping through. Above, the onslaught of rain ceased, but the clouds still hung grey.

"We can't, Snjick."

"You'd abandon one of your own?" he spat back. "During a contract?"

"You have to understand," Ashura said, hesitantly. "We've already lost so many men."

"You're right. And you're willing to lose another." Snjick's brow went deeper into crossness. "It's just pathetic."

"What do you want to do then, kid?" Ashura asked. He inched closer. "Do you want us to scour this forest, *again*?"

Snjick stared, perhaps knowing the stupidity of the search, but stayed determined, nonetheless.

"Whoever's behind this," Ashura began, "they know we're here."

"I know who it is."

Ashura's face receded its anger.

"I have a *strong* idea."

Ashura remained silent.

"On that contract," Snjick said, "I was trapped in that spell by those assailants. If I didn't use *his* magic, then I was to be killed."

"Snjick," Ashura said, firmly. "Who are you speculating?"

The air hung statically, the heat of stares vehement. He exhaled sharply, a stream of images awakening: Cariaah in Zenira's arms. How easy it was for her to touch *him*.

He said his name with disdain. "*Zenira.*"

Ashura hesitated, avoiding any reflexive reaction.

The others stood or sat straighter.

"Are you certain?" Ashura finally asked, fatigue leaking out of his words.

He nodded. "He's a powerful man," Snjick said. "And now it's clear."

That silence was loud. Those trees held no chirping bird or teeming insect.

"It's about the Vantaknights as an order." He recalled that dalaryn's words. "We 'prance around like rats,' is what I was told."

Ashura scoffed.

"He wants to share what we've done—*everything* we've done—with the land above." Snjick dug his nails into his palms, impressing the leather of his gauntlets. "Zenira's through with the Vantaknights." He narrowed his eyes. "He's creating something of his own."

Isaac stood from his leaning against a tree. "When I was a kid, I remember him trying to bring me into his fold." His words leaked through an underlying grimace. "And even though I can cast fire and ice, this 'dark magic' is not something I'm capable of using."

"Never liked his ideas," Ashura said. "He's always been a bastard."

They all shot eyes at him, though not in disagreement.

Benoit was the outlier. "Are we really believing this ridiculous theory?" he asked. "Snjick's just a boy. And what's even worse, he's a half-elf. A *mutt.*"

Snjick looked at the muck below, silence enveloping him. He thought of Zenira—and how Cariaah viewed them both differently. For Zenira was a man. He was just a *boy*.

"Don't say another word," Ashura growled, throwing himself in the dalaryn's face.

Benoit flinched.

"Someone tried to kill *us*, today. That includes you." He shoved a finger into Benoit's cuirass. "Even though some might call you a filthy vulture."

He scoffed through his beak.

They all turned silent, once more.

"Let's move," Ashura commanded. "We've been sitting here for too long, and our backs are painted red. I know we're tired, but we have to make it to the land below."

Snjick sat on the brink of erupting again.

"And if Cariaah's out there," he said, "then we have to trust that she'll find her way back."

Snjick stood on his toes, ignoring the aches of battle.

They trudged away, fatigued and limping. Snjick, as well as the rest of the party, never realized how small the patch of forest truly was, since it had acted as a fiery cage for so long. Their armor had a layer to shed; that of bloody ash and orangey mud. Their gazes encompassed nothing but exhaustion and dread, dwelling upon what was and longing for a warm bed.

They continued, even through the night, Isaac sipping on a much-needed vial of ale that Ashura admonished him for. He chugged it down, hurriedly, before his captain confiscated the empty glass.

They reached the dead forest at midnight. Comprised of ashy, brittle trees that groaned in the wind, it was useless to anyone in the land above. It beckoned no one and harbored not a fiber of life. They filed through the forest, the final steps of their never-ending journey the most difficult.

The half-elf thought not about the steps he took, nor the dry, powdery dirt they fell upon. Instead, the warm presence of Cariaah echoed within. He dwelled on the minute things: her exclusive smell—vibrant and rosy—her mannerisms—the way she always grabbed at her hip—and whip-like rebuttals, even those she deployed for clear defense.

It sat just below the dirt, beneath one hollowed out trunk. Just on the other side of a steel trapdoor the land below resided, opening only to the hand of a Vantaknight.

Snjick longed for it all.

And as the trapdoor squealed open to the hand of Ashura, he begged to no one.

The land below took the anemic party into its jaws, welcoming them into its shadowy embrace.

***

The hall roared with conversation. The sea of black below the loft teemed with energy. The knights sat at their tables, drifting into their usual seats and usual cliques.

"*You* called this meeting, Zenira?" Duke asked as he shuffled onto the loft. "For what?"

"Families need to come together every now and again," Zenira replied. "I love to know that we are all in the same room, fighting for the same cause."

"We have things to work on," Geneva protested.

"Please, stay." His lips turned narrow and eyes into slits. "Have a glass of wine with your sons and daughters."

Geneva looked to his other councilmembers who remained uncertain. "Keep it brief. We're fighting a war," he said. "The largest group we've had on contract is out at *this* moment."

"I'm aware. And it is important for morale to be high during these times."

They all sat on their respective thrones, awaiting Zenira's inevitable dialogue. He poured wine at a small table, the goblets swirling with the grapey mauve.

"The victories may be yet to come," he said as he poured, "however, these victories will be the greatest we've ever had as an order—as a family."

"So confident," Raquel said, dully, flopping her cheek onto a stiff hand.

"To win a war, you must be."

"Zenira," Duke said, "we don't even know who we're fighting."

His glare silenced the dwarf. "We've been fighting them for much longer than we believe."

"What do you mean?" Geneva interjected.

Zenira ignored the dalaryn. He lifted his goblet, rising to his feet and smiling. "Today is the advent of something grander," he called, silencing the mob of noise below. "It is the beginning of a new era for us. The rules have changed."

Perplexity fogged the loft.

"It is up to us to reap what we deserve," he chanted. "For, nothing we have done is in vain." He lowered his brow. "The land above is indebted to the Vantaknights. And I say this to end the darkest of times, thank you my sons and daughters. Thank you for being my martyrs."

Duke propelled himself to his feet. "*What?*"

Steel sliced through flesh. Some knights had risen from their seats, slicing the throats of those who sat beside them. A fountain of blood had taken form, springing its hot crimson about. It stained the wood of the tables and soaked into the carpet below.

"A bird of fire is promised." Zenira spun to his once-councilmates, taking them all under his spell with a ferocious grip. "One to cleanse the land of its *filth*."

They tried to fight, squirming within the confines of his grasp.

Geneva befell to the dark thrall of the spell. His skull caved, fragmenting into sharp pieces. He fell to the loft's floor. Lifeless.

It spread like a virus to Duke who hit the floor like a crack of thunder, his wine spilling onto the stone.

Korbin's blood was shed next.

Though, Raquel revolted against the spell. Her toes dipped into the cold abyss of death, but head remained in the realm of the living. The slaughtering of her subordinates—her family—was cloistered in her ears. Her breath thinned into a whistle.

"There's nothing left for this family here," Zenira said. "I'm sending you all to the same place."

Raquel bit down on nothing, tightening her jaw until it hurt. She spat through the grasp of death beset upon her, "Fuck you."

Zenira's eyes fell agape at the sight of Raquel's glowing fist. He had her for the present moment, then didn't the next. The elf veiled herself behind a cloud of smoke.

And when it abated, thinning into the morose air, the elf no longer stood before him.

Even after Raquel had vanished, the bloodshed continued, erasing life.

Zenira sipped his wine—which he had spilt none of as he killed. He surveyed the cacophony below, his eyes feasting.

***

The labyrinth of corridors sat empty. Sounds lacked in the air. Everything was still. The already tired and confused and disheveled party limped through the land below, wandering through desolation.

"I don't believe this," Ashura said.

"Could they have fled?" Benoit asked.

"And gone where?" Snjick replied with another question.

"Anywhere with people," Ashura answered. He observed the walls, searching for any possible detail. "Take away the armor and we're normal people—just more capable with a blade."

They arrived at the crimson doors. And when they opened them, an extra layer of paint had been applied. It dripped onto the carpet below, seeping, soaking. The doors glared with their towering stature, beckoning them to take yet another step of dread.

Iz took Isaac's hand.

Benoit's feathers puffed.

Snjick clenched his fists.

And Ashura's stomach revolted.

Strewn about were men and women and children, all at one point donning the black embrace of armor. Their parts jumbled together, creating a marinade of lifelessness. Not a soul stirred. A message, drawn with the blood of their fallen siblings, glared from upon the walls with a spectral eye:

She is mine.

The half-elf froze—in unison with the rest of the group—allowing the bloody ink to sink in. That image of her, dazed from the spell scorching the side of her face but vigilant enough to run for Zenira with open arms…it burned him.

She was so timid. So fragile. Every time Snjick placed a hand on her—even in attempts of comfort or consolation—she flinched. But for Zenira, *she* instigated the contact.

Snjick was only a boy. A half-elf. He didn't have anything to belong to, not a race nor an order. *Not anymore.* Moreover, Zenira appeared like a god. His allure captured her.

Ashura shook the room with his shiver. His teeth clacked and his eyes turned listless, drowning in the blood right along with the dead.

They all looked to Ashura for an order. The party placed their hopes in his. Yet, it remained unclear if he had any left.

He spun back toward the entrance, marching through the bloody carpet and into the corridors again. "We have to go," he said. "I can't look at this."

"What are we planning on doing?" Benoit asked.

"We just need to leave," Ashura replied. "This isn't our home. Not anymore." He tightened his face into a knot, halting his march. "We're going to drown these traitors in their own blood, *somehow*."

They followed his lead through the vacancy of the corridors.

"This place," Iz said, her grip tight around Isaac's fingers, "has always been a jail cell."

They sat on her words, their footsteps the only noise.

Isaac's throat grew heavy. "I don't know how this could've happened," he said, fighting tears away. "But now I know for sure that this is Zenira's doing. He treated her differently."

"You mean Cariaah?" Snjick asked.

"Yes," he replied, nodding. "I should've warned her about him."

Snjick thought of that night—the one after the first contract. He shut his eyes.

"It's not this place I'm going to miss," Ashura said, his back turned to the rest of the group as they walked. "It's what the place says."

"What do you mean?" Benoit asked.

"We tried. This order—the family we made—tried to mend things we ultimately couldn't. But we tried," Ashura said. "I tried."

The dead forest greeted them again for the last time. They left behind its greyness. It escorted them into the emerald utopia that was the land above. The sun shone upon everything through the steady breeze, ignoring the desperation and brokenness of the party. The beauty of the day mocked them as they made their languid way through it.

***

Xardiil, as the capitol of the land, bustled as long as the days and nights lasted. The nobles flipped their coin to the grimy hands of beggars, who would supply the rooking merchants with their daily wage. However, those nobles also gave their gold *directly* to the merchants, sometimes making appointments around expensive items.

Patel was a young elf—clean and approachable—donning a long, braided beard. At midday, he—who sold leather trinkets and the occasional historical piece—prepared himself for an appointment with a man of wealth.

Known as Abraham, the nobleman made Patel aware in advance

that he was moving into a new homestead. He needed décor, so, he set up an appointment to acquire a special blade for mounting.

"Patel," Abraham said upon arrival, practically yelling overtop the noisy marketplace. "How is the coin coming in, today?" His head's baldness reflected the sunlight, and his fatness reflected his loin intake.

"It's certainly been worse," Patel replied.

"Well, I suppose that's good to hear."

"It's definitely different in quality from the other news about the land."

"I beg your pardon?" Abraham asked, his demeanor turning from casual to fervent.

"You haven't heard?"

He awaited Patel's next words.

"Of this mysterious group marching through the land?"

"I haven't heard of this, no, I haven't." Abraham's vigilance about the situation turned to franticness. "I haven't," he said again, unnecessarily.

"From what I hear," Patel began, unveiling the blade which Abraham came for, "they're this cloaked group of marauders. But their numbers are *massive*."

Abraham wiped a veneer of sweat from his forehead. "Oh, dear. That sure is scary."

"At any rate, here is the blade, my good sir." Patel held it across his arms. "It is in mint condition."

"Yes, yes, very nice," he said, dismissively. "Now, where are these marauders you speak of, exactly?"

"Oh, I can't be certain. It is just a rumor after all." Patel transferred the item to Abraham. "Now, I know we originally settled on a price of seven-fifty, but sales are a bit slow as of late, so, would we mind bumping it to eight?"

He hesitated, the production of sweat ramping. "Oh, that's perfectly fine." Abraham dug through his pockets, handing him a leather coin purse, plus a couple extra pieces of gold.

"Abraham?"

"Y-yes?" he said, frantically.

"Eight-fifty."

"Oh, that's right, that's right." He coughed up two more coins, shuffling them into Patel's elven hands. "Now, I must be going,

Patel. Thank you for this."

Patel smiled.

Abraham sped through the marketplace, hurrying toward the security district's gate. Therein, he ignored the sights and casual greetings from others. He just carried the blade in his arms like it was a poisonous creature.

He found the guard offices, hurried in, and asked for the captain.

"He's down the hall," said the man at the front desk, who scrawled upon a piece of parchment with a wet quill. "Just knock before you enter."

Abraham nodded and followed the man's instructions.

"Come in," said the guard captain, who sat rigidly in his large seat, reading from the pages of a thick book.

"Flynn," Abraham said, out of breath.

"Abraham!" he exclaimed, excitedly. "What a pleasant surprise."

He struggled to swallow through a dry throat. "Surely," he said, heaving. "Surely you've heard."

"Heard?" he asked. "Of what? That ridiculous looking blade you've got, there?"

"N-no," he said, ignoring the captain's jest. "This group."

"What are you talking about?" Flynn asked, growing concerned. "Have a seat, have a seat." He pointed to the pair of empty, wooden chairs opposite the desk he sat at.

Abraham did, giving his full weight to his seat. The wood groaned upon receiving him.

"Now, once you catch your breath," Flynn said, "explain to me what you are blabbering on about."

"Well, apparently, a bandit troupe is marching through the land," he said. "Although, they don't appear like bandits."

"What do they look like then?"

"I'm not sure," he said, still panting.

Flynn scoffed as another knock came about drumming on his door. "Yes?" he called out.

The door creaked open, unveiling a pair of guards holding a woman by the arms. She only wore a tattered drape of cloth which masqueraded a dirt-covered, pale frame. Her panting conversed Abraham's. While his emerged out of exhaustion, hers whistled because of something else.

Dehydration, hunger, and *terror*.

NIGHT'S GRASP

"By the gods!" exclaimed Abraham, jumping to his feet, clumsily.

"Abraham," Flynn called, standing. "Get this woman some water from the well outside."

"Wh-where?" he asked.

"The well in the courtyard, now *go!*"

Abraham's franticness hijacked his legs as he dropped the expensive blade to the floor. He rushed outside, through the pair of guards and woman who replaced him.

"Who is this?" Flynn asked.

"She collapsed at the district gate just minutes ago," one of the guards said. "She begged to have us bring her to you."

"But why?"

"My village," the woman said, weakly, "just outside the city of Qualia. It was attacked."

Flynn removed himself from his desk, coming to the woman's side and kneeling. "By whom?"

"I'd never seen anything like it," she said. "They were as large as an army—the ones in the storybooks. They wore black cloaks."

Flynn's focus fleeted, but his eyes remained upon the villager.

"Their leader—"

"Did you recognize him?"

"He looked," she hesitated, quivering. "He looked like a god with a head of flowing white hair yet a young face, wreaking havoc on us all!" She tore herself away from the guards as Abraham entered, a bucket of water in arms. "Why is it that we are being judged? Have we sinned against the gods so terribly?"

"Abraham." Flynn gestured to the woman, implying a command.

"Here," Abraham said, kneeling to her side with the sloshing bucket. He presented it to the woman.

She ripped it from his hands and gulped, the excess water spilling onto the floor. "I don't want to be divinely judged!" she shouted. "Not this way!"

"Get me the captain of the wall!" Flynn commanded the pair of guards, springing to his feet. "They need to know what to look for."

"The eye," the woman whispered. "The eye within the star." She shuddered, curling into a ball upon the cold stone.

Flynn inched closer to Abraham. "We need to set up a bed for her in my office. She is to be brought water and food routinely." He exhaled, collecting his thoughts. "This woman's knowledge is invaluable."

She shook, her eyes agape and teeth clenched, like a tightly wound knot on the floor.

***

While dusk may have approached, the gates to the capitol remained open. Rivers of people—merchants, peasants, and nobility who traveled by servant-operated litter—poured in. The five of them were outliers. Their armor drew enough attention, but the mars of blood upon it piqued more stares.

The scars ran too deep for them to care. Those of battle, of loss, of mourning, and of bitter betrayal. It mocked them exactly like the setting sun and the joy of others around them.

9 THE GIRL

Awaken.

The girl didn't know she slept, nor did she obey the command voluntarily. She only rose from where she lay, observing everything before her.

Him.

The sparkling armor, sheathed fang of a blade, and familiar face that belonged to a god beckoned her. He sat in the dark forest, gazing with the perennial calmness she had longed so vehemently for. At his side snorted that steed of icy white, prepared for a swift mount.

Swathes of memories flooded her, pertaining to that dreadful attack. She thought of Iz, how she stopped everyone with a single remark. Of Ashura, who frantically peered through the forest. "Where are they?" she asked, reaching for the bruise.

All fell silent.

"Lost."

"Then we have to look for them."

"There is no need to look for who will inevitably return." Without a second to absorb her reaction—one of perplexity, worry, but underlying faith—he mounted. And with a single breath, he unveiled his blade from its shimmering cage.

Cariaah stared in awe. The stark realization of her dream—her image of Zenira's adorning appearance—came to magnificent fruition. All the pure hues of him juxtaposed the forest's darkness.

She turned in a slow pivot at the feeling of heat against her backside. And there, before the girl's small, youthful stature, stretched a vast sea of black. A near endless army of cloaked figures, lighting torches in a fiery avalanche, peered at the girl through abyssal hoods. She resorted to Zenira's image again, spinning around once more.

Beside his mare was one anew—one she hadn't noticed—albeit grey in fur. He held the reins in a tender gauntlet, offering the girl an empty saddle right beside him.

She was reeled in—coaxed by such a pedestal. The girl mounted beside Zenira, finally level with the blade he held so passionately.

He turned a slow head to meet her gaze, ensuring Cariaah's certain attention. And with the sighing of the wind, snorting of his mare, and blatant control of the night, Zenira presented a spectral smile.

That black sea—in all its sprawling abyss—rode, galloping from the forest into the plainness of a moonlit clearing. But that moon's face would soon disappear behind a dark veil of clouds, making room for an onslaught of morbid torchlight.

As Cariaah looked up, her mare racing underneath a straddle, a crack of lightning split the darkness, leaving a cannon of blaring thunder. But this light illuminated more than Zenira's pearlescent armor, as billows of hazy smoke laced the sky. She looked ahead once more, at their source: an anemic, wooden village.

The cluster of homes stared at the army—the unrelenting sea of death—with petrification. All those in its confines slept, giving their conscious minds to the peace of the evening. But no such peace would arrive.

Those torches were thrown overhead in orange trails, clashing with the black of the sky. They landed in fiery blazes on those homes, tearing through the brittle timber with voracious jaws. Hooves pounded the dirt like the boom of that thunder, slicing through each stead and every meager defense in place.

The fences—moss-sheathed and rotting—befell to tides of roaring fire. The village mutts barked and growled in futility, struck down by zinging steel that left heaps of flesh. Mothers ran with their children in arms, and farmers took up pitchforks or icepicks or mallets to defend what little they had. Only to be met by bloody fate.

Chaos.

Utter despair.

All of it, in a sweeping, morose storm, assaulted Cariaah and her puny senses. She could do nothing but observe. Her steel remained unsheathed. In fact, she didn't heed its presence until now—until this humble village crumbled around her.

Amidst all the fire and blood and guts she found Zenira with her gaze.

He was upon his saddle, running his blade through those who fought in desperate encroach or fled in frantic escape.

They called for their families—dead already—and begged to be spared from this divine reckoning. Others lay below Zenira's picturesque steed, crushed in impossible forms by the weight of hooves. The breaths they took were hopeless, displaying death in the drawing of life.

Cariaah shut her eye in a desperate squeeze so that her temples ached with lurching pain. But the extinguishment of the sights only amplified the sounds. Cloistered within her skull were the screams—the helpless fates of innocent village folk.

Of houses that resembled a former home for the girl.

Of people who resembled a former version of herself.

She had to get out of this horrendous cage, even if it meant curling into a ball upon the blood-soaked ground. Thus, the girl threw herself from that saddle and into the muck. Fire continued its spree, hissing tufts of black smog into the abyssal sky.

She found herself wandering with covered ears and a shut eye. The only sight was darkness, and the only sound was her heaving breath. Even questions had no relevance in comparison to escape.

But just as she awoke earlier, a pervasive call shot through her defenses and resonated.

"Cariaah!"

The girl shot open her gaze, placed taut hands at her sides, and turned toward the village with wheezing breaths. Her eye was a gaping, fear-stricken hole, nearly bulging from its socket in abject terror.

All of the cloaked figures who once rode mares now stood in the midst of their carnage. Some were knee deep in the blood-soaked mud, abyssally peering from drawn hoods. But Zenira stood at their center, his blade flaunted and gleaming in the orange light.

She approached that scene for no one else but him.

With corpses—some whole, some strewn about in pieces—

paving her walk, she never took her eye off that shimmering piece of steel. Her footsteps squelched in the blood, her heart pounded against her ribcage in ferocity, and the village's dying breath stained every thought. Every sound.

But he didn't stand as the only anomaly. Before him—before the edge of his blade—knelt a woman, panting in horrific dread.

He offered the sword. "Take it."

She curled her brow, silently asking what he meant.

"This blade is yours, Cariaah."

From the point of her awakening, not tonight but five winters ago, she hadn't gone a day without thinking of this mere piece of metal. Everything it symbolized—everything it had done for her—usurped any fear she underwent. The girl outstretched a hand.

"But you must follow one, simple request."

She hesitated, her heart hammering and breath ramping up again. Looking to the woman, briefly, she quickly resorted her glance to Zenira.

He nodded.

The girl didn't want to know what he meant, but every piece of that evening told her in plain words what she must do. The festering homes, the abating screams, and the leaking corpses uttered in profound decree, *Kill her. Slit her throat and let her bleed.*

As her shaking fingers flirted with the hilt, a visceral thought of her father struck her. Of him standing over her as a menacing beast with his unshakable grip, predatory eyes, and massive frame.

Those nights—all of those nights—whispered to her memory. She could recall with vivacity just how those bruises felt on her rail-thin frame. Every piece of every fantasy she ever incepted. The girl wanted, with every fiber she had, to feel the power he felt, then.

And with a wretched, bestial glare, she turned to the woman, flaunting her teeth like fangs. In her grasp she seized the sword—*her* sword—and flaunted it like a demon does its trident.

"Look at how filthy she is," Zenira stated, peering at the wretched woman.

The woman sobbed, despair dripping through tears. The fresh muck of battle stained the garment she wore, and her husband's crimson mark was smeared across her face. "I'm begging you," she pleaded. "You've already taken everything from me."

All the anger, all the frustration, and all the pain came out in a wretched strike. Blood sprayed a fountain, soaking the girl's face in thick red.

The woman's deflating, seeping corpse befell to the muck. Her breaths turned labored—fast and erratic—before succumbing to the jaws of ultimate death.

The wind picked up where her last breaths left off, sighing in a tide of air. It rippled the flames, accentuated the smoke's presence, and punctuated the complete, total loss of life.

A new tide swept over the girl as she held her destined blade. It carried serrations—which sent prickly tingles up her skeleton—and a pair of invisible hands which constricted her airway. The predatory glare fell away, making ample room for reality to assault her. She dropped the bloodied fang into the carnage, ripping at her scalp with tense fingers.

No, she thought, meandering about. *I didn't,* bounced around her skull.

A hand touched her shoulder, pulling.

Cariaah whipped around, and as she did, the flash of Snjick doing the same struck her.

Snjick.

"No!" the girl yelled. "D-don't—I didn't—tell me I didn't!" she screamed.

"Child, calm—"

"*No!*" she exclaimed again, backpedaling. "Leave me alone!" Cariaah continued to dig at her scalp, parting from the violent work she left behind. Her throat had thinned to the size of a needle, causing each heave to whistle.

Cariaah's jaw didn't cease its clench, her eye didn't relent with its gape, and her heart didn't abate its aggressive drum. She followed that drum, with all its fervency, into the blackness of the night.

As Cariaah made greater distance from the cloaks, Zenira, and all who swarmed the village of ash, Hassai dropped his hood to his shoulders. "What should we do?"

"We have to let her discover."

"Discover?"

Zenira sighed. "That the blood she just spilled was everything she ever wanted."

***

Muddy was the new day, desolate was the path, and unrelenting were those sullen thoughts. Cariaah felt as if she was trapped in the night still, regardless of the sun's grey presence.

When someone came in passing, the girl closed her eye and covered her ears. She wanted no temptation to recreate the death she had just imposed. It was as if she awakened a creature, one that controlled her with its darkness.

She walked with arms crossed, afraid to place even one hand on her blade's hilt. Her gaze traveled nowhere, and her focus didn't avert from the air she pulled in and fog she let out. She tried not to blink, for closing her eye brought thought of the night before.

Cariaah didn't know her destination, but she couldn't go back to the Vantaknights. That was certain. Even if some had survived the ambush, she couldn't face Snjick—not after what she had done.

So, the girl continued forward like a walking corpse.

She tried to remove all the sounds from her skull—all the screams.

But those final words of her prey wouldn't leave.

You've already taken everything from me.

She stopped on the road, allowing the day's noises to replace the stifle of her steps. She fell to her knees. The girl peered into the grey sky through the mist of her breath. A sight or sound—a new one—needed to replace the ones she currently had.

And that's when she heard the crying.

Cariaah turned to it, now on all fours.

It belonged to a girl, no older than eight winters. Her skin had a layer of ash, her hair was matted with clumps of dirt, and her hands made little fists to rub her eyes. She too knelt on that road, helpless.

Cariaah crawled to the girl, albeit slowly. It was a sight that, momentarily, distracted the barrage of self-loathing. "Are you alright?" she asked the girl.

The little one continued to sob for a second, before pausing her rubbing. "Me?"

Cariaah nodded.

A pair of passing steps came, crunching on the dirt beside them.

The girl went silent, hugging her knees.

"What's your name?"

"I-it's Mia."

"I'm Cariaah. What happened to you?"

"Nothing happened to me. It's my village. My mommy."

Cariaah's face went blank.

"Everything's gone! Everything burned down!" she cried, burying her face into her ash-covered legs.

Nothing miraculous could change the past. And she couldn't run from the haunt of not only what she'd done, but who she was—*what* she was.

But she could try.

"Come on," Cariaah said, rising to her feet. "We should get you something to eat. I'm sure you're hungry."

It was one thing she could be certain of.

Mia's frame was anemic, further annunciated when she rose to her feet. Her arms were the thickness of a sword's hilt, her face was gaunt—with sunken eye sockets and sharp cheekbones—and her ankles showed only skin, bone, and tendon.

Down the road they happened upon a straw-roofed inn. Its door swung freely on loose hinges, the windows were tiny slits in the thick walls, and the chimney emitted fluffy puffs of white steam. Inside, the stuffy air—lit by glowing candelabras that dripped with wax—welcomed the pair.

The tables were empty with only a teenage, elven inn-keep behind the smooth counter.

Cariaah followed her past predilections as a young child. She liked being against solid, unmoving things, especially when indoors. So, she led Mia to a corner table for two, pulling a chair out for her. "I'll get you something. Just stay here, okay?"

Mia nodded, still sniffling from her earlier sob.

On her way to the counter, she dug in her pockets. The only coin purse therein was from the pit—from that fight she argued the reward of. It made her lips form a half-smile until she thought of Snjick.

"Just need something to eat." Cariaah slid the purse across the counter.

The elf sifted through the clinking coins. "Just for the girl?"

"Just for the girl," she repeated in a lower voice. Cariaah didn't deserve a platter of anything, and she knew it.

The inn-keep nodded, turning her back.

When Cariaah returned to the table, bowl in hand, Mia had fallen asleep. Her head sat on its side, what little cheek she had cushioning her face.

"Hey," Cariaah whispered, sliding the steaming stew across.

Mia darted awake as if a wasp had stung her in the backside.

"It's alright," she assured, stirring with the spoon. "You should eat something."

The little one looked into the dish, eyes adjusting to calmness. She took her utensil and tried a chunk of carrot. "Thank you," Mia said.

"Your mother taught you good manners." Cariaah smiled, resting her chin on open hands. She watched the girl shovel food into her mouth like she'd just discovered sustenance. Cariaah couldn't help but feel she was peeking deep into the past—a familiar, flawed, fraction of her innocence.

"Are you okay?" Mia asked.

Cariaah raised her eyebrows in question.

"You're crying."

She sat up straight, cheek glistening. "Y-yes," she said, wiping her face. "Just eat."

But Mia's gaze lingered. It kept an attentive, studying look that preceded another question. "What happened to your eye?" she asked. "Did your home burn down, too?"

Cariaah sighed. She let the silence seep into the moment. "I'm sorry," she said, "about what happened to you." Cariaah sniffled, now. "And what happened to your—"

That front door swung open, slicing through the candlelight—extinguishing. It slammed into the wall and shook the inn. Mia yelped, dropping the spoon into the stew with a splash.

Cariaah's hand went to her hip first, then her hilt.

The inn-keep ducked, her eyes barely peeking over the counter with trepidation.

A pair of entering, metallic stomps preceded two more. However, those first two steps dominated the noise with aggressive presence.

Cariaah narrowed her eye.

Three orcs, all clad in thick, crude, steel armor marched into the place like it was their very own. Clear as the daylight that spilled through the doorway was the leader of this trio.

"Three little girls," he said. "I was expecting *some* sort of challenge, not an afternoon stroll." The large, brooding piece of muscle cleared his throat. His jaw had the weight of a sledgehammer, and his olive skin shone as if covered in oil. At his hip clung a spiky mace which bounced as he marched. "Give me every piece of gold in these four walls."

Only the haze of the freshly dormant candles swirled.

The inn-keep had latched to the countertop like a child to their parent. Not budging—only flinching—with each word.

"Owen," he called, calmly. "Take the girl—the little one."

A smaller, hunched orc came forth, his steps lighter but more frequent. He unsheathed the longsword at his hip rather ungracefully, and with an outstretched, rusty gauntlet reached for Mia's collar.

"Don't touch her," spat Cariaah.

The hunch-back snickered, nasally.

Mia's sobbing returned again. She looked to Cariaah.

The leader took two, encroaching steps toward them, a smile smeared across his face. "You'll have to repeat that, little *bitch*."

Cariaah clenched her jaw. She tightened her fists—one taut around that hilt. *"Don't touch her."*

The cawing of nearby crows penetrated the windows, echoing.

The leader's smile faded. "Owen." He nodded.

Owen's blade had pressed to Mia's throat before Cariaah could unsheathe. He stole the little girl right from the table, sending her chair into a topple.

"Cariaah!" Mia called immediately.

She shot up from her seat, fingers tied to her blade.

The leader took no heed. He had already diverted focus to the inn-keep, who'd receded further behind the counter in refuge. "All the gold!" he reiterated. "You want a little kid's blood on your hands?"

The elf looked on with a listless, terrified stare.

And that word echoed within Cariaah's skull. *Hands*. She released the hilt, looking to her open palms and empty fingers. Then, the girl's glare shot about the tavern, to the leader who demanded at the counter, the hunched orc holding Mia, and the third orc, who approached Cariaah with a drawn pair of daggers.

The creature—which ran her every morbid action—awakened. It put a smile on her face.

She stared at the dagger wielding orc, her teeth icy.

"What are you smiling—"

Cariaah tightened a claw at her side. She slithered that spell's invisible, slender fingers into her opponent's mind. Every memory came in a flash—every fear—every dream he ever experienced.

The girl took no heed.

He writhed in the spell but could move only his eyes plagued with petrification.

She closed her fist.

Her target fell to the floor in a great thud, his fragmented skull leaving a river of crimson to stain the floor.

"Witchcraft!" shouted Owen, his blade still to Mia's throat. He backpedaled, warning, "Stay—"

A new claw took form, and with it arrived the spell in Owen, seizing his every movement. Without a thought—without heeding Mia's struggle, Cariaah closed her fist once more, unleashing a new crimson fountain.

Mia scampered away, into another corner.

The leader had gone silent, pressing his backside against the counter for stability. His mace was drawn in a shivering hand, and he peered not as a predator but as a weak, puny insect. "Don't," he pleaded. "We can make a deal. *You* can have the gold, you—"

She ceased his shivering with her seizing and took hold of every command he sent to his muscles. "I don't want gold," she proclaimed. "I just want your blood to flow like a river."

Ignoring the thoughts she had within her grasp, the pleas that only she and the orc could hear, Cariaah made one final fist. And as her desire came to blaring, crimson fruition, he fell against the counter as a lifeless piece of flesh.

All was silent.

Only the panting of the shrouded killer filled the air. The smoke from the candles had faded, the crows didn't caw, and Mia didn't call her name.

Mia.

Cariaah whipped around.

The girl sat in the corner of the inn, her hands over her ears and eyes vacant. Nothing graced her face. No relief. No gratitude, hope, or even despair. She was a slate wiped clean.

And when Cariaah approached—even with one tiny step—Mia flinched.

Cariaah scrambled out of the inn, panting from more than just the intensity of the spell. Her throat closed. She fell to the dirt, thunder rolling in the distance, wind spewing brittle leaves about.

She curled up below a lone, bare tree, knees tight to her chest and eye squeezed shut. Her ears rung, leaving only the percuss of her shattering pulse. She drove herself toward crying—to let go of everything in a stream of tears. Tears of empathy. Of grief. Of guilt.

Only no tears ever came.

10 THE BRUTE

A thick film of grey lined the capitol's streets. Only the warm, dancing glow of lanterns upon the city walls permeated the fog. The typical stream of passing tourists—their eyes filled with wonderment at seeing Xardiil for the first time—was nowhere to be found. They had withdrawn indoors due to the impending inclement weather.

The district of commerce held the greatest mix of people, as the businesses were a dice-roll in quality and avariciousness. Some pubs encompassed a cesspool of peasantry and ordinary folk, which created a pandemonium that played out through the pipe-smoky haze. Other taverns displayed less idiocy, hosting nobles and rich folk that drank at a ridiculous price. The latter taverns had smooth wooden counters, hand-crafted goblets, and designated lounges.

However, most had women. And the male customers within—peasants or otherwise—shared a mutual lust.

Isaac insisted they go to The Spotted Mare, a bar that fell within the middle of this scale. Benoit agreed, not to mention the half-elf and their captain. A bar like this—with average architecture, ale, food, carpentry, and everything else—would contain the greatest mix of people. Thus, the Spotted Mare would masquerade them best.

Isaac led the group through the entrance, Iz's hand in his. He had been to this bar on many occasions: some during contracts, others in his free time. However, due to the past five winters of Iz's training, it had been a while.

This tavern typically hopped with energy and, due to the impending storm, today was no exception. Everyone inside had settled into their spots—the counter being the most populated—warming their insides with a lit pipe and foamy pint. A crackling fireplace lingered against the far wall, drawing several groups of people to share drinks over conversation.

The night crowd hadn't arrived with their insanity, yet. Thus, things in the Spotted Mare maintained a certain level of quaintness.

Ashura got them a table, Benoit pulled the necessary number of chairs over, and Isaac went to the bar to order a pentagon of drinks. They all settled thereafter, encircling the unwiped table, remnants of bread crust and drops of ale still present.

Snjick had his arms crossed, slouched.

Benoit toyed with his claws, intermittently picking through his feathers.

Iz kicked her legs, glancing about the tavern.

Isaac gazed at the swirling cloud of pipe smoke that hovered above them.

And Ashura stared into his lap, at nothing.

Things were silent.

Eventually the ale arrived, drinks sliding to their respective owners, including a cup of water for Iz.

Isaac drank first, letting the liquor pour down his open throat. "Shit," he said, following a swallow. "I remember it being better than this."

Nobody acknowledged him.

"By the gods," Isaac continued. "What are we doing here?"

Benoit scoffed through his beak. "I didn't choose this place."

"That's not what I'm saying, *wise-ass*." He narrowed his eyes. "I mean in the land above; what are we doing?" he groaned, turning a glare to Ashura, who still bowed his head. "I mean, one of our brothers or sisters could still be down there, as we speak."

Ashura clenched his jaw and tightened his fists. Those morose images sank into his head, like the pools of blood that seeped into the carpets of the hall. "What would you have done differently?" he asked, picking his head up.

"Well, *captain*," Isaac spat. "I definitely wouldn't've tucked my pecker between my legs and ran the fuck away."

Ashura sharpened his glare. "*Isaac*," he snapped. Nothing came out after as his eyes traveled about the table.

They all watched, Benoit the only one sipping his drink.

"What?"

Ashura let out an exhale as he bit his lip. He drummed his fingers on the wood of the table. "I don't enjoy playing around in the blood of my siblings."

Isaac shook his head. "Do you know what you are, Ashura?" He took a swig of ale. "You're an assassin—a tool. Blood is—or should be—in your nature. If you had set your fears aside, we could've looked for survivors."

He opened his mouth to speak but still said nothing. Just wrapped his fingers around his pint and placed his gaze elsewhere.

Isaac stood, his chair skidding away. "And you can't even look at me? *Pathetic.*" He scoffed. "A captain?" Turning away, he navigated through the hazy tavern.

Iz's explorative eyes fell upon Isaac as he left. They glistened in the warm light before fixing on Ashura. "He's just angry," she said, reaching over. "It's not your fault."

Ashura stood before her hand could touch his, gulping down his ale in an ungraceful chug.

"Leaving already?" Benoit asked facetiously.

Snjick still slouched in his chair, his arms crossed as he peered into his liquor's foam.

Ashura left his empty cup for the table, marching through the crowdedness of the tavern, toward the same door Isaac left swinging. He shoved himself through it, hinges squealing as he stepped onto the cobblestone street.

Isaac had gone off on his own, Ashura knew that, and he wouldn't go searching the fog for him. The captain leaned against the Spotted Mare.

The endless grey sky held his gaze upon tilting his head back. Chills nibbled, leaving him numb with tingles.

He needed another drink.

But he couldn't turn back and face his party again. Not as a coward.

The Black Hog—a tavern on the opposite end of the district—came to mind. It may have been twice the cost of the bar he leaned against, but at least he could surround himself with strangers—with people who cared less of his presence.

With the arrival of a drizzle—its raindrops pecking at his cheeks—Ashura took his weight back, though hesitated after an initial step forward.

Splotches of crimson stained the black of his gauntlets with no underlying wound. He rubbed them with his thumb. But no matter how swift, or with how much pressure, the red remained.

The red remained.

***

Ashura once worked on a contract with another knight—her name being Lillian.

Its details stirred up quite a bit of excitement in the land below, despite the mission's smallness. It contradicted the nature of the Vantaknights, or more precisely, their tendency to fall into the shadows during their work. It was determined by the X—and agreed to by Ashura and Lillian—that their approach should converse previous ones.

The contract's subject, Lex, was a vampire. This typically wouldn't cause any sort of issue, but Lex had a reputation of being conniving. Manipulative. Not to mention his lair brimmed with traps and other forms of security.

It wouldn't take place in his lair, however, as he had rented a mansion in the district of commerce to host a party. This was a common tactic for Lex: befriend several people—this time, seven—and invite them over to his newly bought "home" to be killed and feasted upon. One of them was Lillian, who would bring Ashura along as a plus-one.

Ironically, the pair of them planned to make an evening out of it, as well.

"A couple of drinks, first?" Ashura asked Lillian, who held him by the arm as they strolled. The sun's drenching, orange light peered over the walls of the capitol as it set, emitting a breath of warmth over everything.

"Are we really showing up to this thing drunk?" she replied through a smile.

"I said a *couple* of drinks. One each."

"Okay, let me rephrase." She paused, hovering a finger over her lips, pretending to search for the right words. "Are *you* really showing up to this thing drunk?"

He snickered and shook his head.

Lillian giggled.

"I can take more than one drink. I'm a big guy!" he exclaimed. They were already shouting at each other over the noise of passerby, but Ashura made it a point to be obnoxious.

"Alright then, 'big guy,'" Lillian said, pulling him into the Black Hog. "Let's not miss the turn."

The Black Hog bustled in its typical fashion. The prime hour for drinking had arrived, and with it came a tide of drunkards, already inebriated upon entry. And while the Black Hog attracted nobility, it still held a considerable amount of rambunctiousness during the night hours.

Most of the tables remained empty, however, as the people had crowded the bar like a hive.

The pair of them wandered over to a table—freshly wiped and glistening—after ordering their drinks. Ashura fell into his chair, the wood creaking so loud it almost classified as a crack.

"By the gods, Ash," Lillian said as she sat across from him, giggling. "That wasn't very graceful."

"It's a change of pace tonight," he said, leaning back. "I only have to be skillful in words, not movements."

"You're not really impressing me on either front." Lillian placed her chin on her hand, the elbow of which supporting. "Although, you are looking handsome. I only get to see you in that suit of armor. It's a welcomed change."

He observed himself, briefly. Raquel was originally going to dress him for the contract, but Lillian insisted she do it herself. A black tunic of velvet accompanied burgundy leggings, all draped by a silky, decorative cape. It framed to his figure tightly, as per Ellen's measurements and Don's actual labor.

He snickered, eyes glowing in the warmth of the surrounding noise. "You look lovely," he uttered, almost afraid someone else would hear for whatever reason.

"You mean it?" she asked. Lillian's smooth face didn't reveal her age, let alone the excitement that spilled from her lips.

"I do," he said.

The gravel of his voice coaxed her to blush.

And Ashura fell deeper into her violet eyes, getting lost.

Soon an elven boy came over with their drinks and placed them on the table.

Ashura nodded as a means of thanks, breaking his shared gaze with Lillian. He had begun to study the curvature of her face, something he never grew tired of when he got a moment to simply watch her.

Her cheekbones rested high, yet they weren't so gaunt that their structure was chiseled. The woman's tight neck clung to her jaw, all of which was framed by a head of pin-straight black hair.

"How are they?" he asked, gazing at those features.

"What?"

"Vampires. I know you have a bit of experience with them."

"Manipulative. Witty. They have sharp tongues and an untamable thirst for blood," she took a sip of ale, "kind of like men, really."

"Oh, please," he scoffed, "I'm not *witty*."

They laughed.

Sipping at their drinks, they observed each other and, intermittently, the tavern surrounding them. The nobles ranting about things of fluff grew tiresome. Thus, they returned their eyes to each other. However, a creeping, ulterior feeling reminded Ashura to avert his gaze ever-so-often, resorting to a single red jewel on his goblet. He peered into its glow but thought of the woman across from him.

***

Ashura couldn't remember if there were always whores at the Black Hog. Yet, on this day of grey mugginess, they waltzed about the tavern, flaunting their breasts, carrying platters of hors-d'oeuvres, and seeking coin.

The tavern granted his request to simply sit, drink, and exist. A once occupied stool at the bar freed itself when an oafish nobleman had been coaxed away by a woman.

Ashura fell into the stool. He didn't look at the bartender, though in his periphery he watched him clean a goblet with a rag. "Ale," he commanded, removing his coin purse, and dropping it onto the counter. "Fill my drinks up once they're empty."

"That sure is some strange armor, lad," the bartender uttered, swiping Ashura's purse away.

The hive. The land below. The blood. Her.

"Ale," he commanded, again.

"I'm on it, lad, I'm on it."

Ashura looked at the shelves of liquor as the bartender poured his drink.

"Wait a second," said the bartender. "I've seen ye before."

Ashura wrapped his fingers around the ale, not drinking, only staring. His eyes fixed themselves upon a red jewel embedded in the metal of the goblet.

"Well, I must be honest, I only remember you because of the lass you had at your arm."

He bit down on nothing. His brow twitched.

"A fine one she was!" the bartender exclaimed, laughing, which encouraged the others to do the same.

Silent images sped through his mind as he shook, drowning in his seat. They were all of her; the way she pulled at her bangs in a fidget or giggled at his stupidity. Her presence.

It prompted him to leap to his feet and reach for his blade.

The laughter ceased.

He gritted his teeth, prepared to unsheathe his steel.

A hand—one gentle and soft—greeted his forearm.

Ashura quickened his glare to whomever touched him, ready to pounce.

The person's eyes resembled the hand: soft, conversing Ashura's demeanor. It was one of the women—her hair short and skin dark—who stood before him.

Ashura growled, "What are—"

She drove her heel into his toe, shutting him up. "He's with me. We have something scheduled in one of the beds."

The bartender and every surrounding patron erupted in laughter. "He was just nervous for Aya! What a riot!"

She gripped Ashura's wrist, digging her fingers into his gauntlet as she dragged him away from the bar. Her spell—the allure of her and the unexpected ferocity she demonstrated—silenced any protest. The further she led him along, the thinner the crowd around them got.

The air had changed into something else—fragrant with incense and warm with glowing candlelight. The pair of them walked down a narrow corridor, many women chatting and leading clients into bedrooms. Sensorially, Ashura had little time to comprehend the layout or place the sounds and scents.

This woman yanked him into a vacant room dense with the aromatic feast of the corridor. Paintings accompanied the curtained windows yet nothing busied the room's appearance other than the bed that centralized it. Only smoking sticks of incense and flickering candles breathed the room's air.

She closed the door behind them.

Ashura found the silence to squeeze in a single word. "Who—"

"It doesn't matter *who* I am," she said, placing her hands on his shoulders. "I'm here, now. Just do your thing." The ferocity had fallen away in her eyes, turning into something submissive.

"I don't—"

She guided him to the bed—made with pale green sheets of silk—and sat him down.

"Aya?"

She looked at him, puzzled.

"That's your name, isn't it?"

She hesitated. "Come on." Her fingers reached for the fastenings of his cuirass. "Let's get this off, big guy."

The pace she worked at fell in a decrescendo as the level of interest her client reciprocated became evident. Aya eventually stopped her work, placing her hands on his shoulders at the noise he made.

He befell to a sob, giving his weight to the mattress and rolling on his side. "J-just hold me," he said, curling into a ball. "*Just hold me.*"

***

Lillian's hair danced in the flirtatious breeze as they stood outside the mansion. "Are you ready?" she asked. "I want you to meet some new people, handsome." She stated her presence, using the bronze doorknocker to do so.

The door opened, immediately. And clearly something ailed he who answered. His face appeared gaunt; his pupils resided in grey irises as little ovular slits, and the fangs that lingered amongst his teeth hadn't revealed themselves. "Come in, come in," he said, almost whispering. The vampire strafed away from the door, allowing his prey into the newly outfitted lair.

They shuffled—seemingly oblivious—into the empty monster of

a stead.

"It's quiet," said Lillian as the door locked behind them. "I could've sworn we arrived a bit late. I was going to apologize, in fact."

"I'm a bit embarrassed that you were the only ones to show, Lillian." He turned an eye to her accomplice. "And your name?"

His distractedness at the scenery snapped away. "Oh," he said. "Ashura."

"My, quite a large man, you are." His eyes gaped, predatorially.

Ashura grunted, acknowledging his words. "This is extremely nice." He grazed the nearby wall with his fingertips. "Is this new?"

The mansion was cavernous. Its vacancy, however, revealed the endlessness of it. One room seemed to carry the whole interior, extending from the foyer—a towering alcove—to the living area—filled anemically with three cushioned chairs—and to the dining space—which encompassed a puny circular table. The place was soulless.

"Yes," Lex said. "This party—or what should have been a party—was designed to be a housewarming event. Though, I'm only modestly equipped for such a thing."

"I think it's lovely," Lillian said, exhuming false intrigue. "So much potential!"

Lex's face remained listless. "Come sit." He roamed over to the table which had four glasses of wine and a large bottle upon it.

They granted his request, shuffling into their chairs. Ashura glanced at Lillian ever-so-briefly as the vampire poured the wine. She, ultimately, was the leader of this contract.

Her gaze did not avert from their opponent's.

An alarm echoed in Ashura's head.

Lex had poured wine in the fourth glass.

"Is someone else here?" he asked, his fingers flirting with his blade's hilt.

Lex's brow twitched. He hesitated. "No. No, there isn't." He corked the bottle of wine, placing it aside.

Ashura nodded, looking to his wine. Faintly, in the light of the dripping candles, a mark revealed itself upon the brim of the glass: a half-circle of an imperfection. Someone had already drank from it.

"Go on," Lex said. "I'm curious to see what you think. It's imported."

Ashura took a large, languid breath of air. "From where?"

"Across the sea. Mira."

He scoffed. He leaned into the conversation, his chair groaning. "Who else is here, Lex?" His hand gripped the hilt, tightly.

Lex raised his eyebrows, taken aback by the bluntness. He then smiled, revealing his fangs. "The other guests are already dead," he hissed.

Ashura began to rip his blade free from its sheath.

Lillian halted Ashura's drawing wrist with a stiff hand, causing him to raise an eyebrow. Her eyes had turned wide, staring past Lex's shoulder.

When he looked where she did, his heart fell through the floor and into the graves of the other guests.

Another figure—one akin to Lex in appearance—peeled from the ceiling. His frame stretched long and thin, and when his feet greeted the floor, the steps that followed shuffled. "May I join you?"

"Please do, Elliot," said Lex.

He shuffled over, sitting in his seat. Languid. Quiet

Everything fell into silence, calculation and shock filling the air.

"You are a strange pair. Was your name Lillian? I believe that's what I overheard." This vampire already flaunted his fangs. His hair conversed Lex's as it shimmered an icy blonde.

Lillian nodded, her glare sharp.

"The others had realized their fate by this point." He sipped from the fourth glass. The liquid moved like syrup. Thicker than wine.

Ashura's hand hadn't eased on his blade.

"But not you two." He smiled, teeth stained red. "What's different?" Elliot darted his glance to Ashura, cutting into him. "You know, you would make a great beast of the night, like us."

The brute's knuckles turned white.

"As would you, my darling." He looked to Lillian, next.

Ashura ripped the blade out, as if he had uncaged an animal. He lunged for Elliot, flipping the table over. Glass shattered on the smoothness of the floor, red spreading.

Elliot evaded his strike with a strafe, swiping his claws across Ashura's gauntlet.

With a wince, the swordsman sliced the claw-flaunting hand from the creature's wrist, creating a spraying wound.

Elliot hissed, bearing his fangs.

Ashura lunged, burying his blade into the creature's chest, and pinning him to the floor. "A beast of the night?" he asked, hissing like Elliot. "That's what I already am." He buried his steel further into Elliot's heart.

His opponent gasped, nothing but blood arising.

"Ash-Ashura."

He never leapt to his feet faster. And upon turning around, red staining his face, the rage bottomed out into despair.

Lex's fangs had sunken into Lillian's throat, draining her skin of any remote color. He continued to feed, regardless of Lillian's steel driven through his torso. He writhed in the ecstasy of her taste.

Her jaw twitched, struggling to utter a word.

Ashura hurried over and tore Lex away from her, burrowing his blade into the vampire's stomach—alongside Lillian's—and peered into his eyes with blackness. He didn't avert his glare. He *couldn't*.

Lillian fell onto her back. Her throat seeped, leaking onto the floor in a swirling, crimson pool. She gasped and heaved and wheezed, her throat gurgling with the onslaught of red.

Even though Lex was already dead, Ashura kept stabbing, trying to kill a corpse.

Lillian managed a pair of rough, impaling words, "Too fast." Whatever she tried to say next became obscured by death's grasp.

The noises stopped. Thankfully. But too soon.

A single tear—his first tear—rolled from his brooding eyes. He curled into a ball, tightening his figure into a knot, and lying beside her. His gaze faced away, into the emptiness of the mansion.

As he cried, writhing in the marinade of blood, he cradled his torso.

Coward, he mouthed at himself. *You're a coward.*

***

Aya held him tight, squeezing as he recoiled in fervent wretchedness.

"I'm sorry," he murmured through his sob. "I'm sorry."

"I-it's okay," she said, burrowing her face into him.

The door opened. It sliced through the warmness, the gallery of aromas, and the cushioning of their being against each other. "Aya," called a voice. "What in the god's fuck is taking you so long? We need a whore for a *very* special client."

He was a boor—the owner of The Black Hog—with large, droopy jowls and a wiry moustache.

She rose to her feet, taking a blanket from the bedding and covering herself as she approached the oaf. After a slight pause she asserted, "I'm not a fucking whore." She slammed the door so the walls shook. She made a gentle way back to him. She wrapped her arms around the crying man again. "I'm here," she whispered. "I'm here."

Aya held the brute for the rest of the night, the surrounding candles warming that bed.

11 WHAT REMAINS

The girl's new nest was beneath that tree.

Rain poured, shedding grass from dirt to make mud.

A barrage of steps passed her on the adjacent road, yet to whom they belonged she would never know.

She wouldn't dare look.

Cariaah had tightened herself into a knot, knees to her chest and arms hugging her legs. Her cheek had impressed a mold in the mud, serving as the only anomaly of warmth. The only feeling she experienced came in the form of that caked blood on her face.

The girl had no clue who it belonged to.

And the fact that she knew each of those orc's names, fears, dreams, and memories made it even worse.

For all she knew, it could've been the woman's blood.

In the span of one single evening—from midnight to twilight—she'd taken four lives that left devastation. That creature had awakened within, forcing her to enjoy the blood she shed.

Cariaah couldn't run from herself.

But she could *end* herself.

If the girl continued to merely exist then it would lead to inevitable havoc. She would destroy countless lives in a spree of death with that awakened creature at the helm. All she had to do in this moment—as the rain continued to pelt her laying figure—was come to her knees, rip that blade from its sheath, and bury it into her gut.

Then she could enjoy the pouring of her own blood.

She could die knowing she *saved* countless lives.

But her mind ran amok, offering every reason not to bury that sword. It told her that she could continue her spree in her black shroud, immerse fully in that creature's decree, and listen to nothing but morbid desire.

The girl lifted her face from the mud, opened her eye, and unfurled her figure. She rose to her knees in a slow, passionless motion, and stared above. Past those bare branches, the onslaught of rain, and the canopy of an endless, ugly sky, she knew there was a golden one. Where the sun emitted its warm, radiant glow, and promised all life below a fruitful day.

Then Cariaah looked down at the blood-stained, abyssal armor she donned. She wondered if inside her, too, such a scene resided.

That hilt beckoned her grasp. Perhaps it beckoned the golden sky within her to deliver a righteous fate. One good for the lands above and below.

Perhaps *she* was the filth that needed cleansing.

Cariaah gripped her blade with a tight hand. The metal rattled.

But on the near road a pair of squelching, uneven steps metallically rung out. They didn't come in passing but rather in a gradual encroach. "Are you alright, miss?" asked whomever those steps belonged to.

Her grip wavered, abating its tightness. "F-fine."

The rain filled the subsequent void. Until the steps drew nearer.

She didn't draw her blade, instead resting the heel of her palm on its pommel. The girl's breath escalated—just a little—so that her chest recoiled with each exchange of air. Her muscles were sore as if someone had run her over with a horse-drawn cart.

The girl didn't give her attention as the person knelt beside her, a longsword away.

"I like the rain," he said, calmly. "It speaks to the sadder parts in us—our past, our regrets, our emotions. But it brings everything life. *Everything.*"

She removed her hand.

"Think about it. It fills the oceans, rivers, and lakes which harbor fish. Not only that, but it gives life to the plants that surround us. Now, *that* is the key. Because the little critters eat the plants, animals eat the critters, and beasts eat the animals. It's a chain! Beautiful."

A distant clap of thunder echoed.

"Now, what's your name, miss?"

She felt him inch closer. "Cariaah," she said, almost a whisper.

"A very good name. A very different name. *Exotic.*" He hummed. "I'm Jean."

The girl turned her head toward him.

He had a soft face engulfed by a beard—with speckles of rain and grey—and a powdery gaze of blue. Strapped to him was a vest of hefty leather which hosted a smattering of things, some of which Cariaah couldn't decipher. Vials, twine, small daggers, bolts—for a crossbow strapped to his back—and many other tools and trinkets.

However, the fuel of the girl's newfound puzzlement stared with beady eyes of black. On this dwarf's shoulder—perched with sharp talons and dark feathers—sat a raven.

Her eye must have reflected this perplexity.

"Oh," the dwarf said, "this here's Rose." He ran a gloved finger down the bird's chest. "She's a life-saver, that's for sure."

Cariaah's lips parted. She couldn't find proper words, even if she wanted to speak.

"Where are you headed?" he asked.

"I'm—"

"Well, I'll tell you where I'm headed. *The capitol,*" he said as if he were hunting treasure. "Following a rumor about some silver mage."

She was reminded of her breath again. Just how narrow her airway was. "Who?" she asked, nearly interrogating.

"Why, yes," he said, peering into the distance. "Apparently some strange army led by a man adorned in white just...appeared. Truly fascinating. Let's hope he doesn't kill us all!" he exclaimed, heartily laughing.

"So, you're going to the capitol? Is he there?" She reached for her hip, clawing at that bruise.

"Oh, no. I just figure it's the best place for information." He chuckled again. "Anyway, where are you headed again? The capitol?"

"Well—"

"Isn't that just perfect?" He sprung to his feet like he was thirty winters younger. "I'm always happy to share an adventure!"

She scoffed.

"Come on," he said, already beginning on the road. "We can't leave that shithole of a city waiting!"

The girl rose to her feet merely out of obligation. As if she owed this dwarf something of a favor, even though she'd just met him.

Xardiil could be seen as a looming stretch of cityscape, close, but appearing further due to the haze of the rain. The rolling hills—mostly treeless—in their vicinity didn't shine their typical hue of emerald, instead submitting to the rain's sullenness. Their footsteps sloshed the water about, sending minute tides.

"You may be wondering how an old codger like me is still alive, wandering this land for as long I have," he said, breath climbing with every word. "Well, I'll let you guess."

She had tuned him out, assuming he would continue for her.

"Go on, *guess*."

She sighed. "Oh, well, I'm not sure."

"Not a very good response if you want to make conversation."

"I don't know." She shrugged. "You've probably been smart," she settled on. He seemed like the type to boast.

"Nope. I'm a fool if I've ever seen one. The key," he continued as if he were about to unveil a secret, "is Rose, here." He pet the bird. "If she—with her acute senses—detects danger, she'll dart up to the sky and…"

The girl tuned him out once more, focusing on the cityscape ahead. If she lingered around the city, or in its vast sea of districts, where was she to go? Where were her steps leading?

Where could she do it?

The pit.

Perhaps allowing someone else to bury steel into her gut would suffice. It was right for her—a proper farewell to everything she was. After all, such a scenario brought comfort: standing before an armed opponent with a blade to defend her. Only this time, she wouldn't be putting up a defense.

She wouldn't fight for a way out.

"Would you come with me to the pit?" she asked, interrupting whatever he rambled on about.

"The pit?" he repeated in perplexity, humming. "Never understood the appeal. Violence brings pleasure to some people, but not me, that's for sure." He stroked his beard. "But if it's where our journey takes us, then so be it. After all, it's a place I haven't been."

"You'll get to be up close—explore it fully."

"Don't tell me you're going in there to fight." He raised an eyebrow. "Are ye?"

She didn't respond.

"Don't you think you're a little young for a-fighting?"

"And don't you think you're a little old for adventuring?" she snapped back.

He rioted in laughter. "One thing is certain, you sure aren't too young to be talking like that."

It was fitting. Going to the hole. After all, a hole was where the girl belonged. And once they approached the city's massive gates, Xardiil beckoned her with its rampant filth. A storm still lingered above them—dropping rain and thunder—sick people passed them—coughing and sniffling—and an anemic mutt laid beside the road, licking its chops.

But regardless, Jean laughed through it all. His obliviousness came in the form of a shield which deflected all darkness.

Cariaah envied that shield.

She silently led them toward the pit district, through an onslaught of passerby. The district they roamed through now, known as the mediator, brimmed with traps for tourists. Certain beverages—whether it be the juice of native fruits or otherwise—wore ridiculous price-tags. Yet, people awe-struck by the foreignism of the capitol threw their coin purses at merchants.

"I'm curious," Jean said.

Her hand hovered over her the bruise, scared she may reveal something about herself. Something she didn't plan on.

"A girl like you fighting in the—"

She threw a glare at him.

He chuckled. "What would lead you to throw yourself into such a mortal coin toss?"

The crowd roared as the two approached the pit's vibrating shell. They cheered for whomever fought. It was distant and muffled, but the sound beckoned Cariaah into the hole.

With a morbid promise.

Those ever-dripping candles, clinking tankards, and scent of musty stone brought a wave of nostalgia over the girl. A feeling she didn't anticipate. It brought her right to the moment—right to when Snjick touched her shoulder. Only now, in opposition to last night, she shook the thought off. She ventured deeper into the hole.

The girl only recognized two elves who sat in the corner, of which she didn't know the names of. They were strangers. Dahl, however, she remembered with electric vivacity. He sat at his desk, reading from a book.

"I'm going to see if I can get a fight," Cariaah told Jean. "Just wait here."

"Well, there's liquor, why would I want to leave?" He chuckled, parting from her side.

She approached Dahl, the heat of stares searing her back.

Dahl only brought his stare to the girl when she pulled up a chair and sat.

"I want to fight."

He briefly inspected her. "I haven't seen you in quite a while, girl. That armor's new. And you had a spunk about you before. I don't see it now." He looked down at his book, again. "Snjick isn't with you, either. I wonder how the lad's doing."

She tapped her foot against the stone, trying to hurry the conversation away. Expel that thought again.

"I can get you a fight, sure. Right after the one up there. Coin won't be good though, as you're standing in for someone who backed out."

"That's fine. I don't care."

His eyes darted back to her, once again. They lingered longer. "That's not like you, either. You argued about the pay of that last fight."

She hummed similar to how Jean had been doing through their journey. She stayed in her seat, not consciously doing so, but because thought entrapped her. Since her awakening in the forest with Zenira and his mare, Cariaah hadn't drawn her sword. She'd used *his* blade to slaughter the woman. Her hands to kill the orcs in concession. And now, she wouldn't draw it in this fight.

Because it wouldn't be a fight.

It would be the saving of countless lives to come—the killing of that creature within.

"That's it."

Her head perked up, and the girl could hear a shuffling pair of steps pass her seat.

Dahl elaborated, "That's your cue."

She rose from that seat—perhaps awakening once again—and made a direct, slow walk toward the stairs. Toward the pit. Toward her death.

"I've seen this before," Dahl murmured.

She paused.

"Don't do it."

Cariaah exhaled. "I've had every chance," she said, "to *not* do it." The girl continued forward, up the stairs in a march. That blade clinked against her hip. And at the top of those steps, through the bloody trail and haze of muffled rainfall, awaited her very grave.

A tomb with no headstone.

And as she traversed the shadows, awaiting her opponent to come forth from the opposite side of the pit, a voice called to her.

"Cariaah…"

She turned to face the beckon, as it echoed through the stairwell behind her.

It cut through the crowd's roar like a prophetic utterance. "Cariaah…"

As the crowd continued to chant, her opponent presumably ready, she took a step toward the voice behind her.

A figure emerged from the shadowy curtain, stepping into the grey light of the rain. They donned a fluttering, silky black robe which fell to their ankles gracefully. And when they came forth, the dropping of their hood—for the first time since reentering the pit—revealed a face the girl recognized.

Raquel, the elven face of the X.

"Why are you here?"

"This is where you met Snjick, correct?"

She looked to the ground.

"We have to leave. Forget this fight," Raquel said. "Zenira's coming. The land below needs you, all of what's left."

"What do you mean?" Cariaah asked.

"There's been talk of talk of darkly armored people—our brothers and sisters—at the Spotted Mare," she said. "I suspect they're all that remains."

When they emerged from the hole there was a silence amongst them, despite the city's crowded noise. Jean's confusion made him unable to muster a joke—though he gladly tagged along—Raquel's focus was evident in the elf's posture, and Cariaah's angst made the girl a walking epitome of nerves.

However, upon their traversal of the district's gates, Raquel broke the silence. "Cariaah."

Did she know? Like Dahl did? "Y-yes?" She reached for her hip.

"Are you excited to see them? To see your siblings?"

Cariaah couldn't answer the question with a simple yes or no. But she nodded regardless, which made the elf smile.

However, the land below held very little aside from strangers. The girl didn't know which faces awaited her—which faces she'd recognize—at the bar. Cariaah couldn't handle being in a foreign milieu, not for the umpteenth time.

Once they turned the corner on a particular street—filled with vendors selling snack-like foods—the sign of the tavern swayed in the misty breeze. It creaked on its hinges, teasing the trio to draw near.

"The bastard's going to pay," Raquel said. "With more than his life."

Cariaah knew that reverting to her bruise again wouldn't ease her tangling nerves. It raised the question, *What had Zenira truly done?* but furthermore, *which faces—out of the ones she knew—were still alive?*

If any?

The walk toward the tavern's front door proved to be the longest. Cariaah had ignored her surroundings up until then, receding entirely. Her steps had been automatic, maneuvering through the passerby without any related thought. However, in this final stretch of street—from the corner to the Spotted Mare—the girl observed all else.

The cobblestone below. It stretched through the district, winding about, and supporting the steps of those upon it.

The cracks within that stone. Minute like blood vessels, they feathered out in the street, catching rain, and making little rivers.

The sky above. Clouds hung as an endless canvas of grey, pouring nothing but rain.

The other buildings. Most were shops, standing three or four stories tall for residents to dwell with signs outside them. "The Feathered Blacksmith," "Mutton and other Meats," and "Custom Furniture."

Finally, she glanced at the people surrounding them. Nobles passed, one of which scarfed down a chunk of bread beside a beggar who crouched with outstretched hands. But what led her back to her nerves was the sight of an elf who wore chainmail and donned a scimitar at his hip.

They pushed the door open, warm air greeting their skin. It may have been crowded, but the outliers were evident.

Iz's hair was first. That initial sight of icy silk. And Isaac, with a drinking apparatus of some sort in hand, stood at the little one's side. She didn't recognize the dalaryn he conversed with.

Ashura sat across from the half-elf; whose back faced the door. The brute's gaze met Cariaah's, drawing a smile out of him.

She closed her eye out of horror before Snjick could turn to her. The girl dug into her hip with rigid fingertips, for the urge had overwhelmed. Her breath became a pant, just like when she awoke to darkness in the land below.

His approaching steps usurped all other noises.

Those steps stopped, and Cariaah let go of an exhale. "Snjick?" she asked, her eye still shut.

The bar was all but silent, but the pair of them ignored the noise.

He wrapped his arms around her. He squeezed. Tight.

Their embrace generated warmth. Genuine warmth. It swirled between them, leaving tingles and an avalanche of relief. The girl befell to tears—the ones she couldn't find before—as did the half-elf. There couldn't have been a greater moment of connectivity—of silent, mutual understanding.

Ashura stood beside them, as did Iz and Isaac and Benoit. They congregated in the middle of the tavern as Vantaknights once again.

Jean darted glances about the tavern and at his new travelling companions. "I don't know what's happening," he said. "But it seems like a happy time, so I'll order some drinks!"

"I like you already!" Isaac exclaimed, meandering over, and escorting him toward the bar with Benoit, of whom smiled through his beak.

Cariaah found herself overwhelmed. Nothing muted the happiness, guilt, or even the angst. It all combined, churning into a cacophony of feelings.

"We don't have any time left," Raquel said after everyone greeted each other, tears on the fringes. "Zenira is going to invade the city of Qualia, and we need an army." She tightened her brow, anguish and passion emerging. "We need the guard captain."

***

The Spotted Mare had given up a portion of their rooms to the remaining Vantaknights. Everyone had their own room except for Iz and Isaac, who shared one.

Being in her own room again filled the girl with foreignism. A lone candle sat on the nightstand beside her bed—one she peered into as she sat upon her sheets. She hugged her blade, the breeze that coursed through the open window flirting with her skin.

A knock upon her door drew a flinch. She exhaled her fear away. "Come in," she uttered.

In came Snjick, his eyes soft and smile warm. "How are you holding up?" He sat beside her, sure to place his hands in his lap.

"That's a bit of a loaded question," she said, still looking into the candle's flame.

"What's wrong?"

"Nothing." She shook her head.

"Something's on your mind. I can tell."

"How so?"

"You won't look at me."

"I just—" she hesitated. Tears sat behind her gaze. "It's stupid." Cariaah shook her head again.

"It can't be stupid, Cariaah. I promise."

"Well, I know it isn't true."

"What isn't true?"

"Before I came with Raquel, I was with Zenira. I left, I—"

"Cariaah." He placed his hand on hers.

She looked at him with a flinch.

He removed his wrist. "I'm sorry," he said. "I know you don't like that."

She brought her gaze down to his fist, which had turned into a knot. She took it, holding tightly with both hands. "Snjick."

"Yes?"

The candlelight revealed the glassiness of their eyes.

"I'm terrified," she said, defeated by the tears. "I'm terrified." Cariaah spiraled into sobbing and placed her head on his chest. "Terrified of *myself*." Her breath escalated with each recoil in her frame. "Please forgive me."

"You didn't do anything wrong." He held her close. "He can't do anything to you. I won't let it happen. Not again."

The candle stayed awake with them. For the rest of the night.

12 THE FINAL DAY

Fatigue dripped from Flynn. His eyelids had sagged into hammocks. The same suit of armor still hugged his skin and wrapped around his figure with such tightness that it made abrasions. And with each subtle movement he made behind his desk, his skin only grew more irritated.

Greta, the village woman, had been provided a cot in the corner of the room, sleeping upon its cottony surface.

The guard captain would look up from his writings occasionally to ensure the woman's safety and comfort. Between those brief moments, his quill worked on parchment, analyzing each piece of information he had received.

One rumor, which had circulated through the populace with healthy steam, detailed the silver mage's ability to grow curling claws and tusk-like fangs. He didn't need his army, for, a beast of such belligerence could take a village single-handedly.

Another, which baffled the guard captain, described the silver mage's initial friendliness. He had given a struggling town copious amounts of meat and fish and bread, before evincing his morbid intentions. The man had called himself their "savior" before unleashing a display of carnage.

No matter the unbelievability of the tales he heard via proxy, his exhaustion always caused a moment of hesitation.

A knock graced the door.

He exhaled. "Come in."

Richard, the man who worked the desk, stuck his head in. "An elven woman is here," he said. "As well as a group of…others."

"What do they want?" he asked. "I haven't the energy for visitors."

"They say they know the silver mage."

He sat up, scooching his chair toward the desk. "Well, what are you waiting on?" Flynn animated himself. "Let them in."

The elven woman helmed their entering, others behind her. "My name is Raquel," she said. "We don't have time to waste."

Flynn cleared his throat. "What do you know?"

"This 'silver mage' as he's being called, is a man we once worked with."

The tales, in all of their vividness, struck him. Flynn reached for his blade.

Ashura stepped forward. "There's no need for that." His command was well demonstrated. "We wish to kill him just as you do."

Flynn's hand eased but his eyes remained vigilant.

Greta awoke, gasping at the sudden sight of new company.

"It's okay," Flynn said, raising his hand. "Greta is the only known survivor of the silver mage's first village raid outside the city of Qualia."

Isaac was the only one who acknowledged her, doing so with a nod.

"His name is Zenira," Raquel said. "And he is going to attack Qualia. We need to act. *Now*."

"It makes sense for that to be his next move." Flynn scribbled away with his quill.

"Surely you're in touch with the peasantry, no matter how minimally," Raquel uttered, maintaining a rigid posture.

He nodded.

"Then you have certainly heard of the Vantaknights."

Flynn gasped. "You're jesting!" He reached for his hilt, again.

Jean snickered. "Surely you are!" he said, wiping his forehead with a handkerchief he pulled out from somewhere.

"How can I trust any of you?"

Ashura took a small step forward. "If we wanted you dead, you'd already be greeting the gods."

Flynn gulped.

Raquel scoffed, narrowing her eyes. "Either way, it doesn't

matter. Zenira slaughtered all who opposed him. All but us."

Cariaah sealed her eye shut.

"What do you mean by 'opposed?'"

"You aren't going to enjoy this," Isaac said, stepping forward. "But Zenira is the creator of a horrid breed of magic. Now, I don't know about your beliefs on the matter, but regardless, you need to set them aside."

Flynn nodded, hesitantly.

"With proper training, you can control the minds of others," Snjick said. "Their bodies too."

Tales the guard captain had heard carried horror, sure. Yet, the credibility—a name to the figure, his true origin, and all the rest—stirred his insides. The abrasion beneath his armor deepened.

"So," Benoit said, breaking his silence. "I would suggest preparing for the unpreparable."

Flynn's fatigue slipped away. "What do we do?" he asked, burying his face.

"The capitol's army," Raquel nettled. "I don't think it's wise to use all of it, but we need a force to assist Qualia in its defense. The word I received was that Zenira's army had attacked another village on Qualia's southern perimeter."

Flynn scratched his chin, his stubble crunching. "The capitol sits on the northern side of Qualia, albeit quite a distance away."

"I arrived here just yesterday," Raquel said. "That news is only a day old. If we scrounge together a force *today* and leave as soon as we can—"

"We may be able to save Qualia," Ashura interjected.

Flynn sighed, his gaze reverting to the near window. "I can give you a good portion of my men," he said. "But you must know—and I do not say this to ostracize or insult their abilities—that they are *not* battle-hardened fighters."

"What do you mean?" Benoit asked.

"Theis land hasn't seen a war in a century." His words were dirtied with shame. "All of them—even the colonels and officers—have only seen the treacheries of a mere barfight."

"The Vantaknights have prevented war in this land for that long," Isaac said, removing a vial of liquor from his robe. "Perhaps something good will come out of this one."

"It's a juxtaposition in fate," Raquel said. "The gods are testing us."

Cariaah made fists.

"They're asking us a question," she continued. "How strong are we?"

Flynn sighed, shaking his head. "*You*," he said, pointing at Ashura. "You'll straighten my men out."

The brute's gaze remained impregnable. "You want me to lead them?" Ashura's insides twisted in uncertainty.

"There's a duality to their inexperience." He blinked slowly. "They may not be competent with the sword, but their confidence will undoubtedly be toxic."

Ashura didn't faze. "I know the sort." He had *known* the sort.

"I still have general command, you will have field order," Flynn directed. "I'm going to ride out with you all at sunset. Having night ahead of us should mask our march."

Greta broke her silence. "No."

Flynn darted a glare in response.

"You haven't slept in days," she said. "You shouldn't be standing up, let alone commanding an army."

"Know your place," he snapped back. "You're nothing but a village woman."

Greta receded, pulling the cot's blanket close.

"I'll gather the suitable number of troops." He rose to his feet, steadying his dizziness with a hand on his desk. "Everyone else, find a suitable thing to do before sunset."

Cariaah took the opportunity to escape, pushing herself through the door.

Snjick followed, unsure but audacious.

***

Isaac took the day to sit at the bar and sip at his liquor, Iz at his side playing with a dagger he'd let her borrow. Typically, a bartender or inn-keep would admonish someone for having a weapon out, but something about this girl kept the staff distant.

It wasn't the Spotted Mare, however. He preferred the ale at this new bar after perusing quite a few within the past hour. Isaac's focus teetered, wandering about the tavern to get acquainted with the space. However, his gaze consistently reverted to Iz and the dagger.

He had always found difficulty in gauging her mood, desires, and discomforts. Several occasions came to mind as exceptions.

Her speaking—as seldom as it arrived—always exhumed nothing.

No sensitivity.

No fear.

There only resided objectivity—perseverance to achieve whatever Isaac had told her. And when she couldn't achieve an order—even if it had been just for a day—she shut down, failing to confront the humility she fell into.

"Are you scared?" Isaac asked, looking into the metal of the dagger.

She shook her head.

"Why not?"

She rubbed her thumb on the face of the blade. Her brow twitched, something that caused Isaac to widen his eyes. "That's a lie." She exhaled. "Maybe I am a little bit."

He swallowed—not his ale, but his own saliva—and let go of a shaky breath. "And that's okay, kiddo."

She looked to him, a clump of light flickering behind her dark eyes.

The elf hesitated but ultimately smiled. "It's going to be alright."

***

The sun looked down on the city, a golden orb in the likewise sky. Ashura sat upon his made bed in the Spotted Mare. Even though the sheets weren't a silk, they made him think of her. He bemoaned in silence.

A knock came about his door, and upon its opening Ashura rose to his feet.

"A couple hours of sleep have done me nicely," Flynn said, arms crossed and chin high. "Come with me. I need you to meet the men you'll be leading."

He followed the guard captain down the corridor and out of the Spotted Mare. The streets had grown busy, and the whispers that trailed through passerby all related to this "silver mage." Word had already spread about the latest village invasion, and rumors of his abilities had spiraled out of control.

Flynn found himself unbothered. Even if the guard captain were to halt his steps and lecture the small portion of people in the street it wouldn't shift their opinions of these tales. If he told them of their planned aid to Qualia—to prepare for an invasion most people had already inferred—they would then converse about what that meant for the capitol.

Ashura always drew eyes when he walked through the streets. But today he found himself to be a magnet for gazes; all of them speculative and analytical.

The pair wound through the cobblestone streets toward the security district—where Flynn's office sat. However, upon traversing the gates, it proved evident that they wouldn't be headed into that room.

A hive of men—all armored in congruous plates of steel and gold—hummed about the courtyard outside the guard offices. They laughed, chatted, and drank pints of ale. Each man—human, elf, or dwarf—shimmered beneath the sun in their armor. Not a speck of grime blemished their skin or metallic suits.

Ashura heeded the blood that stained his leather.

"Attention!" Flynn called out.

Silence spread like a wave through the soldiers, as did the hawkish peers aimed at the brute. Everyone—from those who leaned against the well in the center of the yard, to the wooden training dummies—shot a pair of eyes at Ashura.

"Sunset is mere hours away," Flynn continued. "and I cannot guarantee your return to this city."

"Let us at them!" yelled a voice from amongst the troops.

A cacophony of cheers followed, trickling throughout the crowd.

"Oy," Flynn yelled, the cheers and cries still echoing. "Everyone!"

Some threw pieces of armor, tankards of ale, or clumps of dirt about. Others even unsheathed their blades.

But one metallic hiss of steel silenced them. The brute impaled the grass with his marred blade. "If you think the steel at your hip will be enough for what marches toward that city, then you will die."

Ashura's words elicited nothing but silence.

"Perhaps you don't understand," the brute continued. "Death is abstract. But believe me when I say your last breaths, or the final breaths of your comrades, will be the marks that scar you forever."

Flynn found himself as attentive as the rest of them.

"This war will not let up. It *will* not be merciful." Ashura tightened his brow. "But it must be fought."

***

The sun gazed at Jean and Raquel as they walked, the dwarf out of breath. Orange seeped into the golden sea of the sky, teasing the inevitability of sunset.

"What does he wish to gain?"

"Control of the capitol."

"Why is that, exactly?" Jean asked as he fed Rose a handful of feed.

"Greed," she said. "In the land below, he always—"

His reflexive perplexity cut her thought off.

"Or the congregation of the Vantaknights," she continued, easing his confusion. "He always pursued gratitude. He desperately wished to be looked up to amongst the X."

"What is—"

"The council of our order's leaders."

"Thank you, thank you."

"Zenira had his conversationalist tendencies, but overall, the man lived as a recluse. He had his own way of receiving the acclaim he sought."

"Which was?"

"The minds of children."

Jean gave the elf his full attention.

"This dark magic—as he calls it—is something he created." She shook her head. "He trained the young with the nature of his craft. Some couldn't muster the spells he forced upon them, but many could."

"How did he train them to conjure such evil?"

"He made them use the spell on *each other*."

Jean's jaw fell agape.

Raquel's lip quivered. "Even though I can't prove it," she said, clenching her jaw. "I know it for certain, now."

Jean took a nervous breath, deep and shaky.

They arrived at their destined district, traversing the gates with a brisk walk. Jean had trouble keeping up. "So, why are we headed back to the pit?"

She exhaled, gathering her thoughts. "Once Zenira commences his attack on this city, we need every able fighter."

Into the hole they went, subjecting themselves to the warm, loquacious air of its interior. Chatter rippled throughout the space, accompanying the clinking of tankards, and rattling of steel. It was dense today, and despite the crowd, Dahl's desk held no man behind it.

He instead sat amongst a pair of elves, conversing. Jean eventually joined this conversation, even sparking his own questionnaire. Raquel had merely sat down, waiting for a ripe opportunity to introduce the topic at hand.

"It's amazing that you two are undefeated," Jean said to the elves. "Perhaps I've heard of you." His fingers had begun petting Rose, which distracted them. "What names do you go by?"

The first was a male elf, his eyes sharp and lips constantly fixed in a smirk. "Akemi," he said. "This's my sister, Hanya. She enjoys calling me a whole gallery of names, though." He looked to the ceiling. "Prick, jackass, bastard; you get the picture."

While everyone else leaned into the conversation—Dahl included—Hanya relaxed in her seat, her feet resting on the table's surface. Her ears were serrated with gold piercings and her eyes emitted a somnolent but vigilant gaze.

"No," Jean said. "I know many faces and names, but not yours."

"Run while you can, before you remember us," Hanya uttered.

Jean erupted in bumptious laughter. "Well, how can I forget now?"

"Nothing like them in this here hole," Dahl said. "A good pair of fighters." He smacked Akemi on the back.

Raquel took the brief moment of silence to interject. "Dahl."

He gave her his attention over a word.

"I'm sure you've heard of the man being called the 'silver mage.'"

"I have," he said, folding his hands. "War excites me."

"Good," she said. "And you've also heard of Flynn, the guard captain."

"Heard of? The man was once a pit-fighter."

Raquel snickered. "The capitol is where this war will end, regardless of the victor."

Everyone paid her close attention.

"What I'm asking you, Dahl—on behalf of the guard captain *and* the land's well-being—is, will you help defend this city?"

"How do you expect me to do that, missy?" Dahl crossed his arms.

"To lead this hole of fighters through Xardiil's darkest hour."

Hanya emerged with bluntness. "The only man these people are willing to follow is him," she said, meaning Dahl. "If you don't have anyone else, you have me."

Akemi chuckled. "He has a silent—but also *loud*—presence here, if you understand."

Raquel nodded.

"While there are some exceptions," Dahl said, "most of the half-wits in here enjoy swinging their steel for glory."

Raquel smiled.

"It's like the elf said," he began, smirking. "I have command here."

***

Within the hour, Snjick and Cariaah would be ordered to exit their seats at the Spotted Mare and join the ride for Qualia. The evening crowd already begun to trickle in, swarming the bar and cozying themselves by the freshly lit fireplace. With the arrival of each new patron—drunk or not—Snjick and Cariaah sensed the sunset's inevitable approach.

Snjick peered into the orangey surface of his ale. "I wouldn't offend you by drinking this, would I?" He bit his lip. "I mean, I can't help but feel—"

"It's fine, Snjick," the girl replied, snickering. "It really is."

"Alright," he said, sipping at his pint with reluctance. "Are you nervous?" He wiped his lips with his gauntlet.

She tapped her toe on the floor as her fingers hovered over her hip, something which persisted all day. "No," she said. "I'm fine."

"Cariaah," the half-elf said, softly. "I've said this before, but I'll say it again; you can trust me."

Cariaah stopped tapping her foot and brought her hands to the table. "I know," she said. "But you shouldn't trust *me*."

He tightened his brow into a perplexed knot.

"I-I—" she wanted to combust with words and emotions and guilt. The girl wanted to apologize again, even though it had brought futility the night previous.

"Did you know?"

She peered into his eyes, tears on the fringes.

"About what he did?"

Cariaah shook her head. And even though that was the truth, it felt as if she had lied. "I didn't."

"It's a lot to take in," he said. "But you have to understand, none of it was your fault."

"I killed her."

"What?"

"The first village he attacked," she said, gazing at nothing. "I was there with him, and I killed her."

He leaned in closer.

"She begged for her life," the girl murmured. "And I did it anyway, for *him*."

"Who was it?"

Cariaah stared at Snjick, her eye a gaping sphere of anguish. "An innocent woman. I slaughtered her. I ran that steel right through her torso and watched her last breaths."

He swallowed nothing. "Cariaah…"

"I can't accept who I am." She didn't avert her eyes. "I've killed so many people."

Snjick couldn't utter a word.

"But that's not what's tearing away at me." She shook her head, her peer still agape and unmoving. "It's that I've *enjoyed* doing it."

To that phrase—to that handful of words—the half-elf didn't know what to say. His paralysis came at the behest of her speaking. For, he couldn't even look away from her.

A pair of shuffling footsteps approached. "Come on, you two. It's sunset." Benoit stood beside them, ignoring the thickness of the air. He tapped his claw on the table as a prompt for them to stand.

Only silence ensued, the sun falling behind the city's walls and casting darkness upon everything.

13 THE STRUGGLE

He couldn't put the liquor down. Not after that training incident.

It started as a branch that stemmed from his love for alcohol. He would drink a couple glasses of wine after working with his new apprentice, perusing labels that were on sale in the hive. On some nights, the hall's tables would accompany him in his sampling, on others he would sit alone in his room and sip away.

Drinking diverged from an explorative hobby to a dangerous habit. He didn't look at the labels anymore—or the price—he would simply grab a random bottle to drown in. The faster he could forget, the better.

But no matter how much Isaac drank, he couldn't forget Mason. He couldn't forgive his own absence during the boy's death.

Isaac had always loathed Zenira's classes.

But Mason found himself interested.

The poor boy always got emotional when met with frustration. Isaac couldn't imagine the pain that boy went through in his final moments.

Isaac's new apprentice, Iz, had been his subordinate for a year, now. The girl conversed Mason entirely. She showed no emotion but maintained a keen level of awareness at all times. She obeyed every command—every order—and succeeded with terrific grace. But there resided more within her besides malleability and blind obedience. The girl's eyes hawked back at their teacher, knowing full well the potential of her learned carnage.

Isaac entered the room where he'd be teaching her, a vial of liquor in hand, and took a final swig. His steps shuffled toward the corner mat—which had become theirs naturally—where Iz already stood.

Her arms were rested at her sides, framing a rigid posture. Iz's grasp on ice had proven to be better than any student—even some mentors—but they hadn't experimented with its counterpart yet:

Fire.

"It's going to be the same as ice," he said, facing the girl's inevitable target: a stone bust of a dead nobleman's face against the wall.

She stared at it too, preparing herself.

"Go on," he said. "Let's see your abilities untampered."

She didn't take an extra breath or change her demeanor. Iz simply conjured a flame, twirling the little ember within her tiny fingertips.

Isaac stripped away the veneer of professional mentor, unveiling vehement awe. His jaw fell open with the hint of a smile. "Incredible," he said. "Very few can use both spells with such ease."

The girl didn't bathe in the praise. She drove her foot forward, like she did with the other spell. Her eyes were narrow and focused, emitting a tight gaze akin to a falcon. Yet as she propelled the flame forward, the embers didn't reach their target, fizzling into a wisp of smoke.

He crossed his arms. "Your breath is the fuel of this spell."

She let go of an exhale, taking a moment to pause. The next summon and release of the fire came concurrently. And while the mechanics she demonstrated were cohesive and concise, the fire evaporated once more.

Isaac knelt beside her, sighing.

She tried to masquerade her escalated breath.

"Everything, visually, is fine." He stroked his chin. "But there's something else missing." The elf searched for the correct words. "Get passionate, Iz. Fire is passion. Think of something that drives you."

She cast that same spell, drove that same foot forward, and *still* met the same results. Again.

And again.

And again.

Iz panted, trying to work through the layer of sweat that

encompassed her. She continued to cast without centering herself. Her fists shot spells in barrages and volleys, that focus slipping away with each conjuring.

"Iz," Isaac said, cautiously.

She stopped. But she didn't look at him.

"Take a break." He stood from his crouch. "Don't tire yourself."

Her demeanor telegraphed no particular feeling toward the command.

Isaac diverged from her, making a languid way toward the exit. With his previous apprentice, he knew how to react when the boy displayed his emotions. The frustration, anger, and self-doubt. But with Iz, she *didn't* display any emotions.

He pushed himself through the crimson doors of the hall, meandering toward a barrel of ale thereafter. The elf had a lukewarm attitude toward the liquor provided here, but it scratched his itch.

A sloshing pint coaxed him to sit—by himself—at a table.

And another cup.

Another tankard.

One more drink.

And then he woke in a nest of mugs and glasses, crust around his eyes. The elf had no conception of the time. He frantically sprung out of his seat, numb to the dizziness—which had reserved a proprietary spot within him—and made a vague way toward the training room.

He bumped into the walls of corridors, tripping over his own feet until he found the room.

Empty.

All except Iz. She still cast that spell, firing it toward that bust in the wall, growling in anger and frustration as the flames evaporated.

He rushed to her side in the most ungraceful form. "Iz?"

Iz planted her feet on the mat, rigid. Her hands made fists, and a veneer of sweat encompassed her face. Those dark eyes were closed. Tight.

However long it had been, Iz was here for all of it.

"I'm sorry," she said. "*I'm sorry.*"

***

The blackness of the night was composed of several parts.

A coating of hazy mist began this marinade. Even in the moon's hiding, they could feel that haze on their skin as they marched, teasing the inevitability of morning. It gave thickness to the air. It mixed with the fog of their collective breath. It made being nervous a chore.

Behind the haze of that veneer, clouds hung. They were merely a black blanket. Though, none of them could be deciphered in the midst of the night or the dizziness of nerves and dread.

Dread was precisely what finished this picture of blackness—what made teeth chatter more than the bite of autumn—and what promised them all the likelihood of death.

Silence plagued the Vantaknights and capitol guards alike. It said what lay ahead of them: a battle between the forces of a land darkly unknown and a land blind to its own darkness.

They rode as one whole army. One force. One entity beneath the command of the brute.

Ashura could tell of Flynn's sudden condition upon leaving the capitol. The man hadn't swung a sword at another person for quite a time.

The guard captain was scared, *terrified*.

But the brute couldn't blame him. He must've looked over at Flynn on three occasions since their departure, and each time he witnessed the man take a heaving breath.

Below the army there thundered a cacophony of hooves that spaded tufts of dirt and dew-coated grass into the air. After the hours of being on a continual, frantic march to Qualia, Ashura's mind had dismissed the orchestra. Yet, one horse's gallop drew nearer. He glanced to the encroaching sound. "What's the matter?"

Snjick bit his lip. "It's Cariaah." He looked to her as she rode alone. "I want her to go into the city."

An amendment to the original plan, which was:

Two groups.

One was to stand to the west with Qualia at their backs and defensive position taken. Zenira's last village attack—to the best of their knowledge—had been west of the city. Thus, they planned to wait for his force there.

The second group consisted of Raquel and Iz and a handful of capitol guards, those of whom would go into the city to notify the count of their arrival. And, if they hadn't received Flynn's courier, to heed them of Zenira's swift attack. Raquel needed to convince Qualia's count to send a support to the outside force—the first group. The rest were to help maintain the city's impregnability from the inside, during the battle.

"Why?" Ashura asked the half-elf.

"I just—" he hesitated. "I want her to be safe, captain."

He let go of an exhale. His finger trailed about his cuirass, rubbing its leather. "It's fine with me. Just make sure you tell her before we arrive."

Sunrise's onset mirrored theirs to Qualia. And, when the cityscape came into their collective view, the glow of the sun made the dew sparkle. It only gazed upon the land for a brief moment before escaping behind the canopy of dark clouds. That was the only breath of warmth—the only tease of comfort—Ashura's army would receive.

In the shadow of the city—taller than it was wide—Ashura signaled for the groups for diverge.

The brute cantered to the city group, where Raquel had already amalgamated the small contingent. His eyes beset upon Snjick, who spoke with Cariaah aside from the group. He summoned a hint of a smile.

"You asked him that?" the girl said.

"Y-yes," he responded.

She dug into her hip. "Why?"

"I just—" Snjick hesitated. Repeating what he said would give her an idea. "I don't know."

"Let's go," Raquel ordered, loudly. "We haven't a moment to lose."

The girl didn't look at the half-elf as she rode away, right along with the rest of that group into the city.

Isaac went to Ashura's side, eyeing them as they galloped away.

"Is she okay?" Ashura questioned.

"Iz doesn't like goodbyes."

"She told you that?"

Isaac shook his head. "There's just a silent understanding…I think." The elf exhaled, sipping on a vial of liquor.

Ashura went to admonish him but befell on a different group of words. "She's going to be fine."

"I know *she* will." He gulped the rest down.

"As will we."

Isaac looked to his captain, biting his lip. He nodded. "Let's take that fucker's head."

***

They waited.

Mist blurred the endless plains. A rear line of Vantaknights—which included Jean and Flynn—overlooked the main force's body. It was sectioned into three adjacent blocks of infantry—blades at hip—and two rows of archers behind them.

"Have they made it into the city?" Flynn asked.

Snjick's head was already turned. "I think so." He averted his focus. "It's strange. I didn't see anyone outside the gates."

"The count must have ordered everyone to shelter." Ashura adjusted himself on his saddle. "Including the guard force."

"Let's just hope *anyone* with a sword and armor comes outside," Benoit said. "Soon."

"If things go sideways in any form," Isaac butted in, "then we'll hurry behind Qualia's thick walls."

"I like the idea of thick walls." Jean chuckled, scratching his immense belly. "I just don't know if I can hurry."

A silence fell upon everything. It seeped into the dew. Plates of armor clinked, chattering with the shivers. Everyone's breath evaporated into mist. They all longed for the sun's warm return.

Though no such luxury would be awarded.

The city behind them emitted no noise or tease of restless populace.

All life—even the grass below—was in question.

Ashura exhaled deeply, rubbing his chest with a finger, again. He wanted to summon that warmth, to bring it back to his figure—to his insides. The captain—whose mind had been on a continual rampage through the night—longed for that feeling.

Emotion took control.

It sped a reel of images through his mind, which distracted him—albeit for a moment—from the mist and the cold and the silence. Lillian's giggles, his siblings' dead upon the red carpets of the hall, and the warmth within The Black Hog. It all brought him back to her.

Her eyes which he remembered so vividly warmed him.

They gave the silence hope.

They injected the assassin with life.

Rose ascended from Jean's shoulder, making an echoing, bumptious cry. That sound—the *only* sound—drew gazes from across the army. She disappeared into the mist, that call turning increasingly dreadful.

"They can't be..." Jean murmured. "Where is Qualia's army?" He looked toward the city's gates. Closed. Empty.

Ashura looked forward into the mist, his glare vehement and unmoving. He drew his blade in a hiss. "Draw!" he commanded. "Archers, notch!"

The three regiments of capitol guards emitted an avalanche of metallic percussion. Their steel was clean in that moment—for the last time.

The brute peered into the darkness. He narrowed his gaze. He bit down on his teeth.

Then came the slim shapes of arrows in the mist, about to fall upon the army like rain.

"*Loose!*"

The arrows from both forces passed in the misty sky, interlocking like fingers, and falling in a storm. The infantry held their shields above their heads, and the majority of the arrows ricocheted off the wood.

Some hit the dirt.

Some shed blood.

"Hold the line!" Ashura called. He turned to those mounted beside him. "Once Zenira's force is visible, we flank." He sliced through the air with his hand. The captain turned to his army once more. "Notch!" he exclaimed. "*Loose!*"

Arrows went soaring again.

"Jean," he said. "Stay here with the other men while we go for their rear."

"Are you sure?" he asked above the sound of falling arrows.

"I know your sort." Ashura hurried through his words. "You're going to keep them safe for us. For *me*."

"I am?"

"You are." He nodded with a smile. Then, the captain turned to the others. "We'll take as many as we can without putting ourselves at risk. Then, we'll fall back and defend Qualia."

Benoit tightened his grip on his reins.

Snjick clenched his jaw.

Isaac lowered his eyes.

As the brute turned his mare toward the mist again, the onslaught of enemies became unveiled. "Okay," he murmured. "Okay!" he growled. "*Move!*"

The thunder of their gallop served as a fuel. It urged each one of them to trudge forward.

"Draw!" Ashura commanded.

Snjick.

Benoit.

Flynn.

Isaac.

Their steel became unveiled as one beast of a weapon.

The eye within the star sat before them as a sea of black.

"If we die," the brute yelled, "it's for *the land!*"

***

Raquel helmed the group's entrance into the city, Cariaah and Iz at her respective sides. A sigh—filled with heavy relief—released from them all.

"Hurry!" called one of the steel-cladding Qualia guards. "Close the gates!" The steel beasts of massive doors groaned to a languid closure, sealing them all inside.

The streets held no civilian. The buildings hosted no flame of a lantern. And typical stands with their respective merchants were nowhere to be found. Not a voice solicited. No rat scurried beneath the steps of beggars.

Only the guards stood before them.

"The count," Raquel said from her mare. "We must speak with him."

"Your courier was received," said the assumed leader of this cohort, a helmetless human with dark hair. "We know of the silver mage's imminent arrival."

"Good." Raquel took a brief, sharp breath. "Our force is ready for the enemy's arrival outside the city."

"We'll need to gather the others." He mounted a near mare,

which had nothing upon its black fur but a bare saddle. "I'll lead you to them."

They were taken beneath his wing and escorted down that empty street. He took the position to Raquel's left, replacing Cariaah, who meandered toward Iz.

The whole of the group didn't gallop ferociously, instead following the pace the guard and his mare set. They cantered, fueled by Raquel's vivid urgency. "Have you heard any news worth our attention?"

"Nothing new." He lowered his brow. "It's a waiting game, now."

Cariaah peered at him, holding her reins with one hand and hip in the other. She dug further, a claw of ulterior thought. What Snjick had done for her—clearly to protect her—stirred more angst with the stress that already surrounded the battle.

Even after what she said to him.

He protected her.

Something dug into her other side. Cariaah darted a glance to a tiny finger, from the hand of Iz.

Her dark eyes had already narrowed beneath her icy hair. They were trying to relay something. Something she couldn't say aloud.

What is it? Cariaah mouthed.

Iz glanced to the guard.

Cariaah couldn't place the exact words, but she knew of the message's nature. "Raquel."

Raquel and the guard looked to her.

She glanced briefly at the guard, attempting to relay the message.

But the guard's steel was already drawn. And before Cariaah or Iz or any of the men could do anything, his blade was buried in Raquel's gut. "Not this time, *elf*."

Cariaah's jaw fell open.

Iz sprung from her mare, falling blade-first onto the assailant. Her blade impaled his chest.

And as he fell limp from the black horse, he uttered, "*notch*."

The streets held the echoes of groans from upon the rooftops, not from men's mouths but from the creaking of bows.

Raquel fell to the cobblestone in a wince, and as the thud of her body echoed, so too did the whizzing of arrows, hissing in the wind. Raquel fought her stomach's wound in order to command. "Put up your shields!" she growled. "Get behind something!"

Her men scrambled to flee, some riding their mares beneath the veil of their shields, others frenzying to gallop out of the city with no other defense. The mounts under them did nothing to help. Those who reached the gates couldn't force them open, and helplessly cried for their mothers. Both of these contingents befell to the thrall of projectiles and wounds and blood.

Raquel had crawled to the cover of a horse's leaking corpse. Her hands plugged the wound in her stomach, drawing grimaces.

Iz and Cariaah crept over to her.

"We need to go, now, while they're occupied." Iz prompted for Raquel's validation.

"Where will we go?" Cariaah asked.

"In the alley," Iz said, gesturing to the one beside them. "Out of the street."

"Can you stand?" Cariaah asked Raquel.

She nodded, fighting off the agony of her abdomen.

The pair of girls helped the elf to her feet, who used one hand to plug the wound and the other to support herself on Cariaah's shoulders. "Thank you."

"You saved me," Cariaah replied as they limped into the shadows of the alley. "I have to do the same for you."

She nodded, obligatorily. "You're a Vantaknight, Cariaah." Raquel smiled, faintly. "But you're more than just a servant of an order—both of you are."

Iz and Cariaah buried their gazes into Raquel's fleeting eyes.

"You're a good pair of girls." She nodded with a more present smile. "I have faith that the two of you will make things proper in this land. I know it."

Cariaah ignored the urges to grab her side. The darkness that always smoldered within her nature. The fears of what was and what could be. The terror of herself. In that moment, there was only hope within the girl. Hope that she could see this through to the end and be alright.

Hope that they would be okay.

Blood.

Raquel's caved skull drenched both of their faces. The elf's corpse became too heavy and dropped to the cobblestone with finality.

That hope vanished.

At the end of that alley, swirled a crackling, hissing, abyssal portal. A figure emerged in a black robe—a century-old creature—a conniving, slithering, abhorrent sight of a monster.

Him.

14 THE REPLACEMENT

Ashura's cohort of cavalry thundered back to the main force. Pandemonium had formed in the muck between the opposing armies. It was a battlefield saturated with blood, lined with flesh, and adorned with steel. Struggle hung in the mist, framing the marinade of soldiers into obligatory carnage.

Arrows zipped through the air and whistled past ears.

Spells glowed in the fog.

And that sigil hung high above Qualia's walls.

Each soldier, upon noticing the enemy's flag, wrote their wills in silence. Any chance of recapturing that initial spark fizzled out.

"What happened?" Ashura yelled upon their return.

Jean shook his head. "Nothing's changed besides the flag!"

"They've beaten us here!" Benoit exclaimed.

"We're stuck in the middle!" Isaac yelled. "We either take Qualia now and risk everything, or we fall back."

"What about Raquel and Iz?" Snjick protested. "What about Cariaah?"

Projectiles interjected, falling in a ferocious flurry. They sliced through the air and percussed in flesh and mud.

The group used their forearms as cover, and Ashura his blade. But as the captain pulled it away from his eyes, he noticed an unsteady elf before him. "Isaac!" Ashura rushed over, stealing him from his horse, blade still in hand. "He's hurt." An arrow jutted from Isaac's side, which stemmed from a dripping wound. "We can't do anything for him here."

Flynn's wrists shook, the intricate plates of steel on his fingers clinking.

Snjick bit his tongue.

"Everyone, fall back!" Ashura commanded through a yell. "They've taken the city!"

***

The girl opened her eye, but blackness served as the only greeting. The air she breathed carried no coolness. No movement. No freshness. It reflected the absence of light, which engulfed her in emptiness.

She couldn't move. Not because of some spell or invisible grasp, but due to her thick, steel restraints. She only realized her standing position after a few moments, but her ankles were pinned too by even thicker, denser steel, which tore at her skin.

When the girl struggled against those cuffs and the flat surface at her back, it only brought splintery discomfort. The restraints were serrated against her bones. She could only be unmoving. There was no way to cope.

The sole thing she could manipulate was her breath. And when she tried to slow it, her lungs disobeyed. The more she fought to find her center, the more she heaved and panted.

"Cariaah?" whispered a voice. "Cariaah?"

A blinding light.

The sun of midday beat down upon her with summer's heat. Here, she had both of her eyes. She had her nest of leaves below that tree on the hill. The trunk twirled toward the sky, bearing a crown of rippling leaves. The girl could sit and blanket herself with dirt beneath it. Safe.

But her village didn't exist.

Nor did her father's house.

Only grass and feeding goats resided.

She looked about in puzzlement. Tingles coursed through her frame, kindling her core and mind. They warmed her in a different form than the sun. The girl stood from her nest, acquainting herself with the breeze. But something made her hesitate before taking a step forward: the familiar tinge from her bruise didn't exist.

For the first time she could reach for it and claw without pain.

Without burden.

"A strange plain?" said a voice.

She looked to her side at the person who spoke. It was Zenira, adorning that suit of sparkling armor. His blade was there, too, gazing at her.

"This is the world without you." He smiled with the same warmth he did on that day. "Or, without those who came before you."

The grass shimmered greener than she remembered. The leaves shook in the breeze with greater purpose. A stillness swam about the air—a lack of urgency or angst or push.

"I've watched over you for a long time, Cariaah." He looked to her with those eyes. He appeared just like he did. *Exactly* how she remembered. "And I know your fate—what you are destined to do." He crouched to her height.

She felt smaller.

"This place—this plain," he said, looking about, "it can be the only land. Serene. Ethereal. Without filth."

She couldn't speak. For, the nostalgia silenced her.

"And you can be in it." He placed his hand upon her shoulder. "You can be its creator."

Darkness returned. It zipped her into that air again. The stuffy, unmoving, stagnant air. She was restrained by the wrists and ankles. She only had one eye again. And breathing reverted into a chore.

She was herself, once more.

"Cariaah?" whispered a voice from the abyss. "Where are you?"

"Iz?"

"What's going on?"

"I don't know. B-but it's going to be okay."

"Raquel's dead."

"I know, Iz, I know."

"I should have just killed him—that guard in the street. I don't need permission from anyone." Iz's inhale was frantic.

"It's okay." Cariaah could hardly form a sentence. "It wasn't your fault."

"Zenira's a filthy *pig*." She heaved. "I'm going to slice him open!" she growled. "I'm going to let him bleed!"

What came out was nothing short of a killer's howl.

Cariaah trembled in those shackles. The darkness Iz spoke of cloistered in Cariaah's ear and scared her own morbidity away. All those morose, self-loathing, abhorrent thoughts receded.

"Iz?"

She panted with Cariaah.

"Where's Zenira?" Cariaah swallowed. "Is he—"

The hinges of a door squealed, and light spilled into the room. But upon the door's immediate closing, a warm glow replaced that light. Torches on the walls were lit in their steel enclosures.

The pair of girls looked at each other in near reflection. Both of them were pinned to upright wooden boards.

Thirst filled the stuffiness of the air.

As did a shadow.

"My children."

After a blink, his face peered inches away from Cariaah's.

"I am glad you have witnessed my garden bear fruit." He spoke through a smile, and even though it was difficult to see upon his face, he showed it through his voice. He looked to Iz, who glared back. "Even if a few flowers have withered."

She flaunted her teeth like fangs. "I'll *kill* you."

"Such a sadness." He inspected her, with hands coupled behind his back. "You're just a mere product."

Iz wasn't fazed.

"The Vantaknights excelled at creating ones like you. Silent. Showing passion only in blood and death." He scoffed. "Killing means nothing to you." He inched closer to her. "Which is why you're neither dead nor alive."

Iz glared with glassy eyes, like a muzzled dog teased with overdue supper.

"You've managed to gain the image of prodigious." His voice dripped into her ears. "A caster of both fire and ice." His eyes grew wider. "But not of a third breed of magic."

Cariaah gulped between heavy breaths from across the room.

"Iz, my child." Zenira smiled. "Do you want a lesson in *true* magic?"

Iz didn't flinch.

Cariaah shivered in her restraints.

"That elven mentor of yours sheltered you too harshly. You never got the opportunity to experiment."

"I'll never betray Isaac." Iz shook her head. "Never."

"You know," Zenira hissed, "he trained a young boy before you."

Iz let go of a weighty exhale. But still glared.

"I believe his name was Mason." He shuffled away from Iz, commencing a pace. "And while Isaac didn't find it in his best interest, I still got the chance to work with this boy." He stroked his chin. "In order to know the spell, you need to know how to defend it. To do so is to expel all dark emotion from you. Because this is what the spell manipulates: all morbid thoughts and emotions."

Cariaah made a pair of shaky fists, the dread that drooled from the walls overwhelming her.

Iz remained unfazed.

"But Mason was a coward. All emotion." He laughed with rasp. "The boy couldn't rid himself of it. So, when it came time for training…"

A silence filled the air. Zenira stopped pacing.

"Other students practiced on him in order to harden the boy's defenses. On one of these occasions, things didn't go in Mason's favor." He sighed. "The boy was killed."

Iz's brow twitched.

"You could hear him call for his mentor as he died—as his bones crunched and his breath got pulled from his lungs."

Cariaah closed her eye. She squeezed it shut until she saw purple.

"He cried for his life. He begged his peers to let him live." His teeth showed in a curling smile. "But they awarded him no such thing."

Cariaah's throat closed, her face turned numb, and the control over her fingers ceased. She couldn't bite down or swallow or cope in any remote form. No thought eased her.

"And so soon after this," Zenira continued, turning to Iz, "Isaac sought a new apprentice. A *replacement*."

Iz's crossness receded. She bowed her head and gave her weight to the restraints. Iz stared at the floor, exhuming no animosity or predatoriness. "I-I'm sorry."

That silence returned. Not even the torches upon the wall crackled. Dust wandered through the density of the air. It swirled in front of Cariaah's face as the only escape she had from the never-ending weight of dread.

"I received word from my subordinates that you couldn't be

casted upon." He scoffed.

Iz didn't flinch, inflate with vigor, or retaliate. She continued to stare at the floor, unmoving.

"I think we'll have to test that ourselves."

Cariaah opened her mouth to speak, but the tingles in her face and limbs ripped the words from her tongue.

"Surely your fate will be different from Mason's." He laughed. "Now, won't it?"

Cariaah's teeth chattered. She wanted Iz to reanimate herself, to do something, perhaps the thing she couldn't bring herself to do. "D-d-don't," she managed to whisper.

"What is fated to happen will happen, my little bird," Zenira said, still glaring at Iz. "This is merely a steppingstone to realizing that fate." He paused. "Remember that plain, Cariaah?"

She shivered.

"Think of how ethereal. How pure." He still peered at Iz. "There was no filth, was there?"

It was true. Zenira, with that armor and blade, those goats free, and that tree, epitomized her fantasy. The cleanest land—above or below—she could dream of. *This* eased her breath.

"That's right." Zenira's smile donned itself proudly. "This is a necessary step." He shuffled back to his original position and looked at Cariaah. "And I want *you* to take it."

Her eye widened.

Iz looked up.

"Wh-what?" Cariaah muttered.

"In order to get to that plain, you must face your rawest darkness." He outstretched his hands toward her. "And I think we *both* know what that is."

Cariaah didn't move.

"Blood excites you." He narrowed his eyes. "Doesn't it?"

She struggled to look at him but couldn't avert her gaze, either. He had trapped her in the truth.

"It's time to face that reality, Cariaah." He nodded. "For the good of the land."

Her shackles broke loose, throwing her for the floor. She panted on her hands and knees, peering at the dust. The girl didn't feel like she owned her body.

"Stand." Zenira spoke, firmly. "Don't be afraid."

I can't accept who I am.
She stood, unleashing a sigh. Her eye shut itself.
I've killed so many people.
"Think about the blood." He coughed. "The flesh peeling from the bone. The skulls caving."
She dug into her hip. The girl felt no pain. Coping was futile.
"Cariaah!" he exclaimed. "This is who you are!"
"Please," Iz uttered. "Cariaah…"
But that's not what's tearing away at me.
Her hand made a claw. She opened her eye, bathed in the sight of her prey as it writhed.
Iz screamed for help. For Isaac.
It's that I enjoy doing it.
Cariaah's made a fist. Never before did she revel beneath the blanket of darkness with such endless, inescapable joy.

***

Arrows and spells laced their retreat. It had been a cage in the form of two hours, but they needed distance. The weight of Isaac on Ashura's saddle grew heavy as the trailing hooves became distant.

They halted once their backs were covered by the veil of trees.

"How is he?" Benoit asked, dismounting, and rushing to Ashura's mare.

"Pale." The brute gave Isaac's shoulders to Snjick, who placed him beneath a nearby tree. "We need to get him more water."

"Here," he said, hurrying to the elf's side. Jean had a waterskin prepared.

"The bleeding hasn't stopped." Ashura's gauntlets were stained red with Isaac's blood.

Flynn paced about, his boots crunching leaves.

"I never got to say it," Isaac whispered.

"Fuck," Ashura murmured. "I'm not letting you die, you drunken piece of shit." He prepared a bandage for the wound, ripping fabric with his teeth and tying it around the elf's torso.

"I never…"

"Dammit!" Ashura exclaimed, his brow lacing with sweat. "He's slipping!"

A horse's thundering hooves interrupted the collective rhythm.

"Hey," Benoit murmured. "Snjick!"

The half-elf rode his mare in a fury, back toward Qualia and its jaws. The girl was the only thing he sought besides Zenira's head.

***

The coolness of sunset whispered to the breeze. Leaves kicked up, skidding, and soaring as night fell. All of them came from the one large tree that hung over the pond. Twilight teased the arrival of stars in the form of little stipples of light. Birds called to their mates and glided with the sigh of the wind. Insects teemed and buzzed and hummed, laying under rocks and moss and ferns.

Serenity never left this place. The sky never swirled with dark clouds. It didn't rain.

It gave the girl with white hair a place to play, explore and wander. She enjoyed skipping stones across the pond and observing the fish dance underwater.

A stream ran through the nearby forest, and in the winter, she found joy in sliding across it. Her feet ended up frozen, but she didn't care all that much. As long as she could warm herself beside the fireplace at the end of the day, nothing stopped her before then.

It was her mission to find a dog because her father's cottage didn't come with one. It did come with books, however, and even though she couldn't read, her father did so for her each night. Whenever a story involved a dog, she wanted to hear it at least twice. This way she could revel in that story before bed, and dream during the day about having one.

Her father promised that one day he would travel to the nearby farmhouse to buy one. That day couldn't come soon enough.

She found herself afraid only of the dark. Whenever she didn't run home fast enough and got caught beneath the moon, her white hair served as a guide. She would rub the tendrils of icy hair with her thumb until she made it home. This also manifested an obsession with candles, and with whatever materials the girl could scrounge up, she would always make them.

Her desk—where she drew and learned to read—was framed by these candles. It was easier in the winter because the frost in the air helped solidify the makeshift wax. Her mother would help after the housework was finished, and they shared many laughs together.

One night, during dinner, her father asked, "Do you want to keep this cottage after your mother and I are gone?"

"Why would you guys be gone?" she replied.

"That's just how life goes, sweetheart."

She thought about it, toying with the food on her plate. "I don't think I can leave home."

"You're still young," he said. "When you get older, you may want to go somewhere else."

"I do like exploring."

"Exactly." He took a sip of water. "Maybe in the city you'll find a husband and want to settle down elsewhere."

"But you don't have to find a husband," her mother said. "Do what you want, my dear. *Whatever you want.*"

The girl nodded with a smile. Her mind filled with aspirations, ideas, and dreams.

"Alright?" her father asked.

"Alright," she said.

All of this—the cottage, the candles, and the dog—existed in a different realm. Another land. A place where that girl with the white hair could dream and shed tears and live. Perhaps one day she could experience it all. But it wouldn't be in the land above or the land below. It would be elsewhere, waiting for the elf to arrive right after her.

15 THE GIRL & THE ELF

"You want a pint?" Bauer asked with raised eyebrows, pouring the ale already.

Snjick's gaze lingered on the stream of amber. "I don't know."

The dwarf released a hardy laugh. "You don't know?" He slid the pewter cup over to the half-elf. "Come on, elf, give it a try."

Snjick glared for a second, murmuring something. But he ultimately took the ale. "I've *tried* it before, Bauer. I just don't know if I want a cup."

"Horse shit." The dwarf took a gulp of his own. "I know that face you're giving. You're full of shit."

Snjick sighed, peering into the frothiness. He took a large—a much too large—gulp. The burning pungency elicited something between a gag and a cough from him. He placed his forehead onto the table in refuge.

Bauer cackled harmoniously. "Oh, what a riot you are, elf!"

"*Half-elf.*"

***

There was no redemption for the things he'd ruined.

He couldn't change what had occurred, nor heal the rippling scars.

But he could save her. He could bring her back. He could *tell* her.

The plains were muddy below the crowded sky, sheathing the

emerald grass in grey.

And as Qualia's vague silhouette approached his narrowed eyes, something else outlined itself. Someone. Snjick unsheathed his dagger, gripping the hilt with white knuckles beneath black gauntlets. He bounced on his saddle, ready to evade an arrow or spell, but also prepared to launch himself toward his target.

Focus lit a fire in him. He exhaled with pursed lips.

Red hair.

Black armor.

Cariaah.

The half-elf yanked the reins, his mare braying as it halted. "Cariaah!" He leapt off the saddle, landing ungracefully onto the grass. Sheathing his dagger, he took an approaching step, one that her demeanor forced him to steal back.

Devoid of the typical inflection that made Cariaah her angst-ridden, sensitive, whip-like self, she gazed into the distance at nothing. Her hair stirred in the wind, clinging to her cheekbones. She stood slouched, vaguely facing him with hands at her sides.

"Cariaah?"

She didn't answer.

He couldn't touch or nudge her. Snjick knew how that would end. "Cari—"

"You need to go back," she murmured, her voice deeper than normal. "Raquel's dead."

The wind howled at the ensuing silence. Grey clouds still loomed above them, teasing a rain that never seemed to fall.

"How did she die?" he asked, lowering his chin. "What happened to Zenira?"

Cariaah didn't look at him.

"Cariaah," he swallowed. "Where's—"

She ripped her steel from its sheath, propelling him into a back pedal. Her elbow rammed Snjick to the ground, the edge of the blade pointed at his face. "Go back!" she yelled. "Tell them I'm dead! It's what you'd want if—" She stopped herself.

He shook his head, back on the grass. "If what?"

"Everyone that walked into that city—that skeleton of a city—is *dead.*" Her jaw trembled. "They're all dead."

He put his weight on his elbows, elevating himself a little. "You're not dead, Cariaah." He rose to a crouch, then to his feet in a cautious motion. "You're here."

She stared at him with saturated eyes. "I know," she said. "And that's what's eating me alive." Her jaw didn't waver from being clenched.

"It's okay." He inched forward.

She drove the steel closer to him. "You need to leave." The girl sniffled. "Zenira left the city. Don't bother going forward."

"I need to bring you back," Snjick said, "where you'll be safe."

"Zenira hasn't killed me yet." She swallowed. "He won't now."

He opened his mouth to speak. To protest.

"It's my choice, Snjick." She lowered her sword and sheathed it. "I don't want to be a part of this anymore." The girl took a longing gaze at him; at the boy who studied her features. "It's not because of you. It's *for* you." The breeze took a tear from her cheekbone. "Thank you for everything you've done."

"Don't thank me."

She bit her lip, hesitant to continue meeting his gaze.

"I've fucked things over—everything over—too many times." He shook his head in rigor. "I dragged you into this. *All* of this." Tears formed on the fringes of his eyes. "It's my job—no, it's my fate—to make this right."

She formed fists.

"Blood is on my hands," he declared. "I twisted my dagger in the stomach of my best friend. I disgraced my father as he died under my watch." A tear fell. "But I won't let you slip away while I can change things; not while you're *still here*."

Leaves kicked about at their feet. They stood in the breeze, under the canopy of greyness, which only now unleashed its first patter of rain.

Cariaah parted her lips but didn't say a word, hesitant. She spun around, leaving her black cape of feathers to gaze at.

He couldn't speak. He couldn't move.

The half-elf could only peer at the fleeting girl's hand at her side, which formed a tight claw. He savored those moments of greyness and rain as she walked away. For, the muddy hues accentuated the girl's fiery head of hair.

***

Night teased the tunnel of brush and trees that encapsulated her. The sun still wasn't visible in the sky; thus, no orange light drenched the land with its warmth. Instead, the air fell into dimness, like the slow trickle of water from a cave ceiling.

Leaves dove from the high branches, twirling in the nippy frost before resting upon the saturated ground. Her steps sloshed. The philosophy of discreetness acquired from the land below showed no evidence in her march.

One of the pale leaves fell upon her shoulder, but she didn't flinch.

She should've felt at ease. The girl didn't have any urge to send her mind racing or grab her hip. Yet, she didn't feel relaxed or starved for any urge at all. She was numb.

If she turned back, she could follow the trail of Snjick's mare to the capitol, turn up at the gates and fall into the collective arms of them all. She could say that Zenira killed Iz, they would mourn, and it would be done.

They would accommodate her in the Spotted Mare, feed her, and try to draw a smile from her lips. They would blindly care for her.

But that, in turn, would make the girl not a girl at all. But rather, a disgusting creature. No, she had already become such a thing. Cariaah—if she did all of those things in deceit—would be nothing more than a leech. A parasite.

The lowest form of life.

Go, the breeze at her back told her. *Exile yourself.*

So, the girl wandered. She couldn't remember the last time she'd eaten, but her stomach didn't cry to her.

Yet she was hungry. And it was after all of these steps that she realized this smoldering desire wasn't for food, but something else.

Cariaah emerged from the wood and paused at the foot of a clearing. Her eye followed a clump of swirling, white smoke into the sky, which dissipated into the sobbing clouds. She looked to the source: a village.

To an ordinary vagabond, a place like this served as a teeming symbol. The livestock meant food, the near stream meant water, and the homes meant rest. All of these things were within this place, regardless of their anemic qualities.

The supposed livestock was a pair of scrawny cows and a pen of hogs.

The stream had a fair membrane of algae.

And the homes were held up by thin wood and the occasional crude brick.

The girl had a different view of this place. To her, the people who lived here meant a cluster of lives, childhoods, and memories. This place was a canvas; vast and white and painted with nothing but purity.

She walked through it—down the muddy path that bisected the village—as eyes peered from behind the veil of curtains or shutters. Whispers echoed. Dogs growled or barked.

All the noises spoke against the rain.

Cariaah continued forward, against the astute attention she gathered. This would typically engulf her in a spiky blanket of anxiety and fears, a blanket that constricted and forced her to be someone else. But here, the numbness was the only thing that smoldered besides that hunger.

A door flung open somewhere, and a pair of uneven steps approaching the girl.

"Nora!" called someone from a house. "Don't!"

That person tugged at her elbow.

Those once-absent feelings surged through Cariaah in the form of a glare.

An old elf—wrinkled and hunched—peered at her. "Miss," she said, "Come with me. I need to ask you a favor."

"No," Cariaah said plainly, stealing her arm back. "Go back inside." She continued to march, pivoting away from the elf.

"Why can't you?" Nora asked, waddling alongside her. "Where are you headed?"

She didn't have an answer or a lie. "Nowhere," came out.

Nora scoffed and took her elbow again. "Come on, dinner is almost ready. I'll fix you a plate."

The girl begrudgingly followed the elf into her home: a wide house with a stone chimney. They entered through the thin, squealy front door, the warm air from a fireplace colliding with their faces.

A woman—slender, young, and human—stood by the door, affrighted.

"What's your issue, Charlotte?" Nora asked. "Make sure that fish doesn't burn."

Cariaah returned her arm to herself, staying by the door as Nora shuffled further into the house. It wasn't much: a rough eating table sat between two single cots made with heavy, wool blankets. The table was set for two, but Nora reached for another plate and shuffled over to prepare a third setting.

"I got these plates in the capitol when I was a girl." She sorted through crude silverware with crooked fingers. "They're two-hundred years old!"

"Yes," Charlotte said, checking the fish that sat over the fire. "We really should sell them to get out of this house."

"Absolutely not! I've had them since I was a girl!" she admonished, half-turning to her.

"I heard you the first time."

"So, tell me, what's your name?" Nora asked.

She curled her toes in her shoes. "Cariaah."

"I'm Nora."

"That's pretty," Cariaah said.

"Not sure about that." She shook her head, taking a seat at the table. "Father gave it to me." Nora pointed at an empty seat.

The girl's weight made the chair groan as she sat down.

"He was a drunk."

Cariaah observed her, more fervently than before. Each mannerism, subtle movement, and every word.

"Where do you come from?" Nora asked.

"Nowhere."

"You're going nowhere, and you come from nowhere?"

Charlotte put a large platter in the center of the table, steaming filets upon it.

"An interesting girl." Nora narrowed her eyes and tucked her lip. "I used to be ashamed of where I came from, too." The elf adjusted herself in her chair—the only cushioned one—which crackled with every little movement. "But in the end—and you can take this from a two-hundred-fifteen-year-old elf—where you come from doesn't matter."

Cariaah dug her nails into her palms.

"It matters where you go from here."

The girl bit her lip.

"The people I live next to were scared when you strolled in here. You could smell it. All because you look different than the rest of us." She snickered. "There're no strange people, dear. None. Only those who you haven't bothered to meet." Nora scanned the table's surface. "Which is why you're having supper with us right now."

Charlotte sat, scooching her chair in a hair.

"I don't come from a place much different than this." Cariaah gazed at the steam emanating from their eventual meal. "The wooden houses, the cows, everything. But something always stuck out to me." She shook her head. Slow. "I was always so hungry, then. Hungry to the point where I could feel my ribs more than my hands. Every day was cold."

Charlotte gazed differently than Nora did.

"I'm glad you're here to eat with us now," Nora said. "It makes me happy."

"You said you needed help?" Cariaah said.

"I'm afraid so." The elf sighed, serving herself a filet.

"You're not going to be able to do anything," Charlotte interjected. "Not alone, at least."

"Marauders." Nora gnawed at a bite of fish. "There's about ten of them who come every now and again. They take whatever they please."

"Our food, our blacksmith's weapons."

Nora glared. "And they killed my husband."

Silence.

The wood of the house creaked in the wind, and the roof percussed with rain. Cariaah's perception was wrong. This place wasn't a pure canvas of white—unscathed and sacred. It had already been soiled with blood and vengeance.

"The next time they come," Cariaah growled, "they won't get the chance to run."

That night, she was given the floor to sleep on, a thick blanket mediating her back and the wooden planks. A lantern dangled from the ceiling, squealing on its hinges from the draft.

The girl hadn't slept in two days, but closing her eye brought no feeling of deflation. It only brought the images of that room—that dungeon—and the childish screams that came with it.

The calls for help.

The *begging* for her to stop.

She sat up, and eventually stood. She needed to look into the stars, bury herself with dirt, or find a tree to curl up under. The girl needed to be anywhere else, anything else. But as she took her initial step toward the door—heel-first as not to wake the others—a distant percussion sounded in introduction—one all too familiar.

Hooves.

"Nora," she said at daytime volume. "They're here." And without heeding the stirs of her hosts, Cariaah marched out. Her heels thundered against the planks below and through the squealing door, allowing a gust of air into the house.

The rain fell in a drench, oversaturating the muddy path into a shallow river. Her steps coasted until she stood in the center, before the onslaught of saddled men on mare. She ripped her blade from its sheath in a hiss, braced. Her cape rippled in the rain-stippled wind, behind her sturdy frame.

The horses were visible now, approaching in ferocious gallops.

Lanterns sparked to life.

Shutters creaked open by the sliver, allowing affrighted eyes to observe.

An undercurrent of whispers hummed beneath the encroaching horses.

Yes, the storm told her. *This is what you're hungry for.*

The riders broke through the border of the village, roaring on the path toward the girl who stood in the center of it. In forming a ring around her, they yanked on their mounts' reins. The horses brayed and swung their necks about, mist emanating from their snouts.

Silence. No hooves. No whispers.

Just the rain.

Just the marauders.

Just the girl.

Her blade was like a sparkling fang, drenched in rain and primed to be soaked in crimson. "Which one, Nora?" she called out.

A shutter opened, slamming against the house. "The human! He's the one!"

There was only one amongst the troupe of dalaryn. His hair ran blonde, and his face held a pair of brooding eyes.

Cariaah didn't allow him to escape from her glare.

"What is this?" that human growled. "The best you could hire was a little girl?"

She didn't move. Unfazed.

"Pathetic." He scoffed. His mare shook as the rain continued to pour. "Go back to the hole you crawled out of."

Cariaah gripped her blade tight, the hilt rattling. She lowered her brow, focusing on her prey.

"Aren't you going to leave?" He yelled.

She twisted her feet, sinking deep into the mud.

"Kill her. Make it quick."

Don't make me.

"Cariaah!" Nora yelled.

Go away.

The frame of marauders narrowed, closing on her like a fist. Blades were flaunted, lascivious laughter rippled. "Mind if we have a little fun with her first?"

Too many thoughts.

Too many fears.

Too much emptiness to care.

A crack of thunder and its inherent lightning split the dark sky above them, interrupting the snapping of rain and bite of wind.

Cariaah dropped her blade into the filth, dark water leaping from the steel.

Her hands were free.

And as she formed a claw, the girl didn't examine her opponents' final breaths.

She only closed her fist.

She only killed.

Blood came in steaming fountains like hot, red springs. The crimson tides soaked into the filthy water, turning it orange. They blinded the girl. Covered her in nothing but red.

And that silence—that silence which clung to their ears like the clouds did the sky—fell away, replaced only by the screams of raw terror.

***

His steps squelched the mud by that spot.

Surely the grass and dirt were stained with Isaac's blood, but the rain had washed it away. All that remained beneath the veil of branches was the elf's dagger and vial of liquor, empty.

Snjick fell to his knees, he pulled at the grass with curled fingers.

The streams of rain soaked into the leather of his gauntlets, piercing his skin with frost. He brought his forehead to the mud and tightened his face into a knot.

Nobody could put him in that moment again. To stay and share his sibling's final breath. He'd missed it, and the half-elf's mind swelled with the blemishes of the past.

He couldn't go back.

But he couldn't live with it, either.

"Snjick?" a voice called out.

He hadn't even looked over to unveil the sleeping figures in the dark forest.

Ashura shuffled out of the brush, his hand swiping away low branches. "Is everything alright? Did you find the others?" The captain knelt before the half-elf, hand on his shoulder and chin low.

Snjick's eyes were still shut tight to the point of needling pain. He left the rain pattering on leaves to speak for him.

"Snjick?"

Ashura couldn't decipher the half-elf's tears from raindrops.

"They're gone," Snjick said. "They're all *gone*."

16 FRINGES

Yuria's council, led by Count Alec—a slender elf—met in the morning. The bright fluorescence of light spilled through the windows. A pair of guards assumed their rigidity on either side of the entrance, listening to the conversations.

"The capitol has sent us a courier. It appears as if this 'silver mage' and his subordinates have not only bested Qualia's army, but a good portion of Xardiil's very own." Alec folded the note and sighed. He interlocked his jewel-adorned fingers and straightened himself. "This is not something we can sweep under the rug."

"What does he even want?" asked a dwarf at the table. "Has it been made clear?"

"Based on various accounts," Alec said, "this outlaw believes the land must be cleansed."

"Who is *he* to mandate such a thing?" added a human, chuckling in flummox. "Besides, he's no savant, slaughtering village folk left and right."

"As I said, he's an outlaw."

"A savage."

"An *intriguing* person."

They turned their attention to who spoke. A courteous stand-in—Lord Duke—who helmed the nearby hold of Timberhill, passing through town.

"Intriguing?" asked Alec. "How is this vermin intriguing?"

"Audacious, I suppose, is the correct word." He spoke into his hand, paying no heed to the heat of stares. "You could classify him as mad, but his skills in battle don't give that assumption any merit."

"You really don't think this man to be mad, my lord?" Alec said.

"And you don't believe *yourself* to be mad?" He glared.

Alec scoffed. "I would tread lightly when you spew such insolence, Lord Duke."

The room turned rigid in posture. Everyone glanced at each other but no one dared say a word.

"Insolence?" A gravel-coated inflection tainted his words. "You speak with such confidence in your own naivety."

"And by that, you mean—"

"I mean you should inspect your own life." His silver—almost ice-white—hair glowed in the windowlight. "Perhaps ripping away this idiotic layer of 'count' would help you."

Stares transferred to Alec.

He gulped, tugging at his silk collar with an index and middle finger. "I don't know what you're referring to."

Lord Duke rose to his feet, the colorful light drenching his black attire. He began a slow walk around the table, hands coupled behind his back. "There are no councils, Alec." His shuffles across the smooth, stone floor echoed as the only sound. "Only groups of people, assuming their superiority."

Alec's forehead stippled with sweat, though he brought no handkerchief to it.

"What separates you from, say, those born in villages?"

He didn't answer.

"I'll tell you, Alec." He stopped his walk, burying a glare in the count.

"Guards, arrest him!"

Those posted at the door didn't move.

"What are you doing?" Alec stood, his chair skidding back on the stone. "Arrest this traitorous—"

"Know when you have power, Count," Duke growled. "*Sit.*"

Alec tore at his collar, obeying the lord's order. He released a shaky breath as his chair settled, too occupied to heed the others.

"There's a distinct difference between those like you and village folk." He scoffed. "Or, if I'm not mistaken, *your* village folk."

Alec clenched his jaw.

"You're equipped with gold, silk, and a stone castle. No one sees your filth." He paced again. "Peasants wear theirs on their skin." He inched closer to Alec. "So, tell your councilmates what it is you refuse to don."

His jaw trembled. "I-I don't think—"

"No." The lord leaned toward him, his face no more than a dagger away. "You lost your opportunity."

There was no sound. Everyone and everything froze at the behest of this man.

"You enjoy your visits to neighboring villages, Alec. Not to feed them for the winters to come, nor to spread your wealth, but instead for the—"

"Don't!"

This lord flaunted his hand before Alec's face as a tightened claw of narrow fingers.

The count couldn't speak. He couldn't move.

The table knew then of this person's truth. Their masqueraded identity.

"I hate nobles. I hate royalty. I detest when they try to open their conniving little mouths." The silver mage let him free from his grip.

The count panted, ripping at his collar more than before.

"Everyone at this table needs to know why you visit your villages." The silver mage scoffed in disgust. "It's because of your lust for the peasant boys. *Children.*"

The panting continued not because of Zenira's spell, but in lieu of that stress.

"Kill him. Kill them all."

The guards came forward in a fury. They ripped steel from scabbard, slitting the throats of those who sat in that exquisite meeting room.

***

Golden sky. The sun soaked the land in its light, allowing no stretch of life to escape its glisten. Yet, it exhumed no warmth. Winter's breath rode the current of the wind, gnawing at faces with serrations.

Nobody led. Everyone's mount loosely moved in a cluster, their hooves thumping against the firm ground. Flynn rode alone in the rear, even his breath quiet. Ashura and Benoit helmed with Snjick and Jean at their center.

Jean hummed.

"Are we going to have enough time for a drink?" Benoit muttered to his captain.

Ashura scoffed. "When you need a pint the most, you never have time."

"Are you certain that Zenira's arrival will be so soon?"

Jean's hum took a higher pitch.

Ashura shook his head. "I hope not. But at this point, only the gods know what his next approach is."

Jean went deeper in tone.

"We only know of his arrival's inevitability," Benoit added.

Ashura eyed the far, looming scape of Xardiil, greyed only by distance. He exhaled, shifting his right hand from the reins to his chest. She seemed so far beyond the capitol, in the furthest reaches of the past.

That gaze.

Jean hummed.

"Is there an *issue?*" Benoit spat, turning his feathery shoulders to the dwarf.

"I'm just thinking." Jean stroked the chest of Rose as he cantered along. "I don't mean to have a negative outlook on things, but if I may, there is a glaring issue."

No one was amused.

"A lot of men perished outside Qualia." He stroked his beard.

Snjick scoffed, in accordance with Benoit who said sarcastically, "You're boosting morale."

"What I'm saying is, our army is hurting." Jean sniffled. "We need soldiers."

"Do you have a *solution?*" Ashura said.

"Perhaps."

They all stopped their march.

"Though, I cannot assure its success."

Snjick interjected, "Nothing's been guaranteed up to this point."

"Neither is this. So, I'll tell you. I've not always had Rose." Jean gathered his fair share of perplexed eyes. "My raven, here. She was a gift."

Ashura deflated. "Do I want to know from whom?"

The dwarf rubbed his leather mitts together. "In my drinking days—which also happened to be my prime days of adventuring—

my wandering couldn't have been more aimless."

Flynn struggled to pay attention.

"I wanted to see the edge of the world for myself. So, I went on and on and—"

"Like your jaw, now," Benoit scolded through his beak.

Jean ignored him, lost in the vastness of his memories. "Met folk of strange—sometimes terrifying—origin, saw incredible cities nobody's ever heard of, and had a run in with a lycanthropic elf whom I cured."

Snjick and Ashura exchanged glances.

"But nothing quite held a candle to Rose's home." Jean snickered in reminisce. "The edge of the land. The *original* dalaryn dwelling—Dunarch."

"That place is a myth!" Benoit exclaimed. "You think dalaryn are treated with *any* respect in this land? Why do you think such a tale came to light?" His feathers puffed.

They fell silent.

"It doesn't exist," Benoit said again. "It doesn't."

Jean cleared his throat. "Well," he said, "I've been there, lad. And I can't shed experiences."

"It must've been a drunken mirage, fatso!" Benoit protested.

Jean raised an eyebrow.

"With all I've experienced," Benoit muttered, "making such a thing up disgusts me."

Jean chuckled. "I'll show ye if you'd like." He glanced to Ashura. "Of course, it isn't up to me."

"If they have men," Ashura said, "who am I to refuse?"

Flynn stroked his chin. "And we're supposed to make it there and back so swiftly?"

"He's right," Snjick said.

They all glanced at him, sparks of hope fizzling out.

"Ashura?"

The brute nodded at the half-elf.

"You're our captain. Our leader." Snjick lowered his brow. "And I'm sure this distant land has one as well."

"A queen," Jean interjected. "No king."

"If we're going for troops," Snjick continued, still peering at Ashura, "then I must ask you something."

"What is it?"

"If someone came running to you, needing an army for *their* cause, would you give us up?"

All eyes fell on the captain.

Ashura gulped. "I get this'll be hard, but we can't hold Xardiil as it stands." He shook his head. "The advantage doesn't belong to us."

Benoit narrowed his eyes.

"Snjick's right. But in order to win this war—a war that's killed too many of our friends and siblings—we have to push ourselves."

The wind picked up, shaking branches of near trees.

"Some of us will stay. Others will go."

Benoit scoffed. "I'm going with the oaf to this place." He picked a loose feather. "If it's real, I must see it."

Jean laughed. "An adventure, it shall be."

"What about you, captain?" Snjick asked.

Ashura brought a hand to his chest. "I'll stay with Flynn. We have a city to protect."

The half-elf shook his head. "I don't like it," he said, "So far, we've split up to no success."

"It's going to be alright, Snjick." Ashura nodded. "Nobody's going to be trapped."

Snjick bit his lip.

"Take care of those two," Ashura said, smiling. "Make sure they don't kill each other."

Snjick snickered, absorbing his captain's expression.

"There isn't a moment to lose," Benoit said. "Flynn. Ashura." He gripped his reins with tight claws. "Don't die."

The guard captain summoned a smile.

They parted as two cohorts, one galloping for the capitol and the other toward the edge of the land—as per Jean's direction.

The half-elf looked back, as always, his eyes lingering on the other half of the group.

Snjick savored the visual of Ashura riding his mare. For, there still existed a possibility for his captain to survive. For the half-elf to redeem himself.

***

Flynn's office served as a reminder of the moments before the battle. When all of them were huddled around his desk, firing ideas and information off the walls. Everything was in his hands. He had had the ultimate decision in how to approach it.

But Flynn had failed, even in his men's final moments.

So much blood on his hands.

He sat behind his desk, across from Ashura, and handed Abraham—who stayed here to help with office affairs—a proper note. "Get that to the wall." He locked his fingers.

"Are they coming?" Abraham asked, that relic sword now attached to his hip. "The enemy? The silver mage?" His fingers trembled as they held the note.

Flynn sighed.

"Get that note to where it belongs," Ashura commanded, his legs folded in his chair.

Abraham nodded and scurried through the door.

The brute sighed. "I see that village woman isn't here."

Flynn stroked his chin. "Before we rode to Qualia, I asked Abraham to put her up in an inn." He glanced out the window, into the courtyard. "She's a good woman."

"That a new opinion?"

"I know how I came off."

"It's bothering you, isn't it?" Ashura tapped the arm of his chair. "The battle?"

"We couldn't do anything."

"Stop trying to deflect. I'm no stranger to the feeling." He shook his head. "Consider me an equal."

"I'm not your equal," Flynn assured.

"Why not? Because I was an assassin? Killing is killing."

"No," he said. "That's not it. You can actually *lead* your people."

He chuckled at the inaccuracy. "Come on." He shook his head vehemently. "I started with thirty. Now, they're dead."

"But you stayed." Flynn buried his face. "I abandoned my own men."

"Under my command." Ashura leaned back in his seat. "There are things I've done, Flynn, that would make your stomach curl. You're better than I am, *fuck* being equal." He gripped the arms of his chair.

Flynn observed. Silent.

"It's no mystery, either. Where I come from, everyone knew about those things I did, the people I let die." He leaned forward, the chair groaning. "I can't keep track of the souls that've slipped through my fingers."

Flynn gulped.

"I would consider yourself lucky."

***

Dusk hummed with the fangs of winter.

Their breath exhumed as fog, their noses turned pink, and they had to flex their fingers every now and again. But they rode, regardless of any preexisting clamps on their journey. Snjick had suggested they stop at nightfall, allowing one of them to stay awake and keep watch. But Benoit insisted they continue, even if it were at a more languid pace.

"Are you sure you're up for that?" the half-elf asked.

"I've been through worse."

"Of course," Jean butted in. "But that doesn't mean you have to push yourself now. Fatigue is the ultimate poison, especially to a warrior."

And when they did settle down, to Benoit's begrudge, it was within a cluster of boulders. They curled up with their blades and bags, Jean's trinkets serving as another rock for them to rest on.

The dwarf volunteered for the first watch, climbing upon the flattest of the surrounding stones and crossing his legs. "The night is cold, yes," he began, letting Rose onto the rock next to him, "but the sky is vast; pure." He sighed, allowing his wispy breath to dissipate. He yawned. "It's why I love wandering."

"I'll be up in an hour," Benoit uttered. "Wake me if you get tired." He rolled over.

Snjick said, "I think he's already asleep."

"What?" The dalaryn sat up, glaring.

Jean emitted a deep snore as he sat with his legs folded.

"Shit." Benoit gave his back to the boulder he'd claimed. "Alright, I'll keep watch. You rest."

The half-elf looked into the stars. "I don't think I'll be able to."

Benoit snickered. "The dwarf's the only one out of us who can—Ashura and Flynn included."

Trees groaned in the wind, and leaves kicked up.

"What happened to her?" Benoit asked. "Everyone else?"

Snjick swallowed, shaking his head to try and wiggle out of the topic. "They're gone."

"Ashura told me the same thing when I asked." He scratched a place beside his beak.

"I know as much as you do about Iz and Raquel," Snjick said.

"And Cariaah?"

He sniffled, both because of the cold and the hijacking emotions. "She's—" He cleared his throat.

"I know you two were—"

"She's alive." Snjick sniffled again. "But Cariaah's dead." He tapped the sheath of his dagger. "I know it sounds…ridiculous, but that girl I carried to the land below—she's gone."

"She worked with Zenira."

"I know." Snjick nodded with vigor. "But this whole thing, Benoit, I can't help but feel responsible. I sent her into Qualia."

"Don't be ridiculous." The dalaryn shook his head. "You've done all you could for that girl. It's as you said, you *carried* her."

Snjick paid heed to Benoit with his gaze. "But I could've—"

"There're things you need to be realistic about." Benoit shook his head. "Granted, going to fucking Dunarch doesn't exactly follow suit."

Snjick snickered.

"Do you know why I am the way I am?" Benoit said.

Snjick shook his head.

He sat straighter. "Because I'm angry. I'm angry at this land, I'm angry that my kind are enslaved, and I'm angry the land below has been destroyed." He scoffed. "The only place where that wasn't the case. Every single friend I've made—*murdered*."

Snjick sighed, deeply and filled with release.

Benoit shook his head. "But Dunarch—if it truly does exist—is a hope worth fighting for."

***

The dark, crimson syrup feathered into the miniscule cracks of the floor. Zenira took a seat at the head of the table where Alec tore at his collar just a moment ago.

"All of them were liars—cowards afraid to wear their identity."

Hassai removed the guard helmet from his feathered head,

finding his seat beside Zenira. "By this point, the city should be ours. We can commence our march for the capitol."

"It's pathetic." Zenira scoffed. "I've come to realize that war is foreign to those in the land above—the former 'land above,' as it were. No amount of training can teach a man how to fight, now can it?"

"That's correct," said Hassai.

"The Vantaknights fought a war for centuries. And with what progress? Look at the *vermin* in such positions of power." He pointed at the dead scattered about the floor. "It's our duty to bring divine rhetoric everywhere."

"And the bird of fire?" Hassai asked.

"The girl's different. That we already knew." He smiled. "But it seems that a fighter was bred in her for one purpose."

"But she's gone."

"Merely wandering, awaiting her fate's inevitable fruition," Zenira corrected. "Seeing her come to terms with her true nature has been rewarding."

"Indeed," Hassai said.

"From the day I sat at that table beside her to now, there hasn't been a doubt in my mind." He snickered, drumming his fingers on the table, and narrowing his eyes. "The girl will return with more power than ever, to cleanse the land of its filth."

17 VULTURES

Benoit detested the capitol, especially its slums, even if the night sky muted the muddiness. The land below radiated warmer than this place, regardless of season. The corridors exuded the glow of torchlight and fireplace, accompanying the comfort of his siblings. He didn't even come to Xardiil to drink, unlike his fellow knights.

Because the streets were lined with filth.

At seventeen winters old, Benoit scurried across those rooftops as nothing but a shadow. The breeze he created coursed through his feathers like capillaries of water after a fresh rain. Below, the slums hummed a low, evening buzz through intermittent coughs, stirring peasantry, and the occasional tattered wanderer.

And the stench. It fueled him to zip forward toward Lance.

This contract contained a target of which he enjoyed assailing: a noble. Even at his age, Benoit lost count of how many like Lance he'd eliminated. But always, there resided an ulterior comfort of chivalry within his work.

All of these men were pigs—Lance, especially.

It made that stench even worse.

"Stop!"

The dalaryn landed onto a brittle rooftop, whipping his gaze about. A flurry of metallic footsteps beckoned him toward a nearby alley, where another voice emerged.

"Yes?"

His curiosity usurped his primary focus. He scurried onto another rooftop and peered over, through the shadows, at the pair of figures below.

A guard, clad in pristine steel, stood in the mouth of the alley. "Hand over what you stole, peasant."

A dalaryn, clothed in a weathered garment, held a lute in arms as he backed away. "Stole nothing. Just want to go home."

"Horse shit, dirty vulture."

Benoit's feathers puffed.

"Put the weapon down." The guard gripped the hilt of his blade.

The dalaryn continued to back-pedal. "I don't have a weapon."

Benoit tightened his claws. He had a contract—a goal—in which to attend. To linger about this situation was to delay his work, and that was illicit. He placed Lance's pompous dwelling within focus and scurried toward his target once more, away from the scene.

What does he mean—a dirty vulture?

Benoit had ventured out of the land below—his own ominous dwelling—to cleanse this slice of the land's filth. Yet, he couldn't ward off the intruding thoughts that followed suit.

That breeze returned with more sharpness as he sped through the dense night. It burned his eyes with serrations. The air had grown cold, turning his feathers into icicles, and freezing his beak in a heap of frost.

He'd traversed the wall into the residential district which held Lance's home: a minute portion of Xardiil with a lifetime's worth of sin. It wasn't difficult to find the house, as it boasted a crimson roof.

Dissonant with each home on that polished street, Lance's displayed the distinct aura of a monument or landmark. Perhaps it was, but Benoit didn't know to what extent. The X—Geneva precisely—hadn't given specific details regarding what Lance had done.

The dalaryn knew of his own youth though he didn't think it would thwart a biography of his target. But Benoit's knowledge carried nothing but the mere surface: Lance's actions carried depravity—unspeakable morbidity.

His talons grounded themselves upon that roof, digging into the shingle of a dormer window. He'd decided something preemptively: if the curtains were drawn shut, he wouldn't bother creating a ruckus. He'd revert to using any back door or ulterior entrance in order to gauge his surroundings.

And drawn they were, with not a flirt of light behind them.

Good, Benoit told himself. *The oaf's asleep.*

But the frame of Lance's stead vibrated—no, it thumped—in a harsh rhythm. Perhaps he was awake, carrying out whatever deed typically occupied his evenings—what Geneva withheld.

So, Benoit decided on that dormer window as an entrance. If Lance truly was in a lower level, then having an owl's eye from above would be of aid. The window's lock proved to be easy work for his claw, as it clicked open with enough pressure.

And uniform with Lance's pretentiousness, the glass's hinge didn't squeal or groan. Someone—hired or otherwise—had applied lubricant to ensure its smooth operation. The curtains fluttered in the icy breeze, allowing the intruder's initial step to be placed on the carpet.

But the oaf snored in that thick, silkily sheeted mattress.

And that thump continued from below, only more sonorously.

Benoit froze.

He knew of his instructions, which detailed nothing but kill. He also knew of what Ashura would say. If the dalaryn was truly nothing but a tool—a faceless, listless shadow—then he would creep toward the sleeping oaf and slice his throat with a sharp edge.

But this percussion from below. It beckoned.

Benoit's claw flirted with his sword's hilt, tracing the seam of the leather. And the thumping grew ferocious in pace, ramming against the house's frame like a blacksmith's hammer.

Yet, Lance still snored.

The dalaryn couldn't help but delve further into the lair.

His trail scurried down a flight of wooden steps, sinking beneath his talons without a groan. Hewn into the walls were candelabras, dormant like the boor who once lit them. And the percussion came in a crescendo, encroaching with each step. The dalaryn wound a curling corner to unveil a door—*steel.*

With each wallop, that door rigorously shook, its handle rattling. A basement. But not a soul—noble, royal, peasant, or otherwise—owned such a crypt in the capitol. *You can turn back,* that noise told him. *You can kill and scurry like always.*

But each sign and every sonic influence ricocheted into vainness. His curiosity triumphed all else. Eager and rapacious, he pushed that door open in a languid sweep.

The value of his surroundings changed.

That air bit with sharp fangs, promising nothing but sorcerous, morbid displeasure. The shadowy abyss which clung to the walls oozed lasciviousness. Torchlight didn't exist. Only black.

And the slamming.

It took a moment for his eyes to adjust—to welcome the embrace of this labyrinth. But his ears—they received that percussion in unfiltered form. Nothing obscured, muffled, or mediated Benoit and the noise.

That rhythm deepened.

And once he traversed that final corner, the noise was raw.

Chains wrapped a slithery, twisting, restraint around he who writhed. In that cellar, across from Benoit stood a dalaryn of black feathers. It peered through the morbid dust, pleading without words.

***

The emerald landscape that bloomed in the morning still buzzed at dusk. Insects teemed, frogs blurted their croaks, and birds sang. All was winter-blind in proximity, going on as if the season existed merely as an option. The grass towered at mare-height, framing lakes and ponds and fluorescent cattails. Trees twisted toward the sky in braids, fettered with rippling leaves.

The dalaryn wore fatigue on his shoulders like spaulders, his somnolent eyes a reflection. His feathers were cold, but not in a sharp manner. The frost nibbled at their stems and branching sinews, sparking a tingle that coursed through his frame. He held those reins with gentle claws and allowed the bounce of each hoof to go its own way.

The black hue of his cuirass had faded. Scathes imperfected the stained leather, darting about as narrow lines. Splotches of once-red blood stippled the chest, peering up as memories. He knew it wasn't his own. It could've been from the half-elf at his right, or the dwarf at his left. But the probable source was that of someone beyond the grave, now lower than the land below.

Luckily, the dalaryn had plenty of distractions. Ahead, that landscape glistened at the behest of the setting sun. And the fog of their collective breath emanated as orange-tinged mist. They needed to move fast, but Benoit felt little pressure from such pure air. Even the mares had abated their restlessness.

"The reach," Jean said.

The other two remained silent, knowing he would carry on anyways.

"That's what they call this place. Nothing of relevance exists beyond our backs." The dwarf chuckled. "At least to them."

"What sort of people are they?" Snjick asked.

Benoit raised an eyebrow in mutual curiosity.

"It's been quite a long time," he replied. "And it should be known that I wasn't sober for most of it…"

Benoit shook his head.

"They contain *multitudes*." Jean smiled, stroking Rose's chest with a finger.

"I never know what's coming out of your mouth," Snjick scoffed.

"I think that's a good quality to have." The dwarf snickered. "Never doubt your wild card."

Benoit followed a buzzing bug with a glance. "Humor me, dwarf. Why shouldn't I doubt you?"

He cleared his throat. "A question I've never gotten, I'll tell ye. Maybe it's because I have the answers to problems nobody detects." He pulled a sealed, leather pouch from somewhere upon his vest. "An answer can come in many forms. Whether it's a prophetic word of advice," he undid the fastenings of that pouch, "or a hidden trick." He poured a handful of pellets into his hand, of which his cohort couldn't identify.

Snjick's eyes lingered.

Rose buried her beak in the pellets, trying to take one for herself. Some other birds even descended, gliding above the party.

"I've been in enough parties to know the nature of them. People have their reserved specialties—their roles—whether they acknowledge them or not." He put the pellets back into their place. "But between those roles, there are gaps to be filled." He sighed. "I'd like to think I fill those gaps."

The sun hid behind the vast ocean of green, bringing the advent of the moon. It lit their journey from hereon and introduced a new orchestra.

A whole new set of noises blared like a war horn.

A brand-new collage of animals scampered.

It was the birth of an environment unseen.

"Should we stop?" Snjick asked, the mares snorting in fatigue.

Jean hummed. "I can't say how far we are from Dunarch's inner coil. But I'm certain this path is the correct one."

"I'm doubting my wild card," Benoit murmured.

The dwarf snickered.

"Regardless, we can't stop." The dalaryn shook his head. "*I* won't, at the very least."

"So be it," Jean said. "We continue!"

The wind picked up as a darker, more brooding sigh. It bared fangs—not nibbling teeth—which sank into their skeletons like cold steel. Its frost elicited a wave of shivers, from more than just their cohort.

Every particle of life withdrew their calls.

Only the wind remained—the wind that rummaged through the towering grass and pearlescent water.

A low, deep growl rung out.

"Jean?" Snjick reached for his dagger.

Benoit's steel beckoned the same.

Jean's eyes fell into wideness. "The beasts," the dwarf whispered. "Those who *wander*."

It sliced through the moonlight like a great sword of cryptic steel. Cracking was its spine as it stood pin-straight. Fanning were its eleven extremities that stretched longer than its slender frame. And wretched was the creature's anemic, curling smile that bared a flurry of yellow, dripping fangs. The beast wore no fur—only pale skin—and a set of gaping eyes.

The mares of Benoit and Jean bucked, launching the pair of them into the foreign muck below. A freakish scurry ensued, as their hooves couldn't gallop fast enough.

Snjick battled his horse under a quivering frame. It brayed and snorted, desperate to free itself from the half-elf's reins.

Rose took flight with spread wings, firing into the sky like the bolt of a crossbow. Her caw echoed vast in that morose wind. It didn't faze the beast.

And that beast growled again. This time, it allowed the three of them to inspect its inherent timbre: clicking, droning, and unwinding. That vocalization taunted and maimed each defense they hadn't prepared. Those two black pits of nothing brought shivers.

The beast conjured a new noise which came subsequent to an

uncanny contortion of the neck. This call pierced ears and shot beyond the clouds.

This freed Snjick's mare, as it launched the half-elf to the ground in a thud.

"What's the plan, wild card?" Benoit uttered, blade rattling in his claws. "Steel good against this thing?"

"We can't kill it." Jean shook his head.

Snjick scurried to them, dagger held high in reactionary defense. "Did I hear that right?"

"If we kill it," he said hurriedly, "the queen will not take kindly to us."

The beast swiped its heap of a hand through the grass, narrowly missing any stray limb or exposed bit of flesh. It created a new wind—one that promised swift death.

"So, do we run?"

Another piercing cry fired from the creature's teeth, along with a slam of the ground.

Jean hummed, louder and harsher than normal. "If it wanted to kill us, it would've already."

The beast peered at them with those pits for eyes, examining. Taunting. Its hands—every single one—held kinked, grey fingers and inherent claws.

They stared back in fervent, terrified vigilance.

But another howl emerged from their backside.

And upon the party's collective, yet involuntary pivot, their guts twisted into knots. Even if Jean had experienced this as a younger dwarf, one-hundred times over, that knot wouldn't abate.

A new creature peered at them.

As tall as the first, and still bared no fur. The encompassing skin glistened a musty orange in the violet of the moon. No lower jaw accompanied its top row of teeth, allowing a curling, slithery tongue to taunt along with unrelenting eyes. Its growl harmonized with the blackness of the night.

And more came in accompaniment. They stomped through their environment, creating a crooked frame around the half-elf, dwarf, and dalaryn.

All went still once more.

Even the breeze.

The only noise left was their pounding hearts.

Those silent, brooding stares paralyzed them.

But hooves arrived in a crescendo, clopping toward the trio of adventurers in confidence.

The outcasts' collective eyes went toward an approaching group of dalaryn.

They were coated in fluorescent feathers and sheathed in ice-white armor, mounted on likewise mares. In their gauntleted claws lay spears, which jutted toward the pariahs in a tepid flaunt. "State your business in being here," their presumed leader commanded. "We wish to avoid blood if we can."

***

Lance's blood stained Benoit's sheathed steel. But when the dalaryn took that final, arbitrary stab, no feeling of redemption swelled. No thirst was quenched.

What Benoit had ultimately done changed nothing. Lance gravely violated unspoken, moral law. His legacy was still the identity of a wretched monster. Those kindred eyes that peered into Benoit's very core would never change. The damage had been dealt.

Benoit scurried across the slum rooftops again, but he took an alternate path. He needed an answer to a new question. His eyes lingered upon what lay below:

Those who coughed and stirred. Those who closed their eyes in a heap of excrement. Those who hadn't a coin to their name and wore nothing but tattered, grime-ridden cloth.

All of them wore feathers as skin and a beak as a face.

He needed to reach that alleyway. Benoit, as more than a mere shadow or tool or blade, ached to discover what had taken place there. As a dalaryn it was his duty was to know, Vantaknight or not.

He leapt with nimble talons to his destination: the rooftop from which he'd observed the alley mere hours ago. Stealth alluded him, painful and nervous desire superseding. And once he reached that rooftop, he peered into the alley below.

What lay there was the corpse of that lute-equipped dalaryn, condensed into a pile of bone and feather and flesh. In pristine, sparkling armor, a guard approached under a torch's flame. He paused at the mouth of the alley, simply gazing, until he spat upon the corpse.

Then he carried on to continue his patrol.

Once the shadows returned to the alley, and the guard had vanished from his sight, Benoit dropped from the rooftop. He scampered to the bloody corpse with agape eyes.

There was no weapon.

There were no stolen goods.

Only the lute, his sole possession, rested atop his mutilated corpse.

Before him was the answer to his question, lifeless and defaced.

Once Benoit left the capitol that night, a child woke from a nightmare. He ran to his mother in refuge, burying his beak into her chest. And to muffle the noises, relieve the stenches, and alleviate the bitter sights, she told him a great tale.

The tale of a place in the far reaches of the land, trees as tall as the sky and fortresses built with nothing but the binds of nature. There, the dalaryn had bright feathers, bathed in the soothing grasp of hot springs, and ate from the largest assortment of fruit. No one dreamt anything of darkness because darkness didn't exist in that place. The sky never turned black.

And a queen—more beautiful than any other—ruled as one of them.

This tale eased the child of his fright and sent him into the deepest of peaceful slumbers.

18 GAUNT

No spell, blade, or otherwise could free them from such a dreadful milieu. The dangling, grotesque smiles of the beasts paired with those unyielding, shimmering spears reminded them of escape's futility.

Benoit didn't bother resting a set of claws on his blade's pommel. Even if the assassin's conscious mind urged him to do so, he wouldn't be able to. The paralysis brought upon him superseded all else.

The riders before him—the natives of this green landscape—donned feathers of unique colors. Dawn hadn't arrived, but even as those dalaryn flaunted steel with animosity, Benoit couldn't help but be in awe at their glow.

"I am Shyke. And you are?"

"Benoit."

"Snjick."

"Jean," the dwarf said in dissonant tone. "I'm not exactly a stranger."

"Yes," Shyke said. "Who could forget such a drunken dwarf?" He signaled his men and women to lower their spears.

"Any more travelers since my last visit?"

He fastened the spear to his back. "Only those who wish to steal or destroy." Shyke clicked with his tongue, loud and firm.

And in reactionary response, the beasts made a languid pivot away, receding toward the trees in a slow march. Their howls called low, echoing in the shadowy distance.

The pariahs unleashed a collective sigh.

"Why is it that you've come?" Shyke asked. "Dunarch only opens its arms for those who do the same."

"My lads and I," Jean began, his arms outstretched, "wish to speak with the queen. It is an urgent matter that not only concerns us, but Dunarch too."

Shyke hummed a perplexed noise.

"We promise," insisted Benoit, "to ensure the safety for every region, Dunarch included."

"It's for the good of everyone," Snjick added.

Shyke lingered his eyes, that hum prevailing through the conversation. "Everyone, continue with your patrol." He took his mare's reins in firm claws. "I will be their escort to the basket."

Snjick and Benoit exchanged puzzled glances.

Their journey ran through the remainder of the night beneath the glassy sky. And upon the sun's rising, that emerald hue arrived once again.

The forest was growing thick around them. And out of solace—not imminent danger—Rose took flight and weaved through the high branches. Other birds—large or small—accompanied her in that soar, cawing their caws.

Below their feet, moss clung to the dirt like foam to a pint of ale. But that soon gave way to a collection of roots that braided like twine. They didn't creak underneath the steps the party took, opting for rigidity. The roots formed a path, paving a clear line through the forest.

Ferns and plants and leaves towered as immense greenery, simply observing those who walked past. They harmonized in the serenity, welcoming the party into the inner coil of Dunarch.

Benoit inhaled that air as a clear, cool, promising vapor. It tasted nostalgic to his lungs, even though his talons had never stepped upon this forest floor. A tension—one he didn't even acknowledge having—released like a dam does its water.

"Aye, we're here," Jean said, "at the basket."

Those roots found a center, swirling in a magnificent spiral below the feet of dozens. Dalaryn—their fluorescent feathers shimmering—chatted over their children, of whom played in frolic. Laughter was this place's undercurrent, erupting intermittently from the alcoves within trunks of trees. But they weren't carved by someone with a steel tool; the trees had grown around its dwellers in a warm embrace.

"You've been here before, Jean," Shyke said, dismounting.

"Aye." Jean nodded. "It's been many years, I'll tell ye."

"But have you, Benoit?"

Benoit wore a smile. "Never," he said. "Only the tales I've heard."

Snjick gave a brief, soft gaze to Benoit, though he asked Shyke, "Where might we find the queen?"

Shyke outstretched a claw, pointing to a massive tree that overshadowed all the bright activity. It glowed with humming, embedded homes. Stoves, furnaces, pots of tea, and pans of food were all heated by natural coals. Visible to the outside eye. There were no doors because, in this place, no one needed to be kept out.

"Beyond the tree is a great root, the artery. It stretches to where she resides, amongst all walks of our family."

Benoit peered above, into the canopy of high branches. "And beyond that?"

"An explorer's question, Benoit," Shyke acknowledged. "From her majesty's dwelling, onward, there exists no border. We haven't destroyed. So, the life surrounding us holds no animosity."

Benoit looked into an open hand—at his wounds—nicked scratched and dull.

All revealed itself through the darkness of his very feathers.

Shyke led them through the basket, his spear sheathed, and demeanor calmed.

The dwellings hewn into that great tree beckoned the outcasts and their collective, awe-struck gaze. But the warmth those hubs exhumed also whispered a promise: *find that of whom you seek,* it said. *There will always be a spot for you, here.*

On they went toward the queen, atop that root.

The artery was thick and bulbous, and it sliced through the vastness of trees. Sheathing the timber was a duvet of moss, which absorbed each ginger step with a soft embrace. It all filled the travelers with wonder, even drawing a childish gasp from Snjick.

The surrounding forest hadn't ceased in its inherent thickness or towering presence. Rather, the trees wore a luscious coat of leaved branches, dripping with the moisture of a fresh rain even though it hadn't. More birds cawed and chirped and sung, soaring from one tree to another in gracious color.

Life—in perhaps its purest form—wrapped its arms around the group.

"Do not be overwhelmed by the sights," Shyke said. "I promise that her majesty is not one to fear, though she may have her hidden thorn."

Benoit raised an eyebrow.

Jean snickered. "I can recall only a brief meeting with her during my visit," he said, following the highly-flying Rose with an eye. "It was when I received my parting gift."

"How long ago was this, Jean?" Snjick asked.

"Too many winters to count."

"Well," Shyke began, "we haven't had a peaceful visitor in four decades. They're an endangered sort."

"Here to break the mold again," Jean murmured.

There was no doubt, when they reached it, that this slice of Dunarch was her majesty's. The trees shimmered with leaves that flaunted hues of violet, the ground was a drape of moss, and flocks of birds came and went in droves. Encircling it all was the purist of water that flowed like a nobleman's gabardine. A throne, comprised of braiding roots, centered it all.

And in it sat a queen more beautiful than any other.

"You approach me like velvet," she said with an equally velvety timbre. "Your steps are careful. They create ripples, not tides." She rose in a gracious ascent, her icy silken garments adjusting to her posture.

The three of them hadn't prepared a formal inquiry, nor a rehearsed introduction. The queen hadn't either, but those words flowed from her beak like languid magma.

Antlers grew from her head of turquoise feather, serving as a quaint host to a handful of hand-sized birds. Her beak shone in the sun's glisten like ruby—color and all—and those incandescent eyes were that of jade.

She made her slow way to the visitors, inspecting through her soft gaze. "I remember you, Jean." Her beak emanated with chuckles. "Who could forget someone of such vibrance?"

He smiled, warmly.

"But I'm afraid these other two are a pair I haven't been acquainted with." She raised her brow in a crescendo. "Black armor. Light steps. Damaged eyes." The queen nodded. "Assassins."

Benoit's eyes fell agape, in concurrence with the half-elf's jaw.

"But you come not by the shadow, which means you seek my aid."

"Your grace," the feathered assassin said, falling to a knee. "I-I know this may sound like jesting, but I cannot fathom this place's existence."

Snjick fell to a knee as well, clumsily, unlike the assassin he was.

"I know our kind have been through many trials," she said. "And it has been my sole, overarching mission to resolve such disparities."

Benoit tightened his claws.

"A tricky endeavor. And it hurts my heart to know that my people, let alone *anyone,* suffers so gravely."

"Re-regardless of that," Benoit stuttered, "The land needs your aid."

"With what sort of matter?" the queen inquired.

"A dark army is sweeping through everything," Jean said, still standing. "Even as we converse now, the capitol could be under siege."

She took a moment, pivoting back toward her seat and pacing.

The forest filled this hole in their conversation with its noise.

"War." The queen shook her head. "A tricky, complicated web of evil." She looked into the sky. "I can't support such a corrupt beast of entanglement."

Their brows laced with a brisk sweat.

"This isn't about land, gold, or glory." Snjick made a frantic way to stand. "It's about what *you* fight for: life itself."

She inspected the half-elf with fervency.

"People have many things inside them." He tightened his fists. "The capacity to do good things—things that create and progress. But evil plagues everyone."

Benoit glanced vaguely at his side, to the half-elf.

"Even yourself, your grace."

Shyke, who stood in idle observation, flinched at such a remark.

Benoit stomped on the half-elf's boot with sharp talons.

"And yes," the half-elf continued, ignoring his comrade, "I may be considered 'just a boy,' but I've known enough people to be certain of this." He reached for his hip and clawed. "Darkness swells and breathes. It's a creature. And on this day it comes in the form of a wretched man."

The queen raised her brow in a swift motion.

"A man who's destroyed too many lives to count—to even process—in the time he's given us to act. And if we don't act, everything will be eaten up by his mission."

"Who is this man?" the queen asked.

Snjick bit his lip, as if his mouth were full of syrup he couldn't allow to spill.

"Zenira," Benoit said in urgency. "The people of the land like to call him 'the silver mage.'"

"What does this mage seek?"

Jean wiped his brow. "Something that I *still* struggle to understand, your grace."

"He wishes to rid the land of its 'filth,'" Snjick said. "Which, our order strived to do. Only his view is—"

"Murdering innocent people equates to cleansing," Benoit interjected. "That is his core philosophy. And it, within itself, is filth."

Her majesty took a slow seat, sighing in concurrence. "A plague," she said. "Rampant and unforgiving, much like your description of this 'Zenira.'"

Snjick held his breath so that his pulse amplified.

"Go to the basket and eat your fill," she said. "It will give me time to think of an approach."

***

The basket welcomed them again with all of its buzz. After Jean scampered away to find a pint of ale, Benoit and Snjick took seats beside one another on jutting roots, eating from a bowl of berries and beans and fern.

"Not what I expected, Snjick."

"I know," he replied, working through a wad of fern.

Benoit let go of a breath, one that oozed with drowsiness. "I never got to apologize."

Snjick glanced at his sibling, who peered into the sky.

"What I said to you after the final contract. How I called you a *mutt*." He shook his head. "It was disgusting."

The half-elf ran a finger down his left ear, acknowledging its sharpness. "It's okay."

"It's not okay. A true Vantaknight should know better than that—better than all the lords and nobles, counts and kings. We need to be."

Snjick sighed through a languid nod.

"My kind has never been filthy. Dalaryn haven't scavenged like vultures or committed acts of heinousness." He allowed the breeze to take his coat in its grasp. "*We've* been scavenged. Ripped from our families, dismissed as nothing but filthy, and stripped of everything but our own feathers."

The half-elf peered into his meal.

"But look around us, Snjick." Benoit brought a smile to his beak. "Even as I think about the land below, now, I know that we were doing something great," he said, making a fist with his claws. "We have to finish what we've begun."

The half-elf narrowed his eyes. "Let's just hope the queen gives us her support."

Jean stumbled into their circle with Rose begrudgingly upon his shoulder. His breath exhumed as a heavy pant, which first filtered through the coarseness of his chest. "She's ready for us."

Snjick and Benoit placed their bowls beside their hips and stood.

The three of them were escorted by Shyke back down the artery and to her majesty's mossy dwelling. Benoit's eyes remained poignant, but vigilant and determined, accompanied by Snjick's nervous gaze.

Jean had his hands folded at his belt, but Rose's chest beckoned his pet intermittently. Otherwise, she may've lost interest and flown off once more.

The queen sat upon her braided throne, motionless as a monument. Her antlers had more birds upon them, but their chirps were silent. Her claws held a coupled position before her face, emphasizing a state of meditation. "My mind navigates through your troubles like a ship does a dark sea," she eventually said. "And in my course of thought, I must heed a duty I inherently have."

"So, you'll send troops to the—"

She held up her claws, gently. "No."

Their hearts dropped.

"My decision comes from the great, dalaryn passion. And our newfound mission is to bring my children home to Dunarch."

"What do you mean, your grace?" Benoit asked, his gaze tight.

"I will not be sending soldiers. I will be leading them at your side." The queen rose to her feet, more birds gathering upon her head. "Fighting for the land we share."

***

The girl found comfort in the shadow.

Its darkness concurred hers in a blissful embrace. *You're hardly even a girl,* it whispered to her. *Not anymore.* There was a swirling, boiling morbidity to this darkness she now called her own. There was no urge for her to cope with the shadow, for it had hijacked her psyche and claimed her insides.

Rain pelted the mud under Cariaah's feet as serrated pellets, though the impressions of her footsteps quickly vanished at the behest of water.

The claps of thunder didn't spark her into a flinch.

Nor did the gleams of lightning that split the sky.

Her vacancy became her fervency.

They wouldn't have to guess her condition, for, anyone who saw the morbidity of her steel, eye, figure, and face would be able to know in an instant.

The only, final thing she wished to change was her hair and its fiery hue.

She wanted to dip it in a large, steaming vat of black stain.

Just to put out that flame.

The girl trudged through a muddy path, the confine of her absent eye, sheathed steel, and black armor.

As well as a galloping horse.

It zipped past, the mare's rider admonishing its hooves to work faster. But upon a shrieking bray, he yanked those reins in lieu of moving forward. For, who was this wandering girl?

"Are you lost?" he called out.

Cariaah kept walking.

The splashing trot that encroached didn't faze the girl. "Are you trying to get to the capitol?"

"Just go."

"Have you caught wind of the siege?"

She stopped walking. "Siege?"

"The wall has been breached," he said, resisting his mare's

restlessness. "A silver mage is behind it, they say."

"The silver mage…"

"I'm riding to the city, now." He nodded. "If you wish to accompany me, you'd better hop on. Otherwise," he said through the rain, "I've got people to save."

Cariaah looked at him for the first time. His narrowed eyes, puffed chest, and natural angst—it all reminded the girl of herself, despite his sex. She felt as if a mirror—unscathed, pristine, and pure—had been placed before her. Though it didn't reflect how she looked now.

Not anymore.

As she continued to ponder, staring into this rider's eyes, Cariaah understood a passing thought with morose clarity.

All the lives that are being lost, right now…

"Climb on," he said, "I can use your help."

They're your fault, and yours alone.

She took his hand and climbed onto that saddle. Yet, no strong feeling swayed her one way or the other. The girl figured that if her infatuation was the causation of this chaos, then she may as well be a witness to it. To think of all the warmth that once swelled within her as something profound.

Love.

Lust.

Hunger.

Terror.

All of the things she once had: those people, that place, and even the bruise at her hip, which hadn't beckoned her in many days.

Those raindrops zipped through the misty air and pricked her skin as the mare beneath them galloped in a fury.

"What's your name, pretty girl?" the man asked through the loudness.

"Mia," Cariaah said.

"I'm Clarke." He whipped the horse's reins. "I just hope the situation isn't as bad as I've been told."

Upon the eclipse of a plateau, Clarke yanked the mare to a halt. The capitol's cityscape spelled out the situation beautifully for them. A black sea of an army had tainted the surrounding land—the farms, homes, and mills—and spilled into the city. The wall had indeed been breached.

And Xardiil as a whole emitted a black smog into the rain. But despite that rain, those flames raged on in a morbid gall that promised nothing but death—that beckoned no one else but the bird of fire.

19 A BLACK RIVER

Ashura finally brought it up. "About last night…"

Aya straightened her legs until they shook. She looked up from his chest, drawing a circle with her finger upon it. "If you're going to apologize, *don't*. You already did last night."

He sighed, avoiding her glance.

"But you weren't apologizing to *me,* were you?"

The brute gripped the sheets with curling fingers, careful to use the hand that wasn't at her hip.

"If you don't want to tell me—"

"You're right," he said, looking to her, "I wasn't."

Falling dust mediated their shared gaze, illuminated by the windowlight. "I hope I did something to help," Aya said, "with whatever it was."

He bit his lip. "You did."

"I'm sorry that bastard interrupted us." Aya closed her eyes, adjusting her head, still tracing that circle. "He's a lout, that one, always ordering me around."

"I didn't hear him."

Calm silence filled the room—one that didn't heed the muffled sounds of the outside street. No desire to move disturbed the pair of them, only the prompt of midday.

Ashura reached to his side, rummaging through trouser pockets until he found his last purse of coins.

"What are you doing?"

"Paying you."

"Absolutely not."

"Well, I can't—"

"And I can't just take gold from you," she said, her face growing close. "I don't want to," she whispered.

"Alright," he said, withdrawing the purse. "But I need to go." Ashura swung his legs overside the bed and sat up.

"Where you headed?" Aya inquired, flopping onto her stomach.

"A battlefield. Soon." The captain slipped his trousers on as he stood, in one fluid motion. "I can feel it." He strapped his blood-stained cuirass to his chest. And that sheathed blade followed suit at his hip. The brute took a lurching exhale.

"Will I see you again?" Aya asked as he made his way to the door.

"Is that what you want?"

She nodded into the nest of blankets.

He conjured a smile.

***

Dust kicked up on the capitol's streets like a storm in a desert. Fire encroached from every direction. Death hung above as a dark, swirling cloud. The screams, whizzing arrows, and flesh peeling from bone—it all created an orchestra of wretched pandemonium.

The chaos told him something simple: *run*.

Ashura held his blade, but it had no wielder. For, the disorientation consumed him. The defense that he and Flynn had made held no candle to the sweeping force of the silver mage. That black sea of once-Vantaknights spilled into the walls, and with each second that arrived and abated, their grasp on the capitol tightened.

The warmth of the sheets became the bite of the wind.

The smoothness of her skin converted into the thickness of blood.

And the light of dawn turned to the blackness of night.

He ran his steel through the flesh of a former sibling, who lunged blade-first from the corpse of a capitol guard.

Blood stained his cuirass, hijacking the endless hue of black that formerly embodied it. The brute's leg cried out with an unchecked wound.

When the wall fell, mere seconds ago, Flynn had disappeared

into the dust. Ashura thought he knew of Zenira's incapability to siege a castle, let alone that of the capitol. But the wall crumbled like a tree in the forest, only with greater, cataclysmic force.

They lunged from the mist as black, lurching silhouettes. It was an undoubted trial of his steel, and the brute's ability to use it.

"Flynn!" he called out through the haze. "Flynn!"

The guard captain heard the cry of the brute but navigating through the thick dust tested all his other senses. Flynn could barely keep his eyes open as the air-riding powder infiltrated them. Akin to this sensation was the assault on his lungs. As he swung his steel to ward off the encroaching swathes of enemies, he also combated a sudden, wretched cough. In his gasping—which strived for fresh air—Flynn's breath emerged only dustier.

Ashura's cries fell into obscurity, and soon enough, the guard captain lost his sense of direction. Flynn's march—albeit unsteady—turned into a meander through that street or alleyway. His setting was a mystery, just like the means of this wall breach.

Doors.

He felt their handles with his gauntlets, but upon several modest yanks, Flynn couldn't muster enough power to break them open. "Help!" he yelled, ignoring the imminence of his enemies. "Open the doors!"

"Hello?" a muffled voice asked.

"It's Flynn!" he called, reinvigorated. "Just let me in!"

The door opened a sliver, and Flynn shoved himself through. He flopped onto the cobblestone with a metallic thud, blade still tightly in hand.

"On your feet," said a gruff voice. "Get on your bloody feet."

Flynn coughed through the dust in his lungs, sucking in the new air of where he traversed. He was outside—in a new district. And upon rising through the aches of his frame, it too was invigorated by that sight.

Dahl smacked him upon the spaulder. "Come on. We've got a pit to defend."

"Ashura's still out there," Flynn said through a pant. "We've got to do something."

"That giant? He'll do just fine, Flynn." The pit-keep snickered. "I've been around swordsmen long enough to know the sort."

And as Ashura, still in that swarm of dust and enemies,

continued to move aimlessly, blood sprouted like fountains. "Aya," the brute said as he sliced his opponents. He coughed through the swirling dust, and continued against the onslaught of screams, "*Aya.*"

His leg cried to him in a throb.

An arrow zipped past.

Another arrow stole his breath.

He choked on each gasp as a wretched, crawling pain tainted the brute's lungs. Upon his looking down, the tip of that arrow jutted from his chest, below his collarbone. Ashura's blade served as a waning support of his weight. He hobbled through that street, struggling to draw any stream of air—clean or otherwise.

Arrows continued to barrage his every meager limp.

He drew that circle upon his chest with a free finger to put himself under those sheets again. Blackness framed his sight. It pulsed like the throbbing flesh that encompassed him. It encroached like the enemies upon the capitol. But ultimately, it whispered to him, *you'll never see her again.*

And as a curtain draped over his eyes—black and unyielding—the brute thought of all those he'd put through a similar fate—a fate that stood at his very doorstep, now.

***

The doors to the pit district whammed in a maddening rhythm until the hinged obstacles gave way.

A river of black trickled into those vacant streets, their weapons stained red with the blood of civilians and guards. And although it couldn't be seen, the spellcasters had blood on their weapons, too.

Hassai traversed from the large group, hood upon his shoulders. His glare was sorcerous and voracious, searching for any trickle of life. "Leave no piece of cobblestone unturned," he hissed through his beak. "Their scent is repulsive."

Scampering ensued, as every sinew of that morbidly armored regiment dispersed. They snaked into alleys, shattered the glass of windowpanes, and penetrated doors with unrelenting weight. And with this new cavalcade of chaos came the poison of that distant noise, now an epicenter in this district.

They spilled over the pit's enclosure like a raging stream, falling onto its fighting floor like dumps of rain. But their avaricious weapons found no prey.

The pit itself was empty.

Hassai curled his talons upon the stone. "They're here somewhere." he sneered, marching toward a fighter's entrance. Upon the dalaryn's hip, a blade clinked in its sheath, which only resided there for secondary use. Otherwise, it was the spell.

However, with each step, the steel beckoned his grasp, dangling before his claws.

He wandered into a dark corridor, but stairs soon forced him to descend. At his backside, his cohort followed close with their respective weapons drawn. Their ears remained vigilant for a command, but regardless of the thick, cavernous silence, their feet kept shuffling.

"I'll kill you all," Hassai hissed. "The land above holds nothing but filth. *Nothing* but—"

In that hole's humming, stuffy, torch-lit air, those fighters—Flynn included—stood with steel in arms. On the fringes, bow-flaunting archers waited with notched arrows, prepared for their pit-keep's inevitable call to release hell.

Dahl stood with a blade, too, a smug smirk smeared upon the old bastard's face. He raised the blade, nice and high.

Tables flipped, glass shattered, and blood poured like sloshing ale. Steel clashed in a spark-filled percussion, fueling the fight—no, the ambush—to take place.

Dahl swung his steel alongside the swordsmen who fought for no one but themselves. Swordsmen who turned up at the behest of nothing and swung their blades for gold and ale and glory. But as they all sliced through the flesh of the enemy, leaving behind leaking corpses, the fighters honed their craft for the only home they had.

The hole took that black river it in its jaws, promising not a single man or woman's escape.

***

Shivering made it worse.

And not even awakening brought serenity. For, Ashura's periphery still encompassed devilish screams. But the dust that plagued the air had receded in its toxicity, eliminating one of the many obstacles for his lungs.

His gaze met a crude, once-white ceiling. In the warm candlelight, it generated a flirt of comfort for the cot-bound brute. He brought a tentative hand to the wound, anticipating the arrow's stark presence, but finding nothing but wet bandage.

"Shit," said a voice.

Ashura tried to dart up and reach for his blade, but the promise of sharp pain finally came to fruition. He squeezed his eyes shut.

A pair of hands guided his backside to the cot. "Careful," that person said. "No need to rush anything."

Upon a coping grimace, and release of his weight, Ashura opened his eyes to the face to which that voice belonged.

He was a young elf, clad in capitol guard armor. "You're lucky I was able to drag you in here."

Ashura paced himself to a successful upright position.

The room was a sponge that soaked up age. Yes, those walls and ceiling had lost their color many years ago, and the dangling candelabra sported a handsome layer of rust, but everything else told the tale.

The dressers in that bedroom must've been five or six decades old, as their timber skin peeled akin to the ascending steps that led to an unseen second story. Several drawers lacked several knobs, paintings clung to the walls under veneers of dust, and other extraneous trinkets barely showed their metallic shine.

"You're the captain, aren't you?" the elf said. "Ashura, right?"

The brute sighed, still navigating the discomfort of his own figure.

"What happened out there?" the elf asked. "Is there anyone—"

"Have you seen Flynn?" Ashura interrupted. "What happened to him?"

The elf wore a puzzled face, briefly, as he gathered his thoughts. "I think I saw him go toward the pit district," he said. "I couldn't tell if he made it inside."

Ashura's beaten, brooding glare cut into the elf. "Who forced your hand?"

"I-I'm sorry?"

The brute sunk rigid fingers into his shoulder wound, unflinchingly. "What's the problem? Have you got lint in your ears?"

The elf looked to the wall.

"Who forced your hand?" the captain yelled.

The guard flinched.

"Who made you stay up here where it's safe?" he asked, the tendons in his neck bulging.

The elf could do nothing but stare at his scolder.

"Have you got no feeling for your dying comrades?" He threw his hands up in front of him, which made the bandage leak. "Or those already dead?"

The elf shook his head, paralyzed.

"Answer me, dammit!"

"I don't know, sir," he finally admitted along with a tear. "I don't—"

Ashura shook his head with a clenched jaw. "Don't call me that."

The elf nodded, averting his gaze to a dust-caked statuette.

"I *hate* when someone calls me that." He cleared his throat. And thereafter, his breaths were sharp and coarse. "People constantly want something—are *expecting* something—when they call me that." The brute scoffed. "Don't expect anything from me. You're not my responsibility."

***

Flynn's gut took the sharpness of that blade.

And when the guard captain's already seeping skull caved, shooting bone about, nobody noticed. They continued their violent cacophony.

Dahl was backed into a corner along with Akemi and Hanya, who sliced through armor and flesh mechanically. Stone pressed against their backs, fatigue ate at their muscles like a ghastly disease, and comrades fell away with each beat of steel. That raging river flooded the hole, turning it into a black lake.

And as the rising tide claimed them with steel, spell, or arrow, a memory etched itself into those walls. It poured with every future pint of ale, roared along with each forthcoming crowd, and would forever serve as an undercurrent for the pit.

Fight for yourself, it said, *because no one else will.*

***

Ashura sobbed. His wound's blood seeped into the sheets like his aching tears, and his curling, red fingers gripped the cotton tight.

"Are you okay?" the elf asked. "Is it your wound?"

"My hands," he said. "There's so much red on them…"

The elf wore a perplexed look.

"I don't know if there's skin left underneath."

The room fell silent around him even though the streets still rippled with fire and screams and death. But the front door just across—bolted shut—hit sharply against its meager frame.

"Someone heard us?" the elf murmured. "But you're in no condition to fight." The elf rose to his feet with sheathed blade in hand. His wrists shook. Those steps toward the door came down heel-first, and the underlying planks groaned.

Another bang on the door.

The elf let go of a concentrated, sharp exhale. The scabbard hit the floor as he unsheathed his blade, removing yet another obstacle from him and his assumed opponent.

The door was the only one left. And it walloped harder, testing the bolt and those rusty, dusty hinges.

Ashura tied himself in a knot, drowning in anguish.

The only armed one between them stood before an intruder unknown. His gauntleted hands gripped that blade with white knuckles, seeking refuge in the steel like Ashura did those sheets.

The bolt snapped, hit the floor, and skipped in a piercing rattle.

"Hello?" The elf said.

Ashura murmured upon that cot to no one.

A wicked squeal and deep groan colluded in the door's opening. Slow, monotonous, and dreadful, it unveiled nothing but a dark silhouette—one that stood against the raging flames, fresh blood, and lurching shadows of the street.

The elf's heart pounded against his ribcage.

"Even if you had quieted down," a voice snarled, "your stench would've served me the same." He took a footstep into the house.

Ashura lifted his gaze, and the presented sight infected his eyes.

"One captain is dead," Hassai hissed. "I crushed his skull myself."

That elf's heart ceased.

"Now, we're just down to *one*."

The brute bit down on nothing. His fingers gripped so tightly that his palms pulsated.

Hassai scoffed. "I could kill you the same way, Ashura."

The elf glanced over his shoulder, at the bleeding man.

"Just look at yourself." Hassai rested a set of claws on his hip-clung blade. "You're broken."

Ashura's fingers withdrew their rigidity. He looked at his hands—at the notches and grooves and imperfections.

"You're a collection of fragments held together by nothing." Hassai took further steps into the stead, his talons drumming against the wood. "And when you do fall apart, those fragments are going to shoot everywhere. They'll slice everyone around you."

Ashura circled his chest. He felt nothing.

"Time is winding down," the dalaryn said. "And when the right sunset graces the sky, you will be the source of a terrible explosion."

The elf brought his eyes to the brute, awaiting anything to exhume from his lips. From his muscles. From *anywhere*.

But Ashura only reveled in the pit Hassai had dug—the curtain he'd pulled back. That was, until he moved, ever-so-languidly. He brought his legs overside the cot, drawing out a coarse grimace. His wound seeped through the bandage, bringing little streams of blood down his arms and onto his hands, which immersed into the already blaring red.

Hassai scoffed again.

He placed his feet onto the floor and stood with a hoist, the glass and trinkets and paintings rattling.

"What are you doing?"

Ashura shuffled over, using the surrounding furniture as supports to his clumsy limp. "You can kill me," he said, "but only if it's on my terms."

The dalaryn tapped his sword's hilt.

Ashura gathered his weight and commenced as rigid of a march as he could. Accompanying those steps was that leaking wound which dripped in a concurrent rhythm. He kept moving, slowly and haggardly, until he passed the elf—until he stood a longsword away from Hassai.

"What is it?" the dalaryn hissed. "How could I humor the traitorous brute?"

"The spell," he said. "That's what I want."

The elf tentatively held his sword with sharp eyes and a sweat-laced brow.

"Go upstairs, boy," Ashura commanded. "It's an order."

Hassai made a fist. He crushed the elf's skull with a simple motion. "No need."

Ashura closed his eyes, tightening them until it hurt.

Screams—albeit distant and intermittent—filled the newfound void. The breath of the street's fire was the undercurrent to their own. And the house didn't make a noise under all that dust.

"You're a stubborn fucker. Even after every assault, you still manage to draw breath."

Ashura only waited.

"And you really wish to die—you're folding."

There wasn't a tense muscle in his body.

"Alright, *coward*." Hassai's tapping claw tightened into a dark grasp. "I'll fulfill your wish."

Like a slithering eel, the spell creeped into Ashura's skull. Its long, slender, gaunt fingers wrapped around his psyche. And the dalaryn's eye peered into his every thought—his every memory—his every regret.

Everything he ever did.

Every single trace of blood on his hands.

It all assaulted Hassai like a black river—one raging and roaring and unyielding.

Hassai collapsed onto the floor, claws to feathered head. His breath ramped into hyperventilation, and his knees shot to his chest.

"You're nothing," Ashura said. "Nothing but a filthy cog."

The dalaryn writhed like the morbid creature he'd beset, as if those distant screams were cloistered within his own skull. His feathers shivered and his beak clacked beneath a listless, petrified stare.

And as the brute turned his back to Hassai, a foreign horn blared from past the city's container. It sliced through the jaded sounds of the street.

He hobbled toward the flight of stairs and made a slow ascension, moving to the nearest window across from him, its curtains drawn to a seal. Those steps he didn't savor, but rather, rushed through in an ungraceful limp.

His wrist ripped the curtains open.

He pressed his face to the glass.

Because over that wall and beyond the black sea, a new ocean came into advent. A canvas of gleaming white and fluorescent feathers which held the only glimpse of moonlight he'd seen.

That army shimmered as a beacon of purity.

20 VESPERTINE

Every reach—every distant crevasse and embedded hue—gathered at the capitol as it burned. That black sea of once-Vantaknights stood with blades at their sides and spells withheld, Xardiil at their backs.

And upon the dying city's wall, donning a glint of icy armor, stood the silver mage. Icy too was his hair, which, in that black breeze, flowed like a silky gabardine. And that blade. He held it as a declaration of victory, a silent incantation, but ultimately, a grand invitation.

Encroaching, another sea brought its foreign tide as a vast contribution. Within it were those colorfully feathered dalaryn—wrapped in armor of pure white—and two lurching, pin-straight beasts that labored amongst them as creeping towers, donning their cryptic smiles and abyssal stares. Yet, at its helm were a trio of anomalies—two of them assassins that donned deeply scathed, formerly black armor.

The queen's plates encompassed her feathers purely. Her cuirass of white steel was clean. Untouched. And a long, narrow blade of silver clung to her hip that she unsheathed upon eclipsing a final hill.

She led a ferocious example, as all under her command drew their weapons in unison.

And what that hill hid was apocalyptic: the gall of the capitol whimpering with a foot to its throat—the foot of the land below.

They rode forth at the behest of a sharp, echoey caw which shattered the air. The undercurrent of thundering hooves fueled the sea's roaring tide through that field. A gargantuan propel that sliced through the landscape of consuming flame, dripping blood, and decaying bone.

Of voracious death.

Benoit and Snjick looked at each other through the tumble of hooves and promise of chaos. No words were said through the despair-ridden haze, but the exchange of eyes conveyed a mutual feeling.

The half-elf looked ahead toward that deep, black canvas of abyss. It garnered no light except for the mass unsheathing of blades. Each speckle of a soldier stood as a cog in a machine that anticipated what inevitably came.

Remember…

Remember to forget everything…

Everything except how to kill.

The collision of those seas rippled, bringing inherent chaos. Spells shot into the black sky as glows in the haze of smog. Steel clashed through foreign technique, as each force had peeled away from where they dwelled, only to exhume violence.

And all that violence encompassed.

Sopping flesh, snapping bone, and spraying blood filled the air like a painter executing their craft upon a fresh canvas. This pure land—which hadn't seen war in longer than a century—served wonderfully as such. But the artist came not in the form of that eclectic battlefield, instead, in the form of its catalyst:

The silver mage.

Overlooking his chaotic creation, Zenira searched the black night for another glint—a sparkle of fiery red—no matter how tiny it may be.

But it couldn't be overlooked—that battle of gruesome art. The chaos was indiscriminate. No adornment of any sort—no complex idea nor pristine armor protected a single body.

The half-elf hadn't obeyed his father's echoing words. He couldn't stop a surge of feelings and thoughts and memories. His identity swung through his dagger, and every mistake and blip of pain he'd caused shone in the blood he shed. Below, sloshing at his mare's hooves, was a marinade of crimson-soaked mud. Each bit of red reflected another's mistake. Another's inflicted pain. Another's grief.

And the steel.

The onslaught of former siblings didn't distract him from these morose thoughts. No, they encouraged them. He used to revel in this sort of combat during his days of pit-fighting. Right alongside Bauer. For, it was their foundation—the root of their friendship.

And his father. Who would his father have been if it weren't for killing? Who would the half-elf be now?

Blades.

Blood.

Death.

The end result of everything in his life.

An enemy's swing knocked him from his horse. The half-elf had to kick away an oncoming soldier and rip his head through a spell, of which he couldn't place the caster. Once he spiraled to his feet in a swift leap, he glanced about in a fury.

His surroundings were no different than a wicked storm. Horses galloped, arrows whizzed, and swords sliced through the stained air. Even one of those beasts collapsed thunderously at the behest of a fiery spell. Fatigue boiled beneath the rush of battle within him, promising his eventual collapse.

Snjick needed fuel—kindling for his ravenous fire.

Her.

She rode on with the stranger, the thinning trees turning to blurs in her periphery as they glided past. The girl's eye pierced the night, matching the beacon of flames that consumed Xardiil. A final hill sat before them—one that masqueraded the sounds of battle.

"Leave me here," Cariaah said.

"Are you sure?" he asked, yanking the reins.

"Yes, I'm—"

Clarke rammed an elbow into her side, stealing her breath and her seat.

She fell upon the dirt, back-first.

"Good, pretty girl," he sneered. "I was going to leave you to the crows anyway." Clarke dismounted, unsheathing his longsword with one hand, and loosening his trousers with the other. "Once I'm finished with you."

The girl inhumed a desperate heave, crawling backward on her wrists until she reached for her blade. She looked to him—his façade. While Clarke—or whatever his name may have been—reflected her, it was not her former self.

Because he had connived, and manipulated, and executed. He

masqueraded his true intentions with dignity and courage. Clarke felt no guilt as he marched toward her laying figure. No, he enjoyed what he had done, and longed for what he was about to do.

Their blades collided in a clang. His triumphed as the victor.

She struggled to raise hers again.

He stomped on her wrist.

Even though the pain shot about, the girl didn't wince or grimace. She only peered into his eyes. She only studied his face.

"Is something the matter, girl?" he barked. "Doesn't this hurt?" He dug further with his heel, twisting, pressing, and driving.

She didn't answer. She only stared.

"Come on!" he yelled. "Aren't you going to fight back?"

Cariaah shook her head.

He grazed her cheek with his fingertips.

"Go on," she said.

His aggression receded.

"Go on!" she yelled. "Maybe then, I'll feel something!"

Clarke's brow furrowed into a complex shape. Perplexity, shock, *fear*.

Her eye turned to a gaping, amber hole. "Rape me, you coward!" She scrunched her nose and lowered her brow as the words spilled out.

But Clarke didn't obey despite his initial intentions. He let go of her wrist with his heel and stood, keeping his blade close.

"Come on!" Cariaah screamed as she crawled toward him.

He gathered his mare and mounted with a hoist, averting his gaze. And thereupon, he rode away with whipping reins.

She threw her balance away with her blade. And the steel landed on the tufts of clay his mare had kicked up. "You bastard!" she yelled. The girl collapsed onto that same clay, digging into her wrist with a pair of fingers to try and ignite something. Then she went to her hip, scratching with a claw.

But no feelings arose.

"Help me!" she screamed. "Someone help!" Her eye peered into the dark ground below, and her ears only encompassed the noise of that near battle. "Please!" she yelled. *"Please!"*

The girl's screams soaked into the sounds of steel and of drawn blood.

Of Benoit and Jean, who stood with their backs pressed against each other, their weapons a levee for opponents. Amongst them were a cohort of natives, their spears killing.

"Perhaps it's time for a hidden trick," Jean whispered, unveiling a pouch from his crowded vest.

"What did you say, dwarf?" Benoit called.

Jean poured the pellets into his free glove.

Rose, upon Jean's subsequent whistle, darted to the sky like a geyser, hovering above in the thick smog.

"Hold on to your ass, Benny!" Jean yelled. "I'm calling them in."

"What are you—"

Jean dropped the pellets into the blood below, which sent another, booming cacophony alight: smoke. It seeped and mixed with the surrounding haze of black, creating a marinade of disorientation.

Benoit gripped his red-doused sword with tighter claws so that his arms became his weapon. He kept his back even closer to Jean's, ensuring no such vulnerability.

And from the abyssal sky, as the sound of steel subsided, albeit for a moment, a caw echoed—one that stole attention. Ripping through the fog was a flock of raven, led by Rose. They took flesh in beak and claw upon a diving swoop, drawing blood like the cohort below.

Those whose throats and limbs remained under that guise of black used their spells in a more belligerent fury. Their grasps searched for birds, and their steel sought after any other aggressor. Thirst for cleansing turned into mortal defense—at least for that particular sect of this orchestra of chaos.

However, in another corner of the raging battle, the antithesis transpired.

A white sparkle walked amongst them.

His narrow blade—although an avid participant—did not host an imperfection upon its steel. Nor did his armor which sparkled despite the absence of the moon.

And he sliced his way through—with that pristine sword—toward the pandemonium's center where the half-elf stood shin-deep in bloody muck.

Snjick couldn't feel his arms. They'd given themselves to the machine that were his natural proclivities. Combating the spells that sunk into his mind grew exhausting. That ulterior battle, which tore at him like the slender, black claws, was gaining ground. As if the sullen sorcery toyed with him like a cat does its mouse.

His greaves and gauntlets held not a trace of black. That foundation of an abyssal hue made way for crimson. For, the half-elf's dagger dripped with fresh blood, which seeped into the marinade below.

Those thoughts of her trailed.

They fell back. They fell into a time when he could sit beside her.

When he could look into her soft, sensitive, but lively gaze.

A time when potential pulsated within the two of them.

And with such a precise thought, there were no more to kill. Corpses framed him, yes, but beyond that frame was another border. His condemned siblings surrounded that pit of death where he struggled. They were wrapped in perfect black, blades in hand.

Snjick peered about, his breath a pant and his wrists trembling. Winter stained the fog of his exhale, and the adrenaline-fueled foundation commenced its crumble. He couldn't move fast enough through the thickness at his feet. He awaited someone to lurch or lunge, shaking dagger in hard.

But only one sloshing pair of trudges gathered his focus.

His free hand beckoned his attention. It pulled strings. It tempted.

Snjick's grip on that dagger coiled tight. He bit down on the taste of blood. A growl slithered through his teeth. For, the sight doused the half-elf's flame in oil, enraging it once again.

The sight of *him*.

"I told you something a while ago," he said, his blade rattling in its scabbard. "You drip with nothing but talent, boy."

Snjick made a fist out of his free hand.

"But I also gave you a warning." All of the gravel had risen to the surface in his voice, leaving no veneer atop his words. "Fall in with your dark talents," he recited, *"or you will face an inescapable death."*

Snjick let go of an uneven breath. He twisted his feet further, ensuring nothing could shove him into a topple. Only the whites of his eyes and knuckles remained pure. All else was scathed or doused.

"But in death, there is dignity." Zenira reached for his blade and grasped it tenderly, like a fragile antique. "And I will give you this much, my rotten fruit." His steel rolled out of its scabbard gradually. Rhythmically.

The smog swirled around them. It exiled all else.

Zenira lowered his blade, displaying his chest in lieu. "Unless you wish to kill me now, with the talent you've naturally been given."

Each hand gave him an option.

In one hand was the dagger his father had given to him all those winters ago. It was an inescapable death. And in the other was something he couldn't see but could undoubtedly feel: the spell. It lay within that fist he made, beckoning him to let it fly, whispering to him, *kill the fucker.*

"I know you can, Snjick," Zenira hissed. "*I* taught you how."

All Snjick had to do was cast and end. And he knew an imminent death would ensue, yet Zenira would be gone—simple. But if he used the dagger, he would die, and Zenira would still walk.

What else could he do?

The half-elf looked about, amongst the carnage—amongst the desolation. But nothing emerged from that smog as a resort or even a mirage. He was alone—alone with nothing but his own filth. And upon a hazy breath he wrapped both hands around that dagger.

"Steel it is, then." Zenira raised his sword. "As your father would've wanted."

Snjick peered. It was to be one strike, after one parry at most. Zenira wouldn't waste any opportunity.

But the silver mage didn't draw near.

The half-elf had to move first.

Snjick had to shatter that foundation he'd created for himself. So, the boy took his first step forward. Heavy. The muck weighed him down.

Zenira conjured that wretched smile. Where his lips curled into little slivers and the corners of his mouth dimpled. But those eyes—those unrelenting eyes—remained unfazed. They pierced.

The half-elf took another step.

The distant, virgin sunrise eclipsed the far mountain, exhuming its breath as Snjick took a final step.

"It can be over," Zenira taunted, "without that shiny little dagger."

Snjick's breath steamed. "Hold your tongue."

"No," he said. "The Vantaknights befell to its sharpness, and so will you."

"If you were wise—"

"Just think of all I've done."

Snjick bit down until his temples throbbed.

"I had you assailed on a contract," he growled. "I betrayed your father's wishes."

"Hold your *tongue*."

"And I held her in my arms."

Snjick lunged, his dagger ferocious as the lead of his weight. But his dagger met nothing, not even the bite of Zenira's blade.

He had dodged the half elf's strike, burrowing his steel into the boy's gut, and impaling through and out his back. The blade shimmered in the freshness of the sun, its fine craftsmanship on display.

Snjick inhaled. No air came to his lungs. Only blood to his lips.

Zenira withdrew his sword with a rip, allowing his opponent to fall to his knees.

The half-elf reached about for his dagger, searching the pool of crimson for that sparkle of steel. But in it, he found no success, only the thickness of that ever-increasing pool. His fingers continued to mix that muck in a swirl until something interrupted his desperate hunt:

Her.

The boy turned to face those encroaching steps. He gazed right through Cariaah's shell.

He saw her smile.

Her eyes.

Her laugh.

Her voice.

Her cry.

Her warmth.

Every flaw.

Every piece of her.

It lingered within him for far beyond that single moment.

The girl crouched before the boy as he collapsed. She took his heavy head in her gauntlet, supporting it with a tender touch. No words. Only the glimpse of a smile and his soft, warm eyes as they befell to darkness.

The wind chilled the beams of warm sun: a reminder of winter's presence.

It left nothing but a biting, sure silence.

"You've finally come," Zenira eventually said, "and graced us with your flame. The bird of fire."

Cariaah rose, easing the boy's lifeless corpse to the steaming blood.

"And you've come a long way, my—"

"Filth," she said. "Filth is why you've latched onto me for so long."

The wind dissipated what was left of the haze, howling through the echoes of fading battle. It rippled the liquid below and swayed the girl's fiery hair.

"To rid the land of its filth?"

All expression faded from his face. Zenira only observed. He only listened.

"I was born in filth," she said. "My home was nothing but filth. The person who raised me held nothing in his heart but filth." The girl shook her head. "And now, with all I've done, *I am filth.*"

His brow twitched.

"And so are you." Cariaah peered. She outstretched her hand so that he could see her bloodied gauntlet. Her fingers tightened into that distinct claw and the spell slithered into his skull with a morose grasp.

His eyes didn't glare, and that curling smile abated. "Is that how you view me, Cariaah?" he murmured, coarsely. "after all I've—"

She closed her fist, ending the words.

And as he fell to the filth below, defenseless, his pristine armor drowned in crimson. His body turned into a carcass, and his glow fell away with the night.

Those bystanders flaunted their weapons and converged upon the girl in ferocity. Their scurries squished and kicked up the vulgar water.

But the girl let every barrier disappear. All boundaries—all hopes of avenging herself—vanished. She cast upon each of them in a fury, crushing skulls and spilling blood like the conductor of death she was. That blade fell from her hip in the abrupt chaos and was buried below the onslaught of fresh corpses—inertly still. She didn't heed it, nor her aching wrist, nor her hip. All the bloodlust and fear and anger unleashed in ultimate catharsis.

One that drained her everything.

And as blood continued to leak from the bodies, the wind placed something at Cariaah's feet: a twirling, brittle leaf.

It received her gaze.

But it too sunk into the liquid, and as it did, she began her exit.

Cariaah didn't heed the decaying battlefield, the mounds of corpses and fluorescent feathers. She only marched away, toward the eventual, wintery forest.

As a girl, no longer.

***

That mare Ashura rode cantered through the desolation. Its snorting breath emanated as fog, right along with the brute's. He hunted for movement—survivors. His fingers didn't choke the reins with tight knuckles, but rather held them gingerly as he navigated the skeletal field of battle.

He passed the heaps of dead—unmoving. But one, as perhaps the stillest corpse among them, beckoned. Ashura drove his mare forward until a hurried, grimacing dismount ensued.

The dwarf: there he rested with Rose upon his shoulder.

"Jean?" Ashura said. "*Jean?*" he repeated, feeling his face.

Rose pecked the dwarf's unmoving cheek.

Jean opened his crusty eyes, awakening from that slumber. "Aye?" he murmured. "I must've drifted."

They shared a brief laugh until Ashura asked, "Where's Benoit?"

"Don't know if it was a dream or not, but I think I saw him venture right into the capitol." He pointed toward Xardiil's skeleton. "Queen was at his side with the rest of them."

"You weren't lying before, dwarf."

The pair of them mounted that mare, Rose in tow. They rode toward the mouth of the capitol, hooves kicking up the muck. Besides Rose, other birds chirped and cawed. They were distant but echoed in an undoubted approach.

Another call resonated amongst those birds in the form of a distantly beckoning dalaryn.

Ashura veered the reins, heeding the cry. He kept his blade close to his red fingers, of which tapped away at that hilt in a speedy rhythm. The mare's hooves splashed below, navigating through the corpses—those lifeless and those twitching—to reach that call.

"Is anyone alive?" they yelled. "Where is everyone?"

Ashura nudged Jean. "Don't answer," he said. "I want to get there, first." Now, he held those reins tightly. They traversed a mound of bodies—the corpse of a beast topping it off—and peered at the source.

He sat with crossed legs, head in claws and helmet removed. His colorful, indigenous coat gleamed in the sun and blared right along with the red upon everything. Never in his subsequent mannerisms, posture, or murmurings did alertness emerge. He was drenched in delirium.

Ashura rode forth, pulling the reins upon a swift arrival.

There beside the dalaryn stood a saddled mare, grey in coat. It snorted upon the brute's dismount but calmed under Jean's murmured coax.

Ashura knelt beside the dalaryn. "Are you hurt?"

"They're all dead," he muttered. "All of them," he continued, gazing at nothing. The dalaryn hugged his knees, brought them close to his chest, and shook. His armor rattled as he curled into a knot. "Where's the queen?"

The brute adjusted himself, grimacing. "She's in the—"

"Ashura," Jean whispered, stealing their attention.

Ashura's eyes lingered, his lips parted, and his brow receded its heed of pain. For, the sigh of the wind told him not to say a word. Because as the half-elf lay there in a pool of crimson, his face the only white surface, they knew to let him rest.

Right along with the fallen surrounding him.

They split themselves amongst those two horses: Jean and Stearns—as he'd told them his name was—upon the grey mare, and Ashura on the other. The squelch of the bloody mud turned into the clop of ash-layered cobblestone. And upon entering the mouth of Xardiil—as a widowed field of assault—they slowed their ride at the hum of activity.

The queen was a glistening savior as she marched through those streets. The plates she'd worn in battle made way for a silky garment of ice, of which draped to the ash like a great waterfall, drawing city folk near.

What remained of the native army dealt out fruit and pitchers of water in droves. Those covered in ash received a handsome trough-washing. Boards on windows were removed by rigid claw or steel tool, and whatever flickering flame remained was doused and extinguished. All that water soaked the streets purely, uprooting the ash and dirt from the stone.

But all such activity ceased when the brute neared.

With his hands bare and red, holding the drenched corpse of the half-elf in arms, all eyes went to him. Even the children. Even the queen. Even Benoit, who emerged from that bustle in a hurried sprint.

Ashura lowered Snjick's face down to him.

And upon the dalaryn's reception of the boy, Ashura gripped his mare's reins tight and whipped them hard. Without a word from anyone—Benoit, the queen, or the approaching Jean and Stearns—he rode down that street, past the crowd that watched.

The breeze greeted his face along with the promise of tears. He rode with a heavy throat and firm saddle. Only a passing flock of birds drew his glassy eyes to the sparkling, golden sky. The ride was short-lived, yes, but only because he'd arrived at his destination.

The front door was still boarded shut, right along with the windows. Thus, upon a frantic dismount, he kicked and kicked and kicked until the door gave way. And inside, dust rode the streams of spilling sunlight as a pair of women huddled in the corner.

His further steps were ungraceful. His scabbard clinked and his heels thumped against the floor. But he reached that back hallway and collection of closed doors. He made it to *that* door. There he stood, about to pound on its painted wood before he saw his red-stained fingers.

All he said was, "Aya, it's me."

Silence clung to the air—like that dust did the light—until the click of a lock broke it. The door creaked open. And there she stood, looking at him with that gaze he remembered so vividly.

ZACHARYTOOMBS.COM

Made in United States
North Haven, CT
16 October 2023